# ROEBUCK'S
# PRIZE

# ROEBUCK'S
# PRIZE

# MICHAEL
# SHAPIRO

*atmosphere press*

# CHAPTER 1

## September 23, 2035

The Kovaleski Skyway was one of the first sold by the state to a group of investors. They set up some tollbooths and tried to turn it into a profit center, and that actually worked for a while. But soon the security requirements of operating a highway became too expensive and complicated and they found a new buyer, an offshore subsidiary of a subsidiary, the identity of whose principals was almost impossible to determine. They hired a security firm operated by some hard-case former U.S. Marines and staffed with some mercenaries from the U.S. and other countries, and started patrolling the road in earnest.

This seemed to be a good solution until some of the security guys, sensing an opportunity to set up their own profit center, started shaking down motorists for cash and goods when they caught them speeding or with a taillight out, and that's pretty much where we are right now. Duh, what kind of minds would think it's a good idea to turn over a state road to a bunch of professional thugs? Answer: The minds of elected officials who've gotten so bogged down in partisan bickering over how to actually spend the money they've finally appropriated for "infrastructure" they turn in desperation to outsourcing and privatization as the only option.

Yes, it can be treacherous traveling roads like this. But

guys like me monitor the police scanner and some other little not-so-public sites to identify the least-dangerous times. I'd done a little homework and calculated that tonight was as good as any to do my "specialty item" grocery shopping run. More about that later.

I was also looking for a real job and had been scanning the hiring sites when Emily came home, heels clicking on the kitchen tile, carrying a shopping bag from Whole Foods. Leafy tips of celery stalks and the thin, crusty end of a baguette seemed to say, *"Hi. I've just completed a full day's work AND found time to go to the store. What have you been up to?"*

Actually, neither my wife nor her grocery-bag ventriloquist's dummy really said that. What she said was, "I could use some help with what's left in the car, please." And, "Is dinner ready? I've got class tonight."

I'm a husband and father who works from home and does family-support and house stuff whenever I can. Some people would call me a stay-at-home dad, but I prefer my way of saying it because stay-at-home implies you're *staying* somewhere and not *going* anywhere, and the "dad" part makes it sound like the "B" side of "stay-at-home mom." You know, the goofy, second-thought thing on the flip side of a real, main thing.

I've been out of work for about six months now since Omega Financial downsized me. Well, sort of. I had been working the Metro North Jersey region for the previous two and a half years and doing a pretty good job of it, if I say so myself. I'd like to think the clients I worked with would agree. And so would the Financial Advisors who brought me in to do the estate planning work for their most prized sources of revenue. I know my insurance and annuities sales numbers were good, and I brought in some nice additional assets under management as a result of my poking around in their clients' portfolios in places the FAs hadn't thought of yet.

I was looking for something where I could use my experience and pick up where I had left off at Omega. Yeah, right.

It seemed like the offerings were few and not really up to my level of experience or pay grade.

Anyway, back to our kitchen at dinnertime, I went down into the garage and found one lonely bag in the car, half-filled with odds and ends—nothing from which you could make even a single meal. This is what she calls grocery shopping? I came back to the kitchen, still shaking my head, and heated up the sauce (my special puttanesca), boiled water for pasta (Tolerant bean) and tossed the salad (triple-washed and plastic-bagged in California) while Emily changed out of her work clothes. Dinner was going pretty well with Olivia, our eleven-year-old, doing most of the talking about her soccer team and some school play she was going to try out for soon.

Then Emily said, "Tay-o said we should try to bring the spirit of our sessions into our everyday lives."

Roused from my stupor, I said, "Who's Tay-o?" That's how she had pronounced it.

"He's our new yoga instructor. I met him in the prison writing project I worked on last year. He was one of the best writers in the class—really sensitive and intuitive and edgy. Anyway, he took a rap, did some time and he's out on parole now, doing great on the outside."

"Wait a minute. Hold up here a second," I protested. "First, how do you spell Tay-o?"

"It's T-A-O."

"That's pronounced DOW, isn't it? It means 'The Way' in Chinese. Weird that the man can't pronounce his own name. Is that really his name?"

"Sure, it's his name. Hey, he's the one who can decide what his name is and how to pronounce it. Plus, you're taking that tone again—the one where you act like you're the only one who knows anything and everyone else is stupid."

"Second, I don't particularly like the idea of you hanging around with felons."

"He's not really a felon. He just had to do some time is all."

"Since when do you toss around expressions like 'on the outside' and 'do some time?'"

"Since I worked in the program, which you probably don't remember because you never pay any attention to anything I'm saying anyway."

Reassessing the situation, I thought the best approach was to try to get through dinner without a full-on argument. She was going to class soon, I had to get Olivia to bed, and then I had some important things to do.

I stole a glance at Olivia while Emily and I were sparring. Ponytail pulled off to the side and tied with a scrunchie—purple to match the fuzzy purple sweater she'd selected herself—she seemed to have tuned us out, off in her own little world, thinking about who-knows-what. A couple of recent summonses to conferences with her teacher to discuss "self-control issues" suggested that someday in the not-too-distant future that little temporary cat's paw tattoo on her cheek might be replaced by the real thing. Always her own person, deciding for herself what she wore, how she acted, what she thought about and what she said.

With some deep breathing, courtesy of my own Eastern meditation studies, which began and ended with an audio tape (seriously) of an old TM program I found in the attic of a house I lived in a long time ago, and some Western-style lip-zipping I invented myself, dinner was soon over and Emily left the table to get ready for class, Olivia off to get her backpack. I was still clearing the plates when Emily clip-clopped back through the kitchen, jingling her car keys.

"You know, Raf, I didn't ask for this either. I get that you're hurting, but it's affecting us too. You want more support from me, but I have my own things I want to do and I'd appreciate a little understanding from you."

"I know that. And I want to, but it seems like you're drifting away just when I need you closer."

"Not sure what to tell you except that I'm not going to

drown in your unhappiness. Not gonna happen. And that's up to you. I've gotta go. Don't wait up."

"No problem. I've asked Maddie Ackerman to come over to stay with Olivia for a couple of hours after she goes to bed. I have something to do later, and it's ok with Maddie. She can just do her homework over here."

"Whatever," said Emily. On the way out, she added, "Oh, and don't forget we've got the Mambergs here Friday night, and I want to have lamb chops."

"Yo," said I, with a little more enthusiasm (and assurance) than I felt.

The "thing" I have to do after our little one is in bed is go to this place called the Specialty Products Distribution Center—known to us regular patrons as "the Depot"—and pick up the Extras, which are foodstuffs like meat—say, lamb chops for example—and potatoes, any kind of electronics and clothing that are beyond the basic pants, shirt, skirt and blouse.

We have to go out of our way because there's a shortage of these things. They say it's just temporary and nobody's really concerned much about it, beyond the fact that there is a little bit of hassle to get stuff you used to pick up easily at the regular stores. Now that we've got four big Terror Wars going (TW I – IV, called Tee-Dub One, Two, etc. for short) everybody has to sacrifice a little, right?

Anyway, you go online where they have an auction website, like eBay used to be, and you bid on an item—like, for example, lamb chops. If you get the item, you pay for it with a credit card and print out your Chit, which you take to the warehouse—the Depot—and pick up your stuff.

Olivia did her homework on the now-cleared kitchen table while I finished cleaning up the kitchen. Then we put on a video, which we both watched till she fell asleep on the couch. I could tell she was upset by our dinner table conversation because she had a few go-to self-consoling techniques that seemed to work for her. Watching *Back to the Future* was one of them. As the movie wore on, I noticed her frowning and catching her lower lip a couple of times—two more little clues she wasn't letting the increasing tension in her parents' relationship roll off her back. I guess I dozed off about three-quarters into it and she woke me so I could put her to bed.

"Don't worry, honey. It sounds worse than it is. You know your mom and I love each other, right?"

She was in bed now, face scrubbed, her breath minty from the toothpaste. Tears sprang to her eyes, but she bravely fought off a full-on cry, as usual. "I know, but it's just so scary. I don't know what I'd do if you guys broke up."

I smiled and dabbed clumsily at her cheeks with a tissue. "We're fine, O. Really. We're just going through a tough patch right now till your old man gets his feet under him again. Things'll be better soon, I promise. Ok?"

She nodded hesitantly, and I helped her pull the covers up.

"Look, I'm sorry you have to go to school about me again. But I just can't seem to hold back when that Megan Holloway whispers something nasty about me and gets the other girls going on it. Like this last thing—about my cat's paw. I like it and I'm keeping it till it washes off. Mrs. Renfrow didn't hear their comments—just me yelling back at them."

"It's gonna be ok. We'll deal with it tomorrow. You know I'll support you. But you've got to figure out some other ways to handle stuff like this. Otherwise, you'll always wind up looking like the bad guy every time."

"I know. It's just hard..."

She trailed off, apparently willing to let it lie there for the time being.

"You know I have to go out in a few minutes to get a few things. If you wake up, don't be surprised to see Maddy here."

Another nod. "'Night, Dad. I love you."

"Me too, Sweetie."

I flicked off the light and walked out into the hall and into my little work room and fired up my computer. I needed to print out the Chits for this week's Extras so I could go pick them up at the Depot.

Maddie Ackerman arrived and, after exchanging greetings, she said, "Boy, Mr. V, I sure hope the missus and O appreciate these late-night runs you've been making. You always seem to have good stuff in your fridge, which is more than I can say for the other people I sit for. I know it hasn't been easy for you guys since you uh, got downsized or whatever. And I know you're probably tired from the day, but—well, you do it anyway and it means something."

I forced a laugh. "Well, thanks for the vote of confidence, Maddy. I shouldn't be more than an hour or so. I just put her in so she may still be awake."

I walked through the kitchen and into the garage, jumped in my Honda Civic hatchback and headed down the street, onto the main road, onto the Kovaleski Skyway for about twelve miles, over the overpass and down into the industrial park where the Depot was located.

Apparently, my intel had proven correct and the road was temporarily clear of prowling bad guys, and I made it through without incident. The Depot lay just up ahead. Formerly the province of only the people who worked here during the day, the place was somewhat brighter now that a new parking lot had been paved and new LED lights installed so regular folks like me could come and pick up their goods whenever they wanted to, twenty-four/seven.

Stopping at the check-in station, I rolled down my window and worked up a big smile for blonde Margot as I handed her my Chits.

"I'll have one of everything," I said grandly.

Completely side-stepping my clumsy attempt at whatever it was, she machine-scanned my Chits and handed them back to me. "Go down to Loading and see Martín." Just like that, I was sent on my way.

"Yes, ma'am," I said, manfully accepting defeat. I rolled up my window and drove slowly down toward the loading dock where the cars would take their turns backing in while guys loaded the goods into their trunks. When my turn came, I backed into position and Martín approached.

"Holá, mi amigo. ¿Qué tal?" I said in what was intended as a rapport-builder but which came out as affected, over-the-top currying-of-favor, handing over my list and Chits once again.

Looking over my short list of goodies, Martín frowned and said, "Oh, you gotta come inside for this now." Strange. His request for me to disembark from my vehicle and come inside the Depot was the first I had ever received in the many times I had driven down here.

I backed up to the loading dock, popped the hatch, shut off the engine and walked over to the door, pushed it open and went inside the biggest interior space I had ever seen. It was hazy and smoky, and the bright, overhead hanging lights seemed to have halos around them in the murky, cavernous warehouse. Forklifts moved up and down aisle after aisle of goods stacked high on big shelves. It looked like the inside of an old-school Costco store, only the aisles were wider.

In case you're wondering, those big warehouse-type stores just sort of collapsed with the first shortages of the most in-demand products. Now we've still got the specialty stores like Whole Foods and regular supermarkets like Food Lion. But those places are tiny shadows of their former selves—more like corner specialty stores with nothing special to sell—and they don't stock any high-value things right now. Just canned goods, a little produce, and bread.

But for folks who really want the good stuff and are willing to pay more, work the Auction site and make the trip, there's the Depot. I was looking around, trying to figure out what to do next when a guy with a clipboard approached and asked whether he could help me.

I showed him my Chits and he looked at them and muttered. "Half now, half Saturday."

"Say what?"

"Like I said. You get half this stuff now—tonight—and you come back for the rest Saturday. Shortages gettin' tighter, you know."

"Hey, I need these things now. We're having people over Friday night."

My new friend laughed, showing me his best jack-o'-lantern imitation, put a greasy hand on my shoulder and said, "Sounds like you got yourself a personal problem, neighbor. Earl, load 'im up," handing my now-wrinkled and dirty Chits to another of the warehousers nearby.

Earl did indeed load me up, and I was almost out of the building when I thought I heard a muffled sound of laughter and some shouting. I walked down a little hallway in the direction of the noise and pushed back a thick black plastic curtain and saw a small crowd around a makeshift boxing ring in which two men were squaring off. One had blood trickling from his nose, and the other's eye was swelling badly. I thought I recognized the one with the bad eye as Joel Avigdor, one of our neighbors from down the street.

There was also a card game going on over in one corner and several guys were rolling dice in another.

For a few brief moments, trying to take all this in, I honestly thought I was hallucinating.

Recovering and noting that another guy with an embroidered patch that read "Carl" on his Dickies work shirt had followed me in, I said, "What is this, Monte Carlo night at the Depot?"

I thought it sounded jaunty and cool, and that it concealed nicely the fact that I had been disoriented and weirded-out by the scene.

Carl replied, "Depends on how bad you want your goods."

"Meaning?"

"Meaning the Auction's not the only way to get Chits. Meaning these guys really want the finer things in life, so they're willing to gamble and fight for more. You can understand that, can't you?"

I stared at him dumbly for a few seconds, then turned and walked back out to the parking lot.

I checked the hatch of my Honda to make sure my order—or rather the half of my original order they gave me—was still there, and pulled out of the parking lot and made the uneventful drive home.

I checked on Olivia, paid Maddie and stood outside and watched as she walked the half block back to her house, let herself in and signaled me with her porch light.

I unloaded the car, put the perishables away, and checked Olivia again. On the way back to my office room I stopped in the kitchen. My head ached, so I took a couple of Advil with a few swallows from the big cold bottle of white wine that was already open in the refrigerator.

Back in my workroom, I flicked on the TV and surfed the channels. Hundreds of options, but nothing seemed worthy of my attention. All the streaming services had folded. Advertising had basically dried up, and not enough people were willing or had the bucks to pay subscription fees. The whole industry had been replaced by a blizzard of so-called "user-generated content" that consisted mainly of homemade videos, crudely-made amateur dramas and pirated copies of vintage TV shows. I settled on the tail end of an episode of *The Big Bang Theory*. Can it be that this thing actually ran for like twelve seasons? Who knew that a group of video game-playing, comic-book fan-boys—self-proclaimed geeks—could be bona fide researchers at Caltech? Chuck Lorre, that's who. Back in the day, the guy had a golden touch with sitcom concepts that almost never missed.

Now, thoroughly pissed at the idiocy and finding no other diversion on TV, I turned it off. I let my pulse slow down, back to almost normal, and reflected on the events of the past hour. Bad enough that for the past couple of months I'd been special-ordering the good things we wanted, but now to find out the following: A. That to get them I was going to have to actually interact with the boys down at the Depot, B. That they were only going to give me half at a time AND, C. That at least one of my counterpart home-boy dads had upped the ante by gambling and even fighting for Chits to get more goods. (Could that really have been Joel Avigdor in a fight for Chits? The same Joel Avigdor from down the block whose son was in Olivia's class?)

One of two things was happening: Either this was a temporary thing and goods would start flowing again and things would get back to the way they were, in which case I just had to roll with it and wait for things to settle down. Or, today's reality was a harbinger of bigger and more lasting changes, and I would need to make adjustments to make sure we got the things we needed. In a way, I kind of hoped it was the latter because I needed to shake things up.

Which was unusual thinking for me. I couldn't recall a time when I did any serious planning for actions I would have to take or wondering too much about the tools I would need. I guess I just hoped better things would come in some way.

Some might charitably call this a "rich interior life" but I realized only much later that my early years had been spent primarily in a haze of fantasy, fueled by old reruns of Westerns where the lone stranger suddenly comes into town, solves a problem for the people there and then rides out triumphantly. It wasn't till I got to college that I realized the path to a happy life would be considerably less glamorous—as in study like crazy, day and night—and that didn't sit well with me.

If what I saw down at the Depot—and heard at my own dinner table—were any indications, I was going to have to step up my game if I wanted to get my life back together.

I considered my options. I still had connections, relationships from my days at Omega. Conspicuous by his absence from any list of fans of my work would be my sales manager,

John Flanagan. It wasn't a deep, seething hate or anything like that, but more of a calm, smiling indifference, so as soon as he found a replacement he liked well enough for the Hudson Region, he made my territory disappear in a so-called cost-saving reorganization. As far as I can tell, despite all the box-and-wire diagrams, the flowcharts, Power Points and pro-forma worksheets, the only real effects of this corporate flim-flam were to ensure John's position as ass-kisser of the month and put me out on the street. Asking John for anything would be a long shot but, hey, who knows?

My thoughts drifted back to my new and very urgent problem of how to get the rest of the lamb chops as I assumed what the yoga folks might call the ancient "Pretzel Pose" (more of that Eastern influence) and dozed off into an uneasy sleep in my reading chair.

# CHAPTER 2

"My best idea right at this moment is to serve 'em as appe-tizers." I think I said appe-*teasers* to lend a little humor to what was otherwise a tense situation. I glanced over at Emily, half-expecting a chuckle or a half-smile. Even a wince or an eye-roll would have been good enough. She just looked down and away without expression.

We were reviewing our supplies situation: four chops short of a main course for the Mambergs' dinner the next night, which was Friday.

After about three beats, she looked my way and I could feel her look of accusation and disappointment that seemed to burn right through to the back of my head.

"Ok, I'll see what I can do," I said, with what I hoped was an air of confidence but which came out sounding more like resignation.

I got up from the breakfast table, hustled Olivia into the car, hopped in the driver's seat and drove toward Millstone El-ementary. As I was pulling up to the drop-off point, I thought I saw Joel Avigdor helping little Ethan out of the rear passenger's side of their SUV with what looked like his science project. As he turned, I noticed Joel was sporting a little bit of a "science project" himself—a nasty, purplish "mouse" under his left eye.

After the little guy was on his way up the walk, I waved to Joel and asked him what happened to his eye.

He glared back. "Meet me at McD's."

We both pulled in at about the same time and carried steaming coffees to a table with plastic chairs bolted on. He said, "Those Depot guys have been shorting me on the goods for the last couple weeks. I rolled dice about three nights for more Chits but you can roll for two hours and come up with about the same number you started with or maybe a couple more or less. It's not worth it. Then last night I thought I'd try my hand in the ring. You get Chits whether you win or lose, obviously more when you win."

"So that *was* you I saw last night? You're kidding."

"Does this bad boy under my eye look like I'm kidding? These shortages are only gonna get worse, man. Did you hear the news this morning?"

"Uh, I guess not."

"Get a load of this." Joel whipped out his smartphone, launched the browser and got the CNN replay of that morning's address to the nation by President Tawana Ross Stapleton.

"And so, I am asking the American people to join together in making the sacrifices we need to make in order to wipe out terror in our world once and for all. As you know, our pursuit of the terrorists has taken us to yet a new front, this one in the Philippines. Our intelligence—certified by a panel that includes representatives from three well-known conservative and liberal think tanks, the major national news outlets and the Woke People's Liberation Party—confirms the presence of weapons of mass destruction at a bunker forty miles outside Manila. This promises to be the last front we will have to open, and I am confident this operation—which should be over in a matter of days, weeks at the most—will rid the world of the threat of terrorism once and for all."

*The last one.* Right. How exactly do you win a war against "Terror"? President Stapleton had been a very popular talk-show host, then a moderately popular governor of Illinois, and now an even less-popular president. As a talk-show host, she had been considered one of the most influential people in the country, and she rolled into public office on the strength of that. But her star had been on the wane ever since, and she never really regained the power or influence she enjoyed from her old TV bully pulpit. If you asked me, she had burned up most of her energy struggling to get elected and had very little left for the business of actually being president.

Joel had never seemed like the fighting type to me, but now I wondered whether this was some kind of new phase for him.

"So, are you gonna keep up this fighting business?" I asked.

"Depends. There's this guy who heads up the whole thing at the Depot. Name is Roebuck. Kind of a weird guy. All the people there seem to work for him—the Auction people, the geeks in Accounting, the Brokers, the Movers and the muscle in Security."

"Wait a minute. What's all that?"

"How do you think things actually work behind the scenes at the Depot?"

Until last night, all I knew was you drove up to the drive-through window, handed them your Chits and picked up your goods.

He continued, "Can't tell you too much 'cause I had to sign a non-disclosure. But you start spending some time down there, you'll learn. There's money to be made—more Chits to be earned."

"Well, I don't know about the fighting, but I do know I've been doing exactly zilch for the last several months, and Em makes shit money but expects us to live like we did when I was making the big bucks. I could sure use some extra Chits."

"Well, show up at the Depot and maybe you could tell them you want to be a Broker. That's where the real money is."

"What's a Broker do?"

"Connects people and goods. Sounds simple, and it is, but it's hard work. Check it out with the boys down there. Listen,

I gotta go."

Later, as I was walking into our kitchen, I spotted the grocery list on the fridge and took it down.

"*Need wild rice*," had been added to the list of basics already there.

Heck yeah, sure. To go with the lamb chops we also didn't have yet. Simple, right? Just go get some wild rice. Like it was 2025 or something.

Lucky for me it was a short list, because I didn't have time today to screw around with the small stuff. Pulling into the Shop-Rite parking lot, I found a spot pretty quickly. Not too surprising since it was only 9:45 a.m.

I made my way down the produce aisle to the strains of "New World in The Morning" by Roger Whittaker, which brought a strange-yet-comforting Englishman-in-colonial-Kenya kind of sensibility to the shopping experience. Much needed, I'd say. The end result of all the sustainability, buy American and minimum wage legislation was that the shelves were mostly bare, except for those few items that managed to run the gauntlet of prohibitions.

Anyway, after picking up a couple of apples (Vermont), oranges (Florida) and bread (from wheat grown somewhere in the Midwest), I found myself staring at a "dazzling array" of breakfast cereals, trying to hunt down my brand of instant organic oatmeal. Around that time, Dale and Grace came on with "I'm Leaving It All Up To You," a pre-British invasion make-out song from the early 1960s. A pure, rare vestige of a bygone era, this track had been on my vintage QPod from day one, and I loved the twangy, countrified simplicity of it. Which reminded me that whoever was in charge of the playlist here knew there were still plenty of us who were sick of the 100%, wall-to-wall hip-hop that dominated the music scene. I had gone along for a while in high school when rappers plied their skills—like herbs and spices—in a song with a conventional structure to alternate with some real singing. Think Pitbull pairing up with Ne-Yo on "Give Me Everything" and J-Lo ("On The Floor.") Think Gym Class Heroes and Neon Hitch on "Ass Back Home." Hell, listen to Ludacris with Enrique Iglesias on "Tonight I'm Lovin' You." Today's rappers aren't content to share a track, even if it would make it more interesting. Nope. They want all of it, the whole damn three minutes. And I guess enough people like it and there aren't enough of us protesters to hold back the eventual overtaking of the whole of popular music.

I caught a glimpse of Alexis Bonaventura, the mother of another kid in Olivia's class, darting past an endcap heaped with a promotional stack of some new kind of cracker. Alexis of the longish-for-her-age chestnut hair and shockingly-blue eyes, looking good in her athleisure pants. After she passed by and went on to another aisle, there was nobody else around, and I started singing loudly along with the music, staring blankly at the wall of cereals. I guess I must've lapsed into some sort of trance. I pictured myself pulling up broadside with Alexis' shopping cart, gathering her in my arms and rescuing her from her own sinking ship, all the while singing along with Dale and Grace. *"Now, do you want my lo-o-ove. Or are we through?"* And all the while Alexis would be smiling up at me sweetly, and maybe even harmonizing with me a little.

"Excuse me." The voice really was Alexis' and it caught me totally by surprise, rousing me from my reverie.

"Could I get there?" she asked, smiling, but none too sweetly, pointing to the cereal boxes my cart and I were blocking.

"Oh, sure," I stammered.

It didn't seem like she wanted to join in my reverie, to continue our conversation or, for that matter, to even acknowledge that she had any idea who I was, so I pushed on toward the checkout.

It was there that I ran into Hannah Mamberg—or Parvathy, as she recently announced she prefers to be called—one of Emily's yoga buddies.

"Hi, Parvathy," I said, swallowing hard to get it out.

She did not respond with "Namasté," but I got the feeling she wanted to.

"Hi, Raf," she said without much enthusiasm. "How's Emily?"

"Oh, good, sure," said I.

"We're seeing you guys tomorrow, right?"

"Yeah. Looking forward to it," I managed to get out, faking as much energy as I could summon.

I waved "Bye" and sidestepped Hannah—er, Parvathy—and checked out and made my way to the car, loaded up and got back on the road.

I still needed four more lamb chops and the newly requested wild rice, and I had 25 Chits. Not sure how many it would take, but I figured that should do it. Maybe I could apply to be a Broker like Joel said, and they'd give me a signing bonus or something because of my excellent work experience. Never hurts to ask.

Back home for a few hours of scouring the job sites, checking for nibbles on my postings, but finding nada, I was ready to hit the Skyway for the Depot. By this time, it was dusk and I was starting to worry a little about the safety of my journey. I did spot a couple of bogeys about halfway there, off on the side—souped-up near-wrecks, fat, oversized tires, dull finish black undercoat, big shaker scoops dwarfing the old Mustang and Barracuda bodies. But they didn't seem to be going anywhere, the guys just jawing over bulky, tattooed arms resting on open windows.

✕✕✕✕

The Depot was less crowded than the night before as I walked in and back to the action area. I went up to Martín and, after learning that he knew nothing about employment applications, I asked how much for four chops and a pound of wild rice.

"Forty, my freng."

"Geez, last time I checked the website was saying the most recent auction prices were seventeen and four for those two items. What happened?"

"Dos razónes: eenflation and scarceety. Seemple, no?"

I had to think about my options and wandered over to the dice corner. Watching this for about ten minutes and seeing how few Chits were actually changing hands, I checked out the blackjack table. My best calculation was that getting into any of these games, I might wind up with less money than I came with. I guess I looked confused and lost because I felt a hand on my shoulder.

It was Carl. "Hey, Kemo? Back on the action side of things again, huh?"

"Well, my right-now thing is I want my lamb chops and wild rice and the other thing is I'd like to apply to be a Broker."

He smiled broadly and nodded. "We'll see—as to both. Go see Roebuck."

He pointed in the direction of a little table, where sat a swarthy, forty-something guy with a shiny bald dome and a long ponytail. He was wearing a vest with a white sleeveless tee under it. I walked up and he looked me up and down with the bored half-smile of the big or strong man, which surprised me, given the fact that he was not that big and didn't really look that tough.

"Yes?" He said it like a question.

"Who do I see about an application to be a Broker?"

And then looking and pointing, "See Bono over there."

He was pointing at a short, stocky guy with slicked-back hair and wrap-around sunglasses that looked like goggles. I guess he did rather resemble the real Bono a little.

"That guy who sent me—that's Roebuck?" I jerked my thumb in the direction of the vest-and-tee guy.

"It is. What can we do ya for?"

"How do I get in the game?" I asked.

"What game is that, friend?"

"The one where you can earn a whole bunch of Chits. I need lamb chops and wild rice tonight. I wanna be a Broker."

Bono laughed. "I'll bet you do. You and everyone else. You gotta work your way up to that, guy. There's the slow way and the faster way. You want the goods now, I'd choose the faster way. And that starts right over there. There's a match starting in ten minutes. Take a seat and watch."

From where I stood, all I could see were about twelve other thirty-somethings like me milling around, watching a couple of dice games and at least three rock-paper-scissors competitions. (I'm serious.)

Mesmerized by the din and the smoke and the fact that nobody had taken any notice of me, I was shocked back into reality by a clap on the back.

Roebuck appeared suddenly at my side.

"So, I hear you want to play big?" he said. "Come on back."

As I walked along the dark, heavy curtain, I saw that we were headed toward the boxing ring they had set up in back, the same one where I'd seen Joel the night before. Bono and Carl joined us. There was a little makeshift dressing room set off to the side, and they escorted me in. I was given a pair of white trunks and told to strip down.

"Hey, hang on a sec. I'm not here for the fighting. I'd just like to fill out an application to be a Broker."

"That's very sweet, Boo-Boo." Roebuck was leaning into my face and pinching my cheek and cooing as you would to a small child who'd just said something cute. Then, quickly and more urgently, faking a lateral lisp kind of like Sylvester the Cat in the old cartoons, "I believe chsumbody chsed chsumthin' about chsum lamb chopchs. Did I get that right? Yechs?"

He got closer and added quietly and menacingly, "I know why you're here and so do you. Don't think you can bullshit either of us. So, put the fuckin' trunks on, sit down and watch the two goofballs in the ring now. And while you're doin' that you can think about how bad your wife wants her dinner and what you're willing to do to keep peace on the home front."

I didn't have the training, skills or experience to get in any ring with any kind of opponent, but I somehow kept my shit together. Then, barefoot, bare-chested and dressed only in the pair of shorts, I caught a glimpse of myself in the mirror over the sink, and got queasy, immediately wishing my physique was a bit more imposing. I was going to need every edge I could get. Who was it looking back at me with the sense of unreality that creeps over you when you're swept into something you couldn't have anticipated only a few minutes ago? It occurred to me that I looked terrified.

"Knock, knock." It was Carl, wearing his gap-toothed grin, playfully pretending to knock at the soft curtain. "You ready, dude?"

"Sure," I said, not sure exactly what I was saying I was ready for.

Emerging from the dressing room, I saw another guy about my age in blue trunks, looking as scared as I did. Gesturing toward two stools by the ring, Bono said to us, "Sit down and watch. Your bout's next. And don't worry about skills or technique. This is more like Fight Club than a formal boxing match." *Oh, great. Very reassuring. Thank you, Bono.*

Inside the ring, two guys were standing there, looking at each other. No punches or kicks were being thrown. It didn't seem too violent to me. In fact, both guys looked scared, and neither looked like they were much into fighting. That didn't stop the guys crowded around the ring from egging them on. I noticed a lighted board off to the side that showed the odds, which froze when betting stopped at the bell signaling the start of the fight. It struck me as strange that anyone would want to bet on either of two poor guys, clearly non-fighters. But the numbers on the board told a different story. Bono called out quietly, "Come on guys, let's get it on. We've got a full card tonight."

Then Carl walked closer to the ring and said to Gray Trunks, "Hey Snowflake, throw somethin', will ya?"

Nothing happened, and the two guys just continued to stand there, shoulders slumped, jaws slack.

"What exactly is going on here?" The voice was quiet and dignified and belonged to Roebuck, who had just walked up and was looking back and forth between the non-action in the ring and Carl and Bono.

Moving quickly, he reached into what looked like a steamer trunk on the floor and came out with what appeared to be two dog collars. He gave one each to Carl and Bono, who looked down at the collars and then sheepishly at each other.

"Time to get it on, boys," said Roebuck. "String 'em up!"

Carl and Bono entered the ring, each grabbing one of the contestants by the arm and yanking him down to the mat, where the collar was put around his neck and cinched up tight. Then a leash was snapped to a D-ring on each collar, and Carl and Bono stood up, each holding a leash.

"I said get it on!!! Now!" screamed Roebuck.

At this command, Carl and Bono started pushing the two guys at each other, whispering insults at them and tapping their ribs, like they did in those old grainy movies of dog fights. This went on for what seemed like a long two minutes, until tears started welling up in the eyes of Gray Trunks. Neither he nor White seemed to know what to do. While they were standing there, I had a chance to appraise the combatants. Though they had to be comparable in weight to be matched up, they couldn't have been more different in body type. Gray was tall and lanky and clearly had the reach advantage. White Trunks, although shorter, was more powerfully built with muscular arms and thicker legs that could do some damage if he knew what to do with them. Watching them, I couldn't help but compare my own physique to both guys and wonder how I'd stack up against whoever they were going to put up against me. I had the urge to vomit, but somehow held it down.

Suddenly, Gray Trunks lunged forward, launching a half-assed kick at White Trunks, who ducked and countered with a sharp little jab that connected with Gray's right eye, leaving a reddening blotch. Gray let out a yelp and came back with a similarly clumsy kick that caught White on the left side of his head and sent him sprawling. White was back on his feet quickly, but Gray was ready with a snap-kick to White's groin that doubled him over, providing Gray the opportunity to follow with a chop to the left side of his neck.

White was down and obviously hurting. I thought it was over till I saw that Carl was whispering to him and tapping him on the flanks some more. A few moments of this and White was back at Gray, pounding him with a flurry of kicks and punches, till it was obvious we wouldn't see any more action from Gray tonight. All the while, White was crying his eyes out though he seemed to have prevailed.

Finally, Roebuck strode forward, ducked under the ropes and called a halt to the action.

"Good, good. Carl, give them their Chits and get these two escapees from Silver Sneakers out of my sight, puh-lease. Next match!"

Bono dragged me up by the elbow, slapped me on the backside and told me to get in the ring. The other guy seemed to hesitate, but Roebuck wasn't about to wait and said, "Time to get in there, Miss Marple. Time's a wastin'! Hey, hold up." Then, pointing at the guy's glasses, "You need those to see?"

I guess the answer was no, because the guy reluctantly took off his specs and placed them gingerly in Roebuck's already outstretched palm. He stood up and slipped under the ropes.

"Ok, ladies. Time for aerobics class. You know what to do," said Roebuck quietly to us.

Actually, I didn't know what I was supposed to do, but I

knew I didn't want to wait for Carl and Bono to arrive with a reprise of the dog-collar treatment. To his credit, the other guy came at me with a flurry of punches, one of which hit me solidly in the forehead, which had to hurt him more than me, but in truth it did smart a bit. Something told me I had to make a move quickly, and I summoned the little I remembered from my Tae Kwon Do classes, and launched myself furiously at Blue Trunks, landing first a glancing roundhouse kick, then a left jab, a wild right hook, then another awkward round-house kick.

His recovery time was just slow enough for me to unload what resembled a back kick that caught him right in the chest. The air was knocked out of him and he fell back, gasping. I was on top of him, pummeling his head and ears, when I felt myself being pulled off by Roebuck. The whole thing lasted less than maybe thirty seconds. I felt bad for the guy. If he had followed up his first hit, it might have just as easily been me there, lying on my back.

"Not bad for a first-timer. What's your name, Dick?"

"Raf," I managed to say.

"Well, go see Bono and get your Chits. Nice work."

I picked myself up and walked in the direction of the dressing room, put my clothes back on and threw the trunks in a hamper in the corner. Catching another glimpse of myself in the mirror, I wondered whether I actually looked different or just felt that way. I shrugged and headed out of there, stopping to see Bono for thirty Chits. He handed me the little form and one of those short, little eraser-less golf pencils and I somehow managed to scrawl *lamb-chops (4)* and *wild rice (1 cup)* in roughly the right places.

Back in my Honda, I pulled around to the loading dock and handed the Chits to Martín who handed me a package wrapped in butcher paper, along with a small bag of wild rice.

"You're the lamb chops guy, right?" he asked, his smile a

little broader than it was the night before.

"Uh, yeah. Right." I was shaking so badly I could hardly hold them.

# CHAPTER 3

I awoke Friday morning with a massive headache from the shot I had taken to the forehead. I knew better than to look to Emily for consolation, especially since we were hosting the Mambergs for dinner, and I know she starts getting tight and focused in anticipation of anyone entering our living space. I was torn between not wanting to seem like a martyr/wuss on the one hand and expecting some sort of recognition or appreciation for my efforts on the other. But I was kind of surprised she didn't thank me or even seem to notice the knot on my forehead.

I immediately thought of my secret pal, Kayla, with whom I had spent many a clandestine hour, partly for sex and partly because I just like being with her. Going over to her place right now seemed out of the question, since I had so much to do and it would have to be quick, and I knew how much she hated it when I just walked in there with two cups of coffee and a couple of buttered rolls, drank and ate too quickly and then expected her to get all excited about hopping into bed with me.

But it was more than just physical intimacy I was craving. Emily's lack of gratitude for my manly feats had left my ego bruised, and I was in serious need of consolation.

After a few moments' consideration, I headed off in the direction of Kayla's and gave her a call from the car. She would have been well within her rights to tell me to go fuck myself.

I mean, she wasn't the one having the Mambergs for dinner, and my big fighting debut the night before wasn't benefiting her in any way. Just why I expected consolation from Kayla was a mystery in itself.

"Sure," she said. "Come on over. I'd really like to see you." All I needed to hear.

Which is also why Kayla could give lessons to wives, girl-friends and most other women of the world. She knew the magic words—words that would make a man mindlessly risk his marriage, his job, his relationships with his kids and everything else he thought was important to him. The words that wives never seemed to be able to learn or be willing to say. They wouldn't even have to mean them. But Kayla was a member of a tiny secret society, simply by knowing these few words and being able and willing to say them: "I'd really like to see you."

I stopped for the customary coffee and rolls and tooled into the garage under Kayla's building.

Kayla was dressed in a sheath-type thing, and I knew without asking she wasn't wearing anything underneath. I gave her a quick kiss and as we hugged, I got a little lightheaded from her scent. She pushed me to arm's distance to appraise the bruise on my forehead.

"What the hell happened to you?"

I told her about the fight as we sat at her dining room table, sipping our coffee and eating the rolls.

"So, is this something you plan to do again or was it just a one-time thing?"

"Not sure. All I know is that I went in there without a chance in hell of getting lamb chops and, after probably less than a minute in the ring, I walked out of there with what I came for. That's something, isn't it? I wouldn't mind doing it again if I need to."

"I guess so. Seems like a hard way to do it, though. And since when do you have to get your face busted up just so your wife can have what she wants for a dinner party? You don't see me eating lamb chops. I mean how pathetic are you willing to be?"

I felt the blood rush to my temples and my neck flush. "As pathetic as I need to be, I guess. I'd rather get my face bashed than go home to a bunch of bull shit."

"Oh, she gets to give you bullshit when you don't give her what she wants? What about me? What about what I want?"

"Listen, Kayla, you don't get to bust my balls, ok? Somebody else already has that job. You're not my wife or my boss, so just knock it off, ok?"

She turned away and was starting to say something or maybe just pout. I sure had more to say. Instead, we both just sat there. This was not what I had pictured while driving over. Kayla had always been an understanding and supportive friend, willing to get together when our schedules permitted. She was a sales rep traveling all over the world for a chemical company that sold binding agents used by pharma companies in making pills. Five years my senior, she'd been married a couple of times but hadn't had any kids. Never wanted any, she said. She had never voiced any anger or jealousy over my obligations at home. I had grown accustomed to her being happy to see me, to share a meal, to invite me to share her bed. In addition to validating me as an attractive male, the benefits of my relationship with Kayla included stimulating conversation not related to home or work—about movies we'd seen, books we'd read, places we'd been or would like to go. No complaints, no promises, no ultimatums. I sure hoped our thing wasn't changing, but I was starting to worry. She looked about the same as I felt: deflated. It was pretty obvious that no consolation or respite was going to come from today's rendezvous.

Rising and heading for the door, all I could manage was "I'll talk with you soon. Take care." I walked out into the hall and down the stairs and into the garage.

Maybe Kayla's membership in that secret society wasn't so

secure after all.

I got home before Emily that afternoon, and was settling up with Maddie for staying with Olivia.

"Oh wow, those are some awesome roses, Mr. Vella. They were just delivered. Mrs. V's really gonna love them!"

I sure hoped so. I guess I was thinking she'd see them as a sort of peace offering. Wallet still in hand, I walked silently past Maddie into the dining room where there were a dozen red roses in a vase with some water in the center of the table. I picked up the card and noticed the envelope was still sealed.

"I called Mrs. Vella right away when they arrived, and she said put 'em in water and she'd be right home."

"Uh, yeah. Good. Thanks, Maddie. So, it's twenty-two for today, right?"

"Oh, I'm good with twenty. But thanks."

I handed her the bill plus two and walked her to the door and said good-bye.

Olivia was at the kitchen table doing her homework.

"Hi, Dad. Ooh, what the heck happened to your face?"

"Carelessness, essentially. I'll cut to the moral of the story: Don't try to stick your head out the car window with the glass still in it."

She frowned, cutting her eyes to the side and backed up her own little head. I couldn't tell whether it was in sympathetic reenactment of my little story or because she had quickly seen through the flimsy lie. Neither of us said anything for an awkward moment. Then, quickly gathering up her schoolwork, "The roses are really beautiful. Mom's gonna love 'em."

"Hope so."

"Oh, and Mrs. Wallace is coming to pick me up in a few minutes. I'm doing a sleepover with Morgan tonight since you guys are having company for dinner."

Happy to have survived the inquiry, I brightened up a little. "Oh, sure. Great. Anything I can do to help you?"

She was already out of the kitchen and called out on her

way upstairs, "No, thanks. I'm good."

She was barely gone when Emily's car roared into the driveway. She bounded up the front steps, almost knocking me over as she came in the front door.

"Maddie said some flowers came for me."

I nodded in the direction of the dining room and she sprinted to the table, grabbed the envelope, ripped it open and stared at the message.

Her expression broke in slow motion: a frown, mouth tightening, color rising to her cheeks, like in a movie where someone had turned off the sound. We stood there together in a freeze-frame, but clearly in different worlds. She was clearly surprised, and not in a good way. I could feel a lump forming in my throat.

She tossed the card and the hastily ripped envelope on the table and walked slowly to the foot of the stairs, removing her coat as she went.

And said in a soft, slow, deflated voice, "We've got a lot to do before the Mambergs get here."

"Hey, don't I get a thanks? Anything?"

She just stared at me for three beats, said "Sure. Thanks," then looked away and walked upstairs. I heard the bedroom door close.

Fighting to keep it together until the rush of adrenaline subsided, my brain was on fire, a lump forming in my throat. What was that shit about?

I had semi-calmed down when she emerged about fifteen minutes later announcing it was time to start the slicing and dicing prep work for the Mambergs' dinner. I got out two green peppers, a head of garlic, and a Vidalia onion we had purchased the day before. Retrieving my best kitchen knife from the rack and giving it a few strokes on the steel, I was ready to begin.

"Make sure you get all the seeds out of the peppers." Emily's voice seemed to come from far away.

We sautéed and mixed and stirred without saying much, and it wasn't long before the doorbell rang and there were the Mambergs, Mitch and Parvathy. They were dressed in their usual, Parvathy with an authentic sari and Mitch rocking his perpetually sheepish half-grin, one eye half-closed in that look of an old rabbi who has just said something he considered wise and ironic, though nothing Mitch ever said could be described that way.

Together they said, "What happened to your face?"

"I ran into a doorknob," said I with as much deadpan as I could muster. They shrugged and looked at each other, apparently satisfied to drop the subject temporarily.

I poured wine for everyone, a pinot noir we'd saved for the occasion. Emily had some appetizers ready—a hard, sharp cheese, some spicy salami and hummus with plain crackers.

As soon as we sat down, Emily and Parvathy started talking about their newest project, which was to start a book club devoted to sustainability issues. Mitch turned his attention to the lamb chops and I just zoned out for a while.

Then Parvathy piped up. "Mmmm. Lamb chops. We've been about 75% vegan for the last few months, but I have to admit, these are delicious for a treat. You guys are really lucky Emily has that great job so you can still get what you want even after Raf got downsized."

I bit down hard on my lower lip, lowered my head slightly and glanced over at Emily, who just smiled, taking in the misdirected compliment, basking in the admiration from her yoga buddy.

"Oh, it's no big deal, really. We're not trying to go vegan or vegetarian or anything, and lamb chops are delicious once in a while."

After dinner, we all pitched in to clear the table, rinse the dishes and put them in the dishwasher. I did the pots and pans, Emily readied the dessert, which was berries and pound cake with almond cream, and Mitch and Parvathy sat at the counter making small talk with us.

It wasn't until Mitch and I went into the family room that he seized the opportunity to ask me about the "third eye" on my forehead, the women getting into their book club talk in the kitchen.

"Seriously, how'd you get the bruise on your forehead?"

"Fighting at the Depot."

"What are you talking about? What Depot? You mean that drive-through place where you get specialty items? You went *inside* there? What for? Why were you fighting? Who were you fighting with?"

I gave him the short version, and his reaction seemed a combination of confusion and admiration.

"I never pictured you as an MMA fighter."

"Well, I'm not, really. I mean I'm just fighting for food. There's a lot going on in there besides fighting. They've got dice games and cards and, for guys in a hurry, you can even do rock-paper-scissors for a few quick Chits. You could do it too, if you wanted to."

That got a laugh and a disbelieving head shake from Mitch. "I don't, believe me. And who goes inside the Depot? Doesn't everyone just drive through or call the guy and have him deliver what they need?"

"Not for lamb chops, they don't. When was the last time you tried to get any good cuts of meat?"

"Not in a while. Not since Parvathy decided we were going vegan, at least at home. Would you consider doing it again?"

"Sure, if it meant I could get something we wanted. But it seems like it's kind of a rite of passage to becoming a Broker, which is what I really want."

I told him about the guys working at the Depot and Roebuck, the honcho who seemed to run the fighting down there.

While Mitch was not up-to-date on the meat-and-potatoes realities of getting the food we want, he was a certified brainiac, a PhD from University of Chicago-type, Professor of

Geopolitical Studies at Wauquinack State University. He had also established a nice niche as a go-to guy when one of the struggling-on-life-support cable outlets wanted an expert opinion they could afford on some new development in the effects of global realities on our economic challenges.

He nodded, as if to recognize my news as a logical extension of the big picture he already knew. "No surprise. Been building for some time now. You know, this business of 2025 being a watershed year. That's baloney. Nothing really big actually happened that year, unless you count the fact that it was the end of a long, slow wake-up to what had been building for some time: Big infrastructure bill passed several years ago appropriating trillions with no friggin' thought to how to spend it, creating a mad Gold Rush among states, cities and towns, and private profiteers finding new ways to line their own pockets with no benefit to the places it was intended to help. Every year a new mini-war on a new front, resources distracted from the business of running the country. The race for cheap labor for decades had already annihilated any serious manufacturing domestically. And then the flood of new laws and regulations making it impossible to sell goods made offshore using labor paid less than U.S. minimum wage. You bet you're gonna get gray markets, black markets cropping up. Time to re-read *The Decline and Fall of the Roman Empire* if you ask me."

While Mitch and I were conversing, I could barely make out Emily and Parvathy in the next room, talking in hushed tones.

*"And you won't believe...this morning's class...that Nicole-something...skimpy little crop-tops and tight little booty-shorts to class?"* Parvathy was actually whispering.

*"Yeah,"* answered Emily, eager to hear the rest.

*"Well...about to get started, she walks up to Tao and asks, 'Are there any positions you shouldn't go into when you're having your period?'"*

35

*"...really asked him that?"*

*"No shit."*

*"And what did he say?"*

*"He treated it straight-up and said, '...do anything we do, except try not to get into positions where the lower half of your body is higher than the top half.'"*

*"Can you believe that bitch? ...do anything to get him to focus on her 'lower half!'"*

*"Yeah...definitely moving in for the kill."*

I couldn't make out what Emily said because she lowered her volume too, but it was disturbing to note that she had also upped the intensity of her voice at the same time.

While trying to talk with Mitch about what was going on at the Depot, the girl-talk in the next room and Emily's part in it gave me a strange feeling starting at the base of my spine.

Soon it was time for coffee and dessert. We used the Nespresso machine to crank out four perfect cups of "rocket fuel"—decaf at this time of day—and spooned a few thawed blueberries onto slices of pound cake and topped it with almond cream.

There was not much talking during dessert, and the evening wound up soon after. We exchanged good-byes and air kisses and hugs at the door, and the Mambergs were on their way.

"What the fuck, Emily?! Seriously? You and I both know how we got the lamb chops! Jeez, the knot on my forehead's still glowing like a fucking taillight. What would it have cost you to say something?"

"Listen, Raf, I never told you to go get your head kicked in to get lamb chops. That was all you. Don't you dare put that on me!"

We had worked our way into our bedroom. I went to my closet and hung up my slacks. As Emily removed her own, I was surprised to see that instead of her usual "granny panties" she was wearing a black thong. Some unseen force took over my vocal cords:

"I was reading just the other day that ob-gyns are recommending that women shouldn't wear those. Apparently as you walk and move, it flosses back and forth, and can actually transfer bacteria from back there to up there."

Emily seemed surprised as she looked down at what she was wearing, like she was seeing it for the first time. But she recovered quickly. "Well, thank you, Dr. Know-It-All. Is that all you have to say? Here I go to the trouble of trying to give you a little change of scenery, and this is your response? Fuck you, Raf! Fuck you and your half-assed, schoolyard boy-fight you seem to want me to be all impressed about!"

"Oh, I see. I get the lamb chops and wild rice you wanted and now that the dinner's over, I'm dismissed, right?

"Don't start with me, Raf. And what was that stunt with the roses supposed to be about? How much did they set us back?"

"You seemed pretty enthusiastic about the idea when you were charging in the front door. You read the card and, all of a sudden, you're like there's been a death in the family? What the fuck, Em. Seriously? Who did you think they were from—Mr. Can't-Pronounce-His-Own-Name-Yoga-Man?"

"You're hallucinating, Raf. And plus, you're jealous. You see me getting some things going in my own life that don't involve you, and right away you assume there's some other man. I've told you, my relationship with Tao is strictly business. I'm going to need your cooperation, so I hope you can accept it and hold up your end here at home."

"I'd say getting into the ring for lamb chops and rice is pretty supportive, wouldn't you?"

"You want this, Raf? Now? Ok. I marry a law student who then fucking drops out after one semester, gets a job at a damn insurance company, gets fired from that, goes into a tailspin depression, basically ignores me for months and now wants to get lovey-dovey with me? How's that supposed to land with me?"

"Oh, you're the victim, huh? I was the man of your dreams when you pictured me making the big bucks, but then…what, exactly?"

"You don't get it, Raf. I don't know why I should expect you to. Both your parents went to college. Your dad has always worked his ass off, and still does at a time in his life when a lot of men his age have hung it up. You always had everything you needed growing up.

"That's not my story. My parents worked as little as necessary to get by, and not one bit more. My dad at the station, turning down promotion after promotion. ('No way they're gonna hang all that bullshit responsibility on me. They can tell my body what to do but nobody's gonna tell me what to think about. Clock strikes four and I'm outa there.') And Mom worked to try to make up the gap between what he brought home and what we needed. I think you know about that.

"But I don't think you know what the day-to-day was like for my sister and me. Like the time we were sitting there at the table after finishing dinner—such as it was. My sister and me and Mom. Mom had made her vegetable soup. We always called it 'stone soup,' you know, like the fable. We never knew what was going to be in it. This and that. Leftovers, some odds and ends from the produce bin at the store. Mom would always get a little piece of what she called 'starter meat' from the butcher. He knew our situation and always was able to come up with trimmings and whatnot she could use in the bottom of the pot with the onions. I have to give it to her. It was pretty tasty, but it wasn't a real meal.

"Anyway, that night while we were still sitting there, wishing we had some ice cream or pound cake or something, and in walks my father holding this giant bowling trophy and wearing a shit-eating grin like he'd won the Nobel Peace Prize or something.

"Best score outa all of 'em! Practice makes perfect!" he crowed. My mother did a little-girl clap like she always did to celebrate something. My sister and I just sat there. That's his news? You wanna know what my news was? That was the day we got our class pictures—the individual ones. Everyone was trading them and telling each other how cool they looked. Know what they said about mine? 'Emily's setting a new trend in hairstyles: The Bowl Cut.' That was my mom's half-assed attempt to cut my hair so it would look good for picture day. Yeah, right. 'Cause we couldn't afford a stylist or even a barber shop. I still feel the burn in my chest from that day.

"I swore to myself that I'd marry a man who had ambition—who'd get up every day and go out and kick ass and bring home lots of money. That's who I thought you were, Raf.

"So, you wanna know about disappointment? Yeah, I'm disappointed. You're goddamn right, I am!"

I instinctively reached for her— to hold her, comfort her. But she pushed me away, her face contorted in terrible pain, tears rolling down her cheeks. She grabbed the blanket off the foot of the bed and threw it, along with one of my pillows, in the direction of the door. I took that as a signal that our conversation and this part of the evening had reached its conclusion.

Bedding down on the couch in the study, flicking on the TV and finding the UFC channel, I watched the first two rounds of a welterweight bout and dozed off, waking up just as they were declaring the winner of the next match.

I tried to get back to sleep but instead my mind shifted to a replay of our early times together.

We met when we found ourselves sitting at the same table at a wedding reception for some mutual friends. She was about to graduate from nursing school at a hospital near the university where I was an undergrad. She was wearing a shimmery silver-on-white dress and seemed interested. It didn't occur to me that her interest may have been the combination of her sensing it was time for her to find someone and that I had told her that I had been accepted at law school.

We were married soon after we both graduated. She got a job at a doctor's office near where I was enrolled in law school and we took an apartment nearby. Things got off to a rocky start. She didn't really understand why I had to study so much and had little time for decorating our place, food shopping and cooking and cleaning and fun things.

And it didn't help that I dropped out after one semester. She had married a lawyer-in-training and ended up with a drop-out. On more than one occasion since those days she has accused me of "false advertising." Maybe she was right.

# CHAPTER 4

The early light in the family room woke me from a fitful sleep. Olivia was staying the night with Morgan Wallace, so I was free of having to explain why I was sleeping on the couch. I didn't hear any sounds coming from the kitchen or from behind the closed bedroom door, so I assumed Em was still asleep. A hasty exit would give us some much-needed distance, and I didn't want to wake her with the sound of the Nespresso machine. I grabbed my laptop and some exercise clothes out of the dryer, put on my running shoes and then headed out the basement door. I figured I'd start with a cup at Starbucks while checking out the Depot website to see the kinds of items people were selling and seeking, and then hit the gym.

I left a note with my plans and saying I'd pick up Olivia, if necessary.

By the time I got home it was almost noon. Olivia was already at the kitchen table doing her homework, and I could hear Emily in the study tapping on her laptop. If there had been a drone buzzing above our house with a camera that could look through the roof, it would have recorded the three of us going through our Saturday, passing each other and exchanging a word or two from time to time, but moving around in separate orbits, seldom connecting in any way. I was beginning to think the lump in my throat was some kind of health concern that might require a medical intervention.

At five o'clock, it was time to talk about dinner.

"Who else is thinking linguini with white clam sauce?" It came out with counterfeit heartiness, like I'd borrowed the voice of a TV dad, and the truth was I wasn't sure they'd have clams. Might have to settle for aglio e olio—not bad in a pinch. "What about Armando's tonight? They don't take reservations, but if we get going, we probably won't have to wait."

I guess it worked because Em and Olivia managed to pull themselves from whatever they were doing and were soon shuffling toward the door.

The waitress handed us our menus and the first thing I noticed was that this new version already had a few line-throughs. Armando's excellent beef braciole and veal Milanese were by this time a distant memory of menus of days gone by. But eggplant parm and spaghetti primavera were still there; Em had the primavera and Olivia and I got the eggplant.

I guess you'd call our table conversation a poor imitation of family togetherness, Olivia and I breaking long periods of silence with little tidbits of information about the week and questions that got one-word answers or were just left hanging. Emily mostly looked down, picking at her dinner without showing much interest. My mind darted between just trying to get through the meal and sheer panic at imagined potential turns of events in our family situation. For some periods of several seconds, I actually stopped breathing.

When we got home, we retreated to our separate corners of the house, Olivia to her room, Em to the bedroom and me to my new place of exile, stretched out on the couch in the study. I started watching a movie about what began as a routine trip to the international space station but turned nasty. I dozed off somewhere after the second guy bit the dust, and woke up around 3 a.m., fully clothed, lights blazing and another movie called *Nobody* was playing too loudly—released in 2021 but still but packing a punch. A middle-aged husband and father, stalled out in the drudgery and tedium of a dead-end job, fails to defend his family against some home intruders. But then he redeems himself, going shit-wild-crazy on a revenge trip. Message from the cosmos.

I went to the bathroom, brushed my teeth, grabbed a blanket and returned to my post and, after struggling for a good position, finally fell into an unsatisfying sleep.

✕✕✕✕

Em was up first, drinking coffee at the kitchen counter while I was coming to life on the couch in the study. She barely looked up as I folded the blanket and groggily made my way to our bedroom suite. When I emerged, showered and dressed, she was gone. Any hope of a return to normalcy today was put on hold when I read her note: *Headed out to meet Parvathy at the Arboretum. You and O are on your own.*

And that's pretty much how it went. Olivia always had plenty to do on Sundays with a soccer game, homework and communicating with friends. We ordered in for Chinese food and had a quiet day to ourselves. I had a hankering for beef with broccoli and Olivia wanted pork lo mein, but not surprisingly both had vanished from the online menu, so we split a double order of vegetable lo mein and some sesame noodles.

Em finally came home and we exchanged greetings, which I took as a sign of a thaw, though not much more was said as she quickly made her way to the bedroom for the rest of the night, which I spent in my workroom, scrunched up on the love seat.

✕✕✕✕

On Monday, I got some news I interpreted as a sign that things were looking up on the work front. My old boss, John Flanagan, left a message that there might be some consulting for me at Omega Financial. Maybe he wasn't such an asshat after all. I was to come right in and talk about it at a meeting with John and a few others.

In the couple of years since I had left, Omega had been bought by a new consortium called Living Water World Enterprises. I had seen the article quoting Living Water's top guy saying Omega was running very well as it was, and that no organizational changes were anticipated.

I had been thinking about trying to get some work at the Depot, but I was naturally receptive to anything that might put some quick money in the family coffers. I got out my blue suit (a holdover from the old days), and compared the lapels with a picture on the site of a new men's clothing catalog. It could still work.

The first thing I noticed when I got out of the AutoZip car that whisked me there was that there was a new version of the big brass Omega logo on the side of the headquarters building, this one a bit different from the last. This wasn't too surprising in itself since I'd seen the logo change a few times in various harebrained "re-branding initiatives." But while in previous versions, the initial Greek omega letter was always straight up and blocky, in this new one it was thinner and kind of leaning to the right. And inside the "O," almost up against the bottom right, was a tiny little cross, also tilted. Hmm.

A young woman with cotton-candy hair at the front desk greeted me with a smile. She was flanked on each side by a large gentleman wearing a black suit, white shirt and skinny black tie, who did not seem as eager to please and stared at me coldly.

"Yes, John Flanagan, please."

"Sure. Whom shall I say is here?"

I gave my name and she said, "One moment, please."

She punched in a few numbers on her console and spoke quietly into the tiny mouthpiece of her headset.

"LeMichael will escort you up now, Mr. Vella," she said, dealing me a carbon copy of the smile she had flashed just moments before.

And so LeMichael—the big guy to her right—motioned me toward the first elevator, and up we went to the 23rd floor. LeMichael's huge, heavily cologned presence so filled the space that sharing the elevator with him, I felt like a stowaway in a space capsule made just for him as we rocketed skyward. It slowed and stopped, and we got out and walked up to another desk, where we were greeted by another young woman, this one with close-cropped blonde hair and nice features. It was clear she was expecting us.

"Mr. Flanagan will be with you in a moment. Please have a seat. You're just in time for our daily Praise and Worship."

She motioned me to a bank of tub chairs facing a Hollywood Squares-style array of nine mounted monitors where different channels of world events, sports and financial news silently competed for our attention.

As I sat there waiting, all of a sudden, the screens flickered and the different images were replaced by a single large image of a smiling young man wearing a white shirt and shiny black vest, three women and an eight-piece band.

At a signal from Vest-Man, the band kicked into gear with an almost '70s-style Supah-fly beat, trumpets and saxes blaring, guitar chick-a-walking. After a brief intro, the vested guy started singing "Have a blessed day, brother, have a blessed day!" After eight bars of this, the women took over with "Have a blessed day, sister, have a blessed day!" People in the waiting area were watching, and some even mouthed the words. Just as I thought I might have to listen to them go through verses for every member of the family, the singing stopped, the band quieted down and Vest-Man spoke animatedly over the music: "Yes, Living Water wants each and every one of you to have a blessed day. And remember, the work we all do here is in His Holy Name. Hallelujah!"

After one more run-through of the chorus, the band wrapped it up, a huge Omega logo (that tilted O with the little cross in the corner) filled all nine screens, and then they were done.

Moments later the screens went back to showing the various channels of news, sports and financials.

The company may not have been "broken" and maybe they didn't call these actual "fixes" but there sure had been some changes.

Moments later the short-cropped blonde reappeared, smiled and nodded, and then ushered me into a large conference room, and LeMichael took his leave, presumably to re-enter his rocket ship and escort some other visitor to some other meeting elsewhere in this newly spiritualized solar system.

A young woman entered the room wearing an ass-tight skirt and an even tighter smile. The skirt and heavy eye make-up seemed inappropriate to the new faith-based orientation of the company, but she carried it off somehow.

"Barb DeMinter," she said, offering her hand. I took it and returned her perfunctory business glance with one of my own—the best I could come up with on such short notice—picking up on her icy blue eyes and frosty blonde blunt-cut hair.

"I'm John's chief of staff. He'll be along any minute."

I settled in for a bit of a wait but before I got too comfortable, John bounded into the room. I hardly recognized him with his sprayed hair and shiny suit, a five-button number of the type you used to see the on the former-athlete panelists on ESPN years ago. Except while theirs were usually baby-shit brown, John's was corporate navy blue.

"Well, hey there, Raf! Damn, it's good to see you. Glad you could make it." He showed drug-store-whitened teeth.

"Sure, happy to be here. Hope I can be of some help to you guys."

"Well, I'm pretty darned sure you can, Raf. Otherwise, why would I have called you, right? Heh, heh. Come on into the conference room. There are some people you need to meet."

With a little back pressure from John, I found my way to the long table where others were already seated. There were two thirty-something guys in golf shirts and Dockers, a twenty-five-ish woman with a frizzed-out perm, a young and trim woman named Portia, and then the aforementioned Barb came in last, closing the door behind her.

"Let's get started," John said, as Barb tapped on her tablet and the title page of a slide presentation filled the big monitor at one end of the room.

"I think you all know Raf from his time here, and we're happy to have him back today to help us with our little project. Let's go around with some introductions."

The guys were from Systems and Operations, the frizzed-out twenty-something was from Actuarial and Portia was from Marketing.

We all sat in these contoured frame-and-wire chairs with nice armrests. I thought I saw a narrow line of embedded little LEDs flash once on the shiny black armrest under my right forearm.

"Ok, everyone. Let's begin." John turned and said, "Would you lead us in the invocation, Portia?"

"Let us bow our heads in prayer," she began. "We thank you, O Heavenly Father, for this opportunity to be in your service..." She said a few more words and all joined in a murmured "Amen."

Mmm. First time I'd seen a business meeting start with an invocation, but hey, whatever. I was already on notice that some kind of New Day had dawned.

"Barb, can you give us a little summary and background so we all understand what we're doing?"

"Sure, John. As most of you know, we've been trying to break in with the big broker dealers. The key is going to be getting some senior industry thought-leaders like this guy Norm Brancati to make a deal with us."

"We don't need Brancati," interrupted one of the young guys. "He's just a tired old man, with no influence in his own company. He may have held some sway at one time, but now he's just an empty suit."

"Yeah, and that suit seems to be getting emptier all the time," added the other youngster. "I swear the guy is shrinking. He's physically smaller every time I see him. And he's no longer the thought-leader he used to be. I think he just comes in at eleven to look at his mail, goes to lunch and goes home. Nobody cares about what he says."

With that, the little rows of lights on the armrests of their chairs lit up, and the two guys seemed to do a little impromptu dance as their legs and arms jerked wildly, and then just as quickly, they flopped back to their previous sitting positions.

"Whoa! What the...?" said the Operations guy. Both young men seemed momentarily disoriented, though apparently not seriously injured.

John smiled. "Just testing to make sure the systems work. Please continue, Barb." Nobody seemed at all surprised. Me? I was weirded out.

"Thanks. Yes, anyway, he wants us to come to a meeting at his place to discuss our proposal."

"Anyone have any thoughts on that?" asked John.

Blank stares all around. Then Portia said, "I think it would be a gesture of goodwill to go see him. If we like the guy and think he can help us, we'd be connecting with a true statesman of our industry and also send a signal to the young bucks under him who'd like to see him gone that he's still viable. It would help keep that line of influence open to us."

The lights on Portia's armrests flashed—this time it was the green ones—and I thought I saw her ass twitch a little in her seat and Portia got a big smile on her face. This was a different—and apparently much happier—type of chair treatment than the guys got just a few moments ago.

A deep voice from the ceiling speakers said:

*"Be humble...Don't look out only for your own interests, but take an interest in others too. Philippians 2:3–4."*

Nobody seemed surprised or even looked skyward but me. In my work experience, I had certainly seen examples of positive and negative feedback, but this was some new technique

I wasn't familiar with. I had to admit, I was starting to worry about what type of treatment I'd get when it was my turn to weigh in or answer a question, and I glanced apprehensively at the light panel on my own chair.

"What do we know about this Brancati?" asked John. "Is he a 'Kingdom Guy?'"

"I don't see any indication of that, John," said the Friz. "He always seems to be looking out for his own interests."

"Fellas?" said John to the two recently jolted twenty-some-things.

"Nope. The guy's got one foot out of the company," said the Ops guy.

"Right," echoed Systems.

"So, if I understand, you are saying we should not go meet him?"

Dead silence.

"Barb, what about you?" asked John.

I think I saw Barb gulp, but she recovered quickly. The young guys had said no, but she had seen Portia get the Good Vibrations treatment for her little "yes" pitch.

"John, I think you should go!" Barb blurted out. "Regardless of whether or not *he's* a Kingdom guy, *you* are definitely a Kingdom guy, and whether or not the time is right, it's up to you to make the first overture."

Now it was Barb's armrests that lit up, and it was her ass that seemed to get the warm-up treatment: She smiled. The authoritative man's voice from the ceiling speakers intoned:

*"Be prepared, whether the time is favorable or not. 2 Timothy 4:2."*

"That does it," said John. "Make the arrangements, Barb!" He was clearly pleased with the result, and with Barb for having the "right answer."

I took note of the fact that Barb's opinion had been the thing that tipped the scales in favor of concluding that this Norm Brancati may or may not turn out to be a "Kingdom

Guy," but that John should go make a presentation regardless.

Turning to me, John said, "Raf, I'll ask you to work with Barb and Brancati's people to put together an agenda. I'd like you to go with me. I think your experience with how life insurance is sold by Financial Advisors will be critical to our getting this done. So, you get with Barb and have a draft of something to me by end of business tomorrow. Fair enough?"

"Sure," I replied, not so sure at all, but glad to have the work.

Everyone got up to leave, but John motioned for me to remain seated. After everyone else had gone, he said, "Well, what did you think of the meeting?"

"Are these chairs actually rigged to give a shock for a 'wrong' answer and a pleasant vibration for a 'correct' one, the authority being the Bible?"

He laughed heartily. "What was your first clue?" And then he went on. "Raf, these Living Water people we report to now have it figured out. When we try to solve problems by ourselves, we just screw it up. We're always focused on the wrong things, which are our own needs and fears. God is the ultimate problem-solver. When we do it His way, our attention is turned gently and naturally to focus on the solution. And there's no problem too big or too small to let God solve it. That's what we want our people to do here. And when they do it the wrong way, we give 'em a little unpleasant jolt. Not enough to hurt 'em, mind you, but enough to let them know they've strayed from the path. And, when they do it the right way—God's way—we give 'em a little pleasurable vibration and read 'em just what God said about that very thing, so it's reinforced."

It all made perfect sense, the way he explained it. And the drift toward religion in business had started a long time ago: the national chicken sandwich chain that proudly closed on Sundays; the hobby stores company whose medical plan didn't cover abortions; the baker who refused on religious grounds to bake a cake for a same-gender wedding; the tax resolution company that claimed to do business according to "Christian principles"; the HVAC contractor giving notice of its spiritual orientation with a dove in its logo; the car dealership that swapped out the owner's manuals for Bibles in the glove boxes of every car sold; the manufacturing plant that ran mandatory-attendance prayer meetings every Friday morning. It seemed a natural next step to the kind of things I was seeing at Omega.

"Well, reluctant as I am to switch from the divine to the mundane, I guess we should talk about my compensation."

"Right. Sure. I guess I was thinking we'd pay you on an hourly basis comparable to what your salary was at the time you left."

"Yeah, but don't forget my base salary was only about half my total compensation for the year when you factor in my bonus and participation in the long-term incentive plan."

"How about if we work in a bonus of say 25% of the total upon satisfactory completion of the work? How does that sound?"

"That sounds about right."

"Good, good! Let's start with this Brancati deal and go from there. Gotta get to my next thing. I'll expect to see something from you and Barb, right?"

"Ok. Sure. Thanks for the opportunity, John."

He rose from the table and shook my hand, gently leading me out the door and to the bank of elevators. He raised his hand to wave good-bye, but I swear it looked more like he was bestowing some sort of blessing upon me.

As if by magic, I sensed the approach of a hulking presence and LeMichael appeared at my side, smiling as he pressed the down button for the elevator. The door opened and he held it with one massive forearm, while with the other he ushered me in.

The door opened again at the street level and he motioned

me out into the lobby and then into the street with a wave and a smile.

My mind raced as I got into the AutoZip car for the ride home. I spoke the address and off I went. As the car wound through the light mid-morning traffic, I sat back and let my mind review the weird events of the last hour or so.

The way this thing was unfolding, John was thinking the contribution I could make would be similar to the work I did for him when I reported to him. Whenever he had a big, important meeting with a prospective business joint-venturer, he'd always ask me to put together the agenda. And here he was, looking to me to do the same thing again. Only this time, I'd be working with this Barb DeMinter. If he had her, why did he need me? And I had seen enough of her type so many times over so many years, I wondered why I'd want to get tangled up with her bullshit after finally disengaging from that stuff.

Because I needed the money, that was why. We had one of those balloon mortgages where the monthly payments seemed to go up every year. Olivia's school wasn't cheap, and I had to save for the enormous college bills that would start to appear before I knew it.

Like many of her friends, Emily had an executive-type job with a drug company with a fancy title and big office, but she made lousy money and had virtually no real responsibilities.

That was fairly typical, since the cynical corporate response to pressures to promote women and minorities into high-level positions had the paradoxical effect of turning those jobs into mere figurehead positions.

My thoughts about my own future didn't include anything in the corporate world right now. I was intrigued with the idea of becoming a Broker down at the Depot. I wasn't going to play cards or roll dice and, while I guessed I could go back in the ring, I felt my experience and background was better suited to some kind of sales transaction. But in the meantime, if I could do something at Omega to make a little money until I could get up and running with the Brokering, that would be all to the good, right?

# CHAPTER 5

"The thing you've gotta remember is that anything made in China, Viet Nam, Thailand, India or Sri Lanka or any of those countries where they pay their labor less than U.S. minimum wage is considered *Slave goods* and it's illegal to buy 'em or sell 'em. That's where we come in."

I was back at the Depot Saturday morning, and Carl was explaining to me the inside story of the Real Deal Economy (RDE), as it's informally called.

"See, what happened was the Progressive party had this bill they kept trying to bring up for a vote, and the Conservatives kept blocking it. The Progs had become so desperate they reluctantly agreed in a marathon session to add this tiny pledge the Neocons put up at the last minute as a 'poison pill,' thinking nobody'd go for it. Wait, here it is—I keep this card right here to show our guys. It says: 'By casting my vote in the affirmative, I hereby certify that I will purchase for my own use and that of my family ONLY those goods and services produced by workers earning U.S. union or comparable wages, no matter where in the world they are produced.'

"Most of the senators and reps who voted for this thing were run out of office when it came to light they were secretly buying Slave goods for their own use, usually provided by a tiny little rogue operation which just happened to be run by Roebuck and yours truly. Virtually everyone in Congress now is staunchly anti-Slave, in public at least. So, it was a short step to enact another law that made the prohibition applicable to every citizen."

He leaned back and laced his hands behind his head and smiled. "And that was the thing that helped us scale up our enterprise here. We're basically modern-day moonshiners-gone-corporate."

He gave me another of his jack-o'-lantern grins as he fired up a Marlboro red. (I hadn't seen a pack of those in a while.)

"So, you wanna fight again for more Chits?"

Actually, I badly needed the Chits for Olivia's birthday present, which was to be a sequined bomber jacket. I had arrived at the Depot with the full expectation of having to fight for the Chits to get it, but I wasn't looking forward to getting into the ring again.

"I was thinking of becoming a Broker," I said with as much confidence as I could muster.

Carl looked up at me with a sideways smile. "Ya know, a smart guy like you has options. But you gotta work your way up to that shit."

"Like how?"

"Like by becoming a Mover first, for instance."

"How's that different from a Broker?"

"The Broker *finds* things and people who want 'em and connects the dots. That's a real good job, but the goods have to get from Point A to Point B and the money has to be collected. That's where the rubber meets the road, and that's where the Mover comes in. We give him an order for, say, a dozen steaks or a half-dozen beach umbrellas and he gets 'em. We've got a Buyer who's agreed to pay $2,500. And the Broker's identified a Seller willing to take $1,500. You go see him and bring us back the goods for $1,500 and you've just earned Chits worth 10% of the $1,000 difference, or $100. 'Course, out of that you pay the Security guy."

"Security guy? What's he do?"

Carl chuckled on that one. "Well, uh, the Seller you get the umbrellas from might not be the nicest guy you ever met, and he might try to hold you up. Your Security is what's gonna let you make the deal, and keep all your body parts intact."

"Would I get to have Security on my first run?"

"Hell, yeah. Wouldn't want my boy here gettin' all fucked up on his maiden voyage." He reached over and tousled my hair.

"Ok. Let me try one."

"Gotta get the go-ahead from Roebuck. Let's see if he's in."

Carl got up from his chair, gave me the universal "wait-one" finger in the air and left the room. He was back in about ninety seconds and motioned me to follow him down the hall to Roebuck's office, where he sat behind a desk, wearing the same vest over white tee, bald dome reflecting the overhead LEDs, frowning at some spreadsheets on his desk.

Without looking up, he motioned me to a chair and Carl left and closed the door behind him.

He got right to it. "You wanna be a Broker, huh? Well, so does my granny. But that doesn't make her qualified to be on my team of mo-fos that do the job every day. What kinda experience you got?"

"Well, I've bought and sold things. How different can it be?"

He winced. "World of difference. This is a tough environment, getting people to part with things for a price that's lower than they think they're worth."

"Doesn't sound that special to me. It's called commerce."

And so, we drifted into a kind of tennis match: me—fueled by my fervent desire to avoid going back in the ring—serving up reasons why he ought to give me some work, and him slamming back excuses for why he shouldn't. It went on like this for a few volleys, neither of us able to move the other away from the spots where we started.

Finally, things slowed down and we just stared at each

other for a full ten seconds. Roebuck leaned back and smiled.

"Listen, I get dickweeds in here every day telling me why I oughta take a chance on bringing them on board. As far as I can see, you're just another beggar lookin' for a job."

What went through my mind at this particular moment was this: He might be able to intimidate homeboys like me on unfamiliar turf like a fight ring, but buying and selling shit was my briar patch. I figured I might as well go for broke.

"A *job*? Did I just hear you say the word *job*? Is that music from the 1980s I hear—'Eye of The Tiger?' Michael Jackson, maybe? Next thing I know, you'll be using words like 'position' and 'career path' and offering to lend me motivational tapes. This is real simple shit and you know it. The way I see it, you've got work that needs to get done but nobody you trust to do it for you. I'm here to take a chunk of it off your hands."

"As in what?"

"As in right this minute I'm betting you're sitting on an order from somebody willing to pay good money for something that's hard to find. Some job that's been collecting dust in that side drawer of yours because you can't see giving it to one of those lazy-ass smokers, jokers and sports fans you've got out there, taking up space and eating up your overhead. I'm ready to go out and separate that item from its current owner, bring it back here and sell it to your Buyer."

"And...how do you get paid?"

"I'd expect a salary and bonus, with participation in a generous stock options plan and health insurance, of course."

He glared at me through narrowed lids. "Are you serious?"

"Hell, no! I'm jerkin' your chain, of course." And then, purposely mocking the menacing cartoon-Sylvester voice he'd used on me, "Scchumbody didn't have his scchecond cup thicch morning. You're scaring me, Dude! Look, you're focused on the spread between what the Buyer says he wants to pay and what the Seller says he's willing to take. But there's more spread in there if I can get the Seller to take less. You and I split the extra spread. Easy."

"Split, like you get 10%?"

Kinda proud of myself and now clearly on a roll, I continued. "That'll be ok for this little getting-to-know-you experiment, but let's face it: all you're doing is giving me a lead. We don't know what kind of scene will be waiting for me at the Seller's, or what I'm gonna have to do to get him to part with it. Things could get tricky and I expect to be paid for taking on that load. That 10% deal you've fallen in love with might be ok for getting those other shitheads to sleepwalk your run-of-the-mill goods from A to B, but it's nowhere near the right money for really tough assignments. That's where your real profits are, but right now those deals are still in your desk. Trust me, at the other end of this, you'll be happy to take 50% and let me have the 50 I deserve. Think of it this way: I want to be on your team but not on your payroll. Now, after all this talk, my foot's been getting kinda itchy to go kick some ass, so open that drawer and dig out that mystery item we both know is in there, and let me go do what I gotta do."

Damn, that felt good! He reached in the drawer and pulled out an envelope and told me to take it to Carl, who would explain my first assignment. Our meeting over, I got up and left the room without good-byes or other pleasantries. I went immediately to Carl's office, filled him in and handed him the envelope.

He nodded and raised his eyebrows, apparently impressed with my willingness to step up. He handed me the assignment form, which read:

*4 wood-and-canvas beach chairs—$1,450*
*Seller: Jonas Cantrigger*
*427 Beachtree Street*
*Harbrough Glen*

Then he counted out fourteen $100 bills, two twenties and a ten.

"Any questions?"

"I don't think so."

"Good. Good." Then, yelling over my shoulder, "Hey, Le-Mike. You ride with him, ok?"

I turned and saw none other than LeMichael from Omega. Well, I'll be darned! Small world. Only today, he had on a leather jacket and jeans instead of the black suit.

He smiled, showing a serious gap, and said, "We ride when you ready. Car's right outside."

I walked out of the Depot, found the AutoZip and got in and sat for a full minute before I switched on the engine. Then I pulled up out front so LeMike could get in the passenger door.

I switched on the navigation system and started to call out the address, when he said,

"Uh, that's ok. I got 'dis. I will take some AC, though."

I called for the air conditioning and off we went, LeMichael calling directions to the car.

We exited the big Depot parking lot and drove out onto the highway in the direction of Fort Watkins.

"It's just a few miles. We be there shortly," LeMike let me know.

"Sure," I said, not so sure.

After a few more minutes, he pointed to the sign that said Exit 14, Harbrough Glen, and said to our car, "This exit. Now."

Our car activated its turn signal and got in the exit lane, braking into the off-ramp. Sensing my question, LeMichael said to the car, "Next lef' end a' the ramp."

We drove down the large boulevard, and at LeMichael's command, made the third right into a development of small ranch-style homes.

The third street sign said Beachtree, and I wasn't sure whether it was to the left or right and neither was LeMichael. The car's AutoNav had us turn left onto a street where the little ranches and the yards out front were badly run-down. The first house on the left was 300 and the second was 302, so

I figured we got lucky. We slowly made our way into the next block and soon we were in front of 427 on the other side of the street.

"Pull up to the end of the block," said LeMichael.

We crawled to a stop, and our car went into parking mode. When the door opened for me to get out, LeMichael pulled at my forearm. He flashed a grin and pulled back his jacket to show an honest-to-gosh .357 Magnum. "Jus' in case somebody be gettin' ideas."

"Sure. Let's go," I gulped, eager to get on with it.

We walked up to the front door together and pushed the button which activated a nasally buzzer I could hear over a TV game show. A teenage girl came to the door—stringy blonde hair, little blue shorts, a tank top that had once been white and dirty flip-flops. I flashed my best smile. "Hi. Is Mr. Cantrigger at home?"

She rolled her eyes and said, "Wait here."

Turning and walking back toward the kitchen, she yelled into an open door that seemed to lead to a basement, "Hey, Jonas. Some guys to see you."

"Right up," a voice croaked back.

A small, over-smoked, unshaven, weaselly guy with thinning brown hair, wearing a worn lightweight bathrobe, dark socks over pale, scrawny ankles, and beat-up slippers came shuffling toward us from the hallway. He raised a hand woodenly in a half-hearted greeting and said, "Hi, fellas."

The girl glared at him, gave us some more of the eye-roll, then looked away, marching back in the direction of the TV we heard in another room.

I guessed it was up to me, so I said, "You must be Jonas. I'm Raf," and stuck out my hand, which he shook weakly. Then I asked him, "You got the stuff?"

"Oh, yeah. The beach chairs," said Jonas.

He retreated back through the doorway to the basement, back down the steps and, after rummaging around awhile, returned in two trips with four beat-up wood-framed beach chairs with blue canvas backs and seats. He unfolded one of them and set it up on the floor.

"Carl said $1,450 for the four of 'em."

Now, I realized this was my first run, and I knew nothing of the "system" or the "process" or any of the secret conventions of this new Real Deal Economy, blah, blah, blah, but I DID know a shit-ton about beach chairs from my three summers of running an umbrellas-and-chairs concession at Toren Beach.

And my experienced eye told me one thing: These chairs were seriously fucked. The paint on the armrests was worn, rough and chipped in spots, rather than shiny and smooth like it was supposed to be. The canvas was faded and thin, and even torn in the seat from the relentless assault of hundreds of asses over the years. The canvas backrest was stained dark and slick from gallons of Coppertone, Sea and Ski and homebrew baby oil-and-iodine that didn't do shit to protect you from the sun, but did a great job of messing up a beach chair. And here was this guy, holding them out to me like they were pure gold.

Oh, but they did have this one little thing going for them: Real wood-and-canvas chairs like these hadn't been made anywhere in the world in the last fifty years. Even used ones were damned hard to come by. Somebody wanted these chairs and had put in an order for them at a price where Carl figured he could buy them for $1,450, fix them up and still make a good buck on the sale.

Feeling suddenly strong and in control, I said, "Uh, this isn't $1,450 worth of chairs, Cuz. I'm looking at about three hours' worth of labor putting them in some kind of shape to sell 'em. First, you gotta remove all this old canvas, sand and paint the wood, then cut and apply the new canvas which, as you may already know, isn't made here anymore, so I'd have to buy it *Slave* from who knows where, which is going to cost me some serious money, plus involve some serious risk of getting busted."

I was on a roll now, proud that I could use my old beach-stand knowledge and that I had absorbed enough of what Carl had just told me that I was already willing to take a chance on using the *S*-word in an actual business transaction, albeit with a low-life like Jonas. But business is business, right?

I peeled off eight of the hundreds and held them out.

"Are you kidding? Hey, a deal is a deal!" protested Jonas.

"Yeah, well, this is no deal at any price more than $800." I slapped and fanned the bills like I had seen them do in some B-movies, and pushed them his way once again.

"Can't do it. I paid almost that much myself."

"Ok," I said cheerfully, turning to go, really feeling like I could push this a little bit. "No problem. I understand completely."

"No, maybe you don't. Listen, Carl's gonna be pretty pissed when he hears about this. He and I do business together all the time, and he's not gonna take too kindly to you screwing up our deal."

I pulled out my smartphone and took a couple quick pictures of the opened chair that was sitting on the floor. If Jonas wanted to play the Carl Card, I could play it too.

"When Carl sees these photos and hears what I've got to say, he's gonna know you tried to screw him with that price you conned out of him on a sight-unseen, trust-me deal. He also knows I've been known to dabble in the ways of beach chairs in a past life, and that I know what it takes to fix 'em."

At this, I thought I noticed Jonas looking a little deflated.

"Well, how about $1,100?"

"Jonas, you seem like a good man, and you apparently have a good track record with the folks at the Depot." I peeled off another hundred, and curved the stack to make it stand out flat as I offered it to him.

"Last call. LeMichael here and I are ready to go." I thought it wouldn't hurt to remind him that the large man standing to my left and slightly behind me was here for my protection and that, even though he seemed lost in whatever music was being piped into his earbuds, he was very much aware of at least the tone of our conversation. "Take the $900 or we're outa here."

With that, Jonas snatched the cash and motioned to us to take the chairs.

Damn, I'm good!

We walked down to the car. I talked the hatch open and LeMichael set the chairs carefully inside. He said, "Carl gon' be impress wi' what he see an' hear 'bout 'dis shit."

"You mean what you're gonna *tell* him?"

"No, man. What he *see an' hear*," patting the tiny camera clipped to his collar, which I hadn't noticed before. "He gon' wanna see the video we got of the whole scene back there, if he wasn't watching the feed real-time. Uh, you know, first time and all, they wanna be sure they got the right guy on the case. My man really *do* know somethin' 'bout 'dem chairs!"

"Yep. My job history entry about the beach concession was legit."

"Lucky you, man. Hey, I will take some AC, if you don't mind." LeMichael gave me his big smile and sat back in his seat as we pulled away from the curb and rode back toward the Depot.

"Hey, LeMichael. If you don't mind my asking, I gotta tell ya I was surprised to see you show up here for this mission when I thought you worked at Omega."

"Oh, yeah, well, that's my day job. This here my side hustle. Guy's gotta do what he gotta do to make da bread, Cuz."

"Oh, I get that part ok. What I'm curious about is that it's kind of coincidental that your, er, side hustle puts you right alongside me for my first ride as a Mover. You see why I'd wonder about that, right?"

LeMichael nodded slowly and smiled. "Oh, yeah." And then he looked and started fiddling with his smartphone. Something came over me and I figured now was as good a time as any to ask him.

"I can't help but think I've seen you somewhere before. Have you ever been on TV?"

"Well, years ago I was trying to get my acting gig going, and I did a few commercials."

"No shit?"

"Yeah, one of 'em was for a weight loss company, not under my Christian name. I guess they didn't like LeMichael, so they were looking for something else. They was tryin' this an' that and then asked me where I was born. I said 'Atlanta,' but they said nobody would have that name. They asked what county and I said 'Fulton' and they liked that better, so I became 'Fulton' for the commercial."

"Yeah, you know, I do remember that one. You lost about forty pounds, right? You were good, man."

"Damn, you got a good mem'ry! I really did 'eat the food, lose the weight,' but nothin' big came of it. Not much more acting work was comin' my way and I had bills to pay, so I went back to security." Adding with a chuckle, "Started back eatin' what I like, and the weight came back too."

"Probably for the best. Entertainment business is fickle. One day they love you, next day they don't know you."

"You got that right. Insurance business not much better. Look like the same in every business, you ask me. Uh, can I aks you somethin'? It's a personal matter."

"Sure. Go ahead."

"You seem like a guy who might know somebody help a brutha out. Well, I got a problem with the law."

"What kinda problem?"

"I was in this place—you wouldn't know about it. It's an after-hours club folks hang out called the Renaissance Lounge. I'm there about a week ago, and met this young lady. Well, I had seen her around before. She beautiful and we had kinda looked each other over a few times before, but no connection till that night. Anyway, we got to talkin' and had a couple drinks and she aks do I want to come back to her place. I say sure. An' so we did. We had more drinks and things got a little hot an' heavy on the couch an' I suggested we go in the nex' room, but I guess she wasn't ready for that, which made me kinda mad, and I admit I got a little rough and, first thing you know, my piece—you know, my weapon—fell outa my holster and came clatterin' onto her coffee table. An' well, you know, it's kinda large and she got all big-eyed and scared and well, she pee'd herself, which made her embarrassed and she screamed at me to get out, which I did. I didn't think too much more about it till the nex' night when two officers of the law come around to my place to arrest me for assault with a deadly weapon."

"Do you happen to remember the names of the cops who arrested you?"

"Well, yeah, I got it here somewhere."

He fished around in one pocket of his sport coat, then another and finally found two business cards and handed them over.

They were both from the county detectives' unit—Cantrell and Stingone. The latter name was unfamiliar to me, but Cantrell and I had crossed paths a couple of years ago when I was the victim of identity theft. That whole thing was a shitstorm nightmare, and they never caught the fraudsters, but Cantrell followed up every lead he could find and kept me informed. He seemed like a straight shooter, and I thought he might remember me.

"Well, what happened next?"

"I called Roebuck and he put up my bail so I could go home, which I 'preciate. But now I'm lookin' at charges. I gotta meet court next week. I no more pull a gun on this woman than the man in the moon, but it's gonna be her word against mine. I know she jus' lookin' for some money..."

"Wait, did she actually try to shake you down for money?"

"She didn't, but her attorney called me. He's this guy, Gerry Weintraub. You've probably seen him around or maybe on TV. Does his own cheesy-ass TV commercials. Wear a wacky lookin' wig—look like a bird nes' up on his head."

I was indeed familiar with Counselor Weintraub. "So, you figure she'll drop the charges if you lay a little money on her?"

"'Zakly right. Plus, cover Weintraub fees on top 'a that."

I actually believed LeMike. The idea that he pulled a gun on the woman didn't hold up, and I hoped the Common Pleas judge would agree. But the thing was serious enough that he needed representation.

"I'm not a lawyer, but I can talk with someone about it. Would you mind if I try to reach this Cantrell and see how serious they are about this? Then we'll see about a lawyer."

Giving me a big grin, he said, "Gee, I'd sure 'preciate that. Thanks, man."

Holding up my hand, I replied, "Don't thank me yet, Le-Mike. Let me see whether I can get someone to help you out of this mess. Then you can bring all the thank-yous you want."

Our AutoZip was just pulling up to the Depot, so we got out and walked in to see Carl to deliver a post-mortem report on our successful scavenger hunt. Only Carl wasn't in his office and nobody seemed to know where he was, so we had to hold our big news till the next day.

# CHAPTER 6

There was still plenty of Tuesday remaining, and I had to get a draft agenda to Barb DeMinter for John Flanagan's meeting with Brancati's people. I don't usually have caffeine in the afternoon, but I figured I could use a boost so I fixed myself a Nespresso before sitting down to work.

It had been a while since I had done one of these but, while I wasn't exactly sure where to start, I was pretty sure the process would be about the same as before. My usual cure for drafter's block was to start typing.

After banging away for a few minutes, I had a rough outline that included introductions, expectations, deliverables and dates, measures of success, financial, monitoring, reporting and recordkeeping, staffing, communications and points of contact, next steps.

Then I spent a few minutes building out the "Omega delivers" part. As the former sales manager for the Estate Planning Consultants, I had an idea how this ought to go, and knocked out a page of notes describing how our guys would work with Brancati's financial advisers, get some information about the client's assets, introduce the concept of estate planning by showing the so-called "Trainwreck Scenario"—the tax burden if things were left as they were—and then propose some remedial work.

The plan would include a hefty dose of life insurance that

would mean some decent commissions for the Financial Advisors (FAs), and the inquiry itself would reveal some assets heretofore unknown to the FAs. In separate follow-up discussions, the FAs could initiate a conversation about how those assets could be better managed if moved over to Brancati from wherever they were currently held.

It was a pretty simple approach we had used successfully at Omega. I was convinced it delivered real value to the clients, and it helped fortify the FAs' relationships with them.

Satisfied with my first draft, I figured I deserved another espresso as a reward, and sipped it gratefully while I thought about the right corporate protocol to get this out of my computer and into Barb's. I typed her name in the "To" line of an email, and clicked to attach my draft. Then I typed a quick explanatory note:

> "Hey, Barb. As promised, here's my first draft of an agenda for the meeting with Brancati. I wanted to get something over to you so we could discuss and send to John by close of business. I also sent you an invitation for a short call later today to finalize. If the time doesn't work for you, please feel free to propose an alternate. Looking forward to working with you on this project."

I thought I had done a pretty good job on the agenda and that the cover note had just the right tone, so I hit Send. Feeling a sense of satisfaction at doing some familiar work, I closed down and packed my laptop and headed out to the Depot, presenting myself in Carl's doorway.

"What up, Kemo Sabe? How's the new fresh-from-the-kill Mover and soon-to-be Broker? Puttin' a little butter on that bread!"

"There's gotta be some kind of catch. It can't be that easy."

Carl had indeed viewed the video LeMichael had taken with his tiny lapel camera.

He held up a hand. "Hold up, buddy. First things first. You done good. Handled that beach chairs deal like a pro. I think you could easily move to the Broker job. There's no catch to it. You sit at your computer at home or at Starbuck's and look at the lists of stuff people have ordered and then you go online, buy one and make arrangements to have it picked up and brought here. Then you put in a requisition to a Mover and they do the rest which, as you just learned, is actually picking it up and delivering it to us. Fuck, if an asshole like Jonas can do it, you sure can."

"Uh, that Jonas-guy I just saw is a Broker?"

"Now what did you think a dickwad like him was doing with four beach chairs from the '70s, Dude?"

"And that's it? You just buy and sell shit?"

"Yep, that's it."

I had already collected my Chits from the work the night before and given them up for the jacket for Olivia. I had given LeMichael $50 plus an extra $50 even though he hadn't done much besides ride along. Well, just having him and his hand cannon along was definitely a factor in the persuasion department, and his clandestine video of the transaction had gotten me in really good with Carl. Per my agreement with Roebuck, I got to keep half the money I saved on the deal, which was $175 when all was said and done. Not bad for a night's work.

I heard the buzz of a silenced cell phone, and Carl reached into the inside pocket of his leather jacket and retrieved it. "Yo?"

He blinked a couple of times and glanced up at me and said, "Yeah, he's right here. You want me to bring him in right now?" More blinking. "Be right there."

"Uh, Roebuck wants to see you. For what, I have no idea, but when he wants to see somebody, I say 'Ok.' Lez go."

He rose and I followed him back through the cavernous hallway into a small office that at first seemed empty. It took a full five seconds for me to notice Roebuck seated almost motionless at a large oak desk—actually, it was a worktable with stacks of files and papers, a few Post-Its of different colors stuck here and there with terse notations in surprisingly neat hand lettering.

His eyes and eyebrows came up but everything else stayed where it was. "So, this is the master dealmaker," he said, smiling and extending his hand. "I watched LeMichael's video. You sure know your way around beach chairs. Let's talk a minute." He motioned toward the scarred round oak chair in front of his desk, and I sat down.

Same vest. Same white tee. Same bald head. Something about the economy and efficiency of his movements gave off an aura of quiet confidence that more than made up for his average size. He produced a blister pack of Nicorette gum from his pocket and, using the blade of a tiny Swiss Army knife on his key ring, carefully cut into the foil backing to reveal the gum, then stabbed it with the point of his knife, popped it into his mouth and started chewing appreciatively.

"Y'know. Price and lack of availability of the gaspers was never a big issue for me. And I always liked to smoke. But it got to the point where there was no place you could do it legally, so this works better for me."

Smiling with satisfaction at either the flavor, the nicotine hit, the enjoyment of the little ritual or some combination of all three, and still chewing, he said, "I need more guys that can do what you do. Fighters, I can get easily. Guys that can bring in merchandise at a bargain are harder to come by. Where'd you learn?"

"I'm not sure I really know anything. I just reacted, is all. Plus, I actually know something about beach chairs from my old days."

At this, he nodded vigorously and rocked back and forth in his chair. "Well, that's good. Maybe you know a little about some other stuff, too. That's what I'm talking about! Carl explained how the Mover pay works, right? You eat what you kill. You want in?"

"Well, I really want to be a Broker."

"You show you can handle the Mover job and you'll move up to Broker in no time. I guarantee it. Don't blow this opportunity, man. This is exactly what you should be doing." He smiled broadly and punched the air with his forefinger as he said it.

"But, ya know. I'm kinda wondering why a smart guy like you hasn't asked more questions about this place—why we're here in the first place."

"Well, Carl told me some. But sure, I'd like to hear more."

"The government and businesses—I'm talkin' the President, Congress, big corporations, everyone—the last many years what have they been thinking about? Redefining progress as anything that makes sure all these fringe elements get a seat AT the table. But fuck, that's not progress. Progress is making shit and buying and selling it—putting food and goods ON the table. And nobody's stopped to notice there's less and less of the things people really want going up on the table. That's where we come in. That's ALL we care about—giving guys a chance to bring home the good stuff for their families. You do good with us, you're helping Americans get the stuff they want and need. But you gotta be committed."

At this, he leaned over practically into my face. "You committed, guy?"

"Well, yeah. That's what I wanna do."

He smiled broadly. "We'll see." Standing up now, gesturing toward the door, he signaled the end of our little meeting and my little tutorial.

XXXX

I walked back out with Carl and then back to my car. I tossed the bag with my fighting tape and bandages in the back seat, glad I wasn't going to have to use them tonight, fired up the engine and drove home.

Emily's car was in the driveway and the side window of the house was wide open, and I could hear her talking on the phone and giggling girlishly. I couldn't make out any of what she said, and I really didn't have the patience or the heart to even try to eavesdrop.

I parked and went in through the garage and up to my little office. I wanted to get started on LeMichael's legal problem. My first thought was to call Joel Avigdor because I knew him well and he did criminal work, but I wanted to talk to Detective Cantrell first.

I called the number on the card and he picked up on the first ring.

"Cantrell."

"Hi, Detective Cantrell. This is Raf Vella. You may not remember me, but you helped me out a couple years ago with an ID theft."

"Yeah, well, we get those about every fifteen minutes, so... you know. What can I do for you today, sir?"

I told him I was a friend of LeMichael's calling about the matter with the woman, and he said he couldn't say much since I wasn't LeMike's lawyer. After a couple minutes of back and forth, with me finally convincing him I was not going to burn him if he told me something, he allowed that he didn't think the woman had much of a case.

"So, you think this was basically your garden-variety, man-woman situation that got out of hand? The woman got embarrassed and feels she has to vindicate herself by pressing charges. Am I getting you right?"

"That's about the size of it, yeah." He thought the prosecutor would probably want to go ahead with it anyway because the complaining witness was so adamant, but said he'd put in a good word for LeMike, who had no priors. I thanked him and hung up and immediately dialed Joel Avigdor after all.

I guess he was surprised. "On my day off? Seriously?"

"You know you're glad to hear from me."

"Spit it out, bitch. I know you've got something you think is important, and I want to get back to my leaf blower before I lose my momentum completely and then, more importantly, to the one last Carlsberg I'm nursing before it gets warm. I hate yard work and I've been saving this bad boy for when I needed a special incentive—like now."

I filled him in on LeMichael's predicament and gave him the names of the two officers. He said he'd call them in the morning and enter his appearance for LeMike at the arraignment. I would have liked to continue the conversation, but I could see he was itching to get back to his precious brewster.

I hadn't heard anything from Barb DeMinter about my draft, so I found her number in the contacts directory on my phone and punched it to connect.

"Miss DeMinter's office," said a twenty-something female voice.

"Yes, is she in, please?"

"One moment and I'll check. Who shall I say is calling?"

"Just tell her Raf Vella."

"Sure, one minute, Mr. Vella."

Three beats passed, and then, "Barb DeMinter."

"Oh, hi Barb. It's Raf Vella."

Dead silence for a beat. Then, "Oh-h-kay. How can I help you?" Like it really wasn't ok, or she had no recollection of having met me.

"I was in last week when we talked about the Norm Brancati trip. How are you?" Another beat of silence. "I was wondering whether you got my draft agenda and when we could talk about who's gonna do what to finalize something for John's big presentation."

"Uh, oh, yes, sure, I remember. Well, you know, I just sort of threw something together and whatya know, John really liked it, so that was that."

"You mean it's done?"

"Yep. One and done! One more thing off the to-do list." She

said it real breezy-like.

"Oh, well I guess I got the impression John wanted you and I to be working on it together..."

"Well, like I said, it turned out to be easier for me to just knock it out myself and get it over to him."

"Was my stuff helpful?"

Two beats this time. "Um, well, I'm not really sure we actually got it. When did you send it? You know, to be honest, I'm not sure why John bugged you about this in the first place. I usually do that stuff and I had this handled. Ok?"

"Well, I'd like to talk with John. I'm sure he expects something from me."

"That's up to you. Like I said, he's got what he needs for the trip. Hey, listen I've gotta get to my next thing. Take care. Have an awesome day!" And with that she hung up.

Ohh-kay. "Nasty, nasty, nasty," I said aloud to myself, punching my thigh for emphasis on the first syllable of each 'Nasty.' Fuck you very much, too. Outmaneuvered and aced-out before we even got started. Message dee-livered. Some things were just like the old days at Omega.

I was starting to feel like I needed a little TLC, and I really didn't think walking in on Em's giggly phone call was going to lead to anything good, so I backed up the car and drove off in the direction of Kayla's, thinking I might drop by. "Dropping by" was not something I normally did with her, but I figured this was kind of an emergency.

I parked in front of her building and walked into the lobby and pressed the intercom button for L6. "Yes," said a female voice I initially assumed was Kayla's, but something was different.

"Uh, Kayla. It's Raf."

"Well, this is Ashley, her new roommate. Kayla's not here."

I hadn't heard anything about a new roommate.

"Come on up. She'll probably be back in a while."

She buzzed me in, and I took the elevator up.

When I got out on her floor and started down the hallway toward Kayla's, a short blonde in a shift was standing by Kayla's door, holding it open.

"Hi," she said, smiling at me and, once I got past the glasses that made her eyes look bulgy, I noticed she had a decent smile over large white teeth. She came in behind me and closed the door.

As she passed, I caught her scent, which had notes of girly soap on top of something mildly musky underneath.

"Can I get you something to drink?"

"I'd take a beer. When did you move in?"

"Day before yesterday."

"Ok. Hey, so where's Kayla?"

"Well, she's playing bridge tonight, and won't be back till after ten."

She had poured the beer in a frosted glass and walked toward me with it in her outstretched hand.

"Thanks. What about you?"

"I've got a nice cab going. I'll get it."

She walked back into the little kitchen and came back with her half-filled wine glass. She motioned me to the join her on the couch, and when I did, she moved a little closer so I could feel the warmth of her thigh.

We talked for a few minutes, or rather she went on animatedly about this and that: her last apartment, the cat she had to leave with her old roommate 'cause Kayla didn't like pets and the building didn't permit them anyway, her boss at work who's "a real geezer and a lech and makes sleazy comments all the time," and then she turned toward me, brushing her left breast against my arm.

"I understand you're a consultant."

"Yeah, I guess you could say that. I was downsized a few months ago, and I've been trying to get my own thing going, and it's happening slowly."

"So, where do you do this...consulting work?"

Not wanting to give her too much info, I said, "Well, here and there."

"Yeah, you've got that look. That down-sized-and-in-transition look."

"Is it that obvious?"

She giggled. "Kinda. I mean that's pretty much the norm with guys of a certain age."

"Ouch. So, what do you do?"

"I'm a Marketing VP at an insurance company."

"Which one?"

"Omega. You know it?"

"Uh, yeah, sorta. I used to work there—till I was...down-sized. What do you do there?"

"I'm in charge of a marketing team. I've been there about six months. I'm making sixty grand, and I'm gonna need to get a promotion to make five K more. They better make me a Senior VP in the next couple months or I'm outa there. I'm not gonna fuck around with these people. I went into my EVP's office last week, and told her she'd better make some shit happen pretty soon or I was gonna have to start talking with HR. I think she got the message this time. We'll see."

Sooo, if I was reading this right, Ashley basically had a job at the level I used to have, but for about half the pay.

She noticed my beer glass was empty, so she took it and got up to go to the kitchen.

"Keep talking. I'm listening," she called over her shoulder. "Gotta get you a refill. You and me both, actually."

When she returned with our drinks, rather than hand mine to me, she put them both on the table and sat on my lap, put her arms around my neck and to my surprise, kissed me full on the lips.

"Hey, what if Kayla walks in?"

"Not gonna happen for at least an hour."

The invitation was unmistakable, but my brain immediately ran that little loop of "aftermath video" I had stored up there.

*Maybe we'd both have dozed off and I'd awaken first and take a moment to look at her lying there. Is that really what she looks like? Did we really just do what I think we did?* **This** *is the person who was designated by the universe today to revalidate my membership in the informal club called Men A Woman Would Be Willing To Have Sex With? No, actually she's just a woman you happened to sleep with, and when she wakes up, her first thought is going to be "What was I thinking?" What in the world would ever lead me to think that a few minutes of coupling would do more than put a flimsy store-brand bandage on a deep aching wound? Dumb shithead.*

She tried to decode my hesitancy. "Oh, you've got one of those DamnRight Cards, huh?"

"Nope, but I'm thinking of getting one. I've been through this a few times and don't like the way I feel at the end."

The Card was an actual thing, started on a lark in the wake of the #MeToo movement by two sorority women at one of the prestigious New England universities. The idea was to head off awkward situations by giving guys some reassurance of their desirability so they wouldn't have to resort to high-risk, low-probability chances of hitting on women. The panel voted on guys they knew or saw on campus. If a majority voted "Yes" to "Would-you-have-sex-with-this-guy?" a delegation would tromp over to his dorm or fraternity house and present the card in a little impromptu ceremony. It got so popular the two founders took the thing off campus and brought it to Shark Tank. The Sharks got a good laugh, but none of them would bite. Too bad for them because the thing really caught on. They're selling for $120 now and going like hotcakes. Middle-aged guys and geezers are snapping them up faster than the young guys.

She shrugged and smiled. "I guess. But if I were a guy, a card signed by some random women would seem like a poor substitute for a little free sex now and then."

"Yeah, well, in my experience it's never really free, is it?"

She tried a brave little smile, but the corners suddenly turned down, her eyes abruptly red and wet. A single, big tear escaped and rolled down her cheek. She caught her lower lip, fighting the slide to a full-on cry.

I impulsively reached for her and she leaned into my shoulder, warm tears on my neck. "Hey, what's going on?"

"I'm such a mess. I can't even do this right."

"You're a damned attractive woman and you know it."

"Yeah, well, go tell my boyfriend—er, ex-boyfriend. The one who threw me out after we've been living together for a year. One day we're talking about honeymoon destinations and the next he's telling me to pack my shit and go. What kind of girl gets that treatment?"

"Everybody, that's who. Nobody's immune. Except maybe the ones who are too scared to put themselves out there and commit to a relationship in the first place. This is the tough time and it sucks. It'll get better, I promise."

We both just sat there, staring straight ahead for a few moments.

She sniffed and dabbed her eyes with a tissue, composing herself. She looked at her watch and broke the awkward silence. "You know, you can save us both an unpleasant conversation with Kayla by getting the hell out of here."

A woman doesn't need to tell me that twice. I got up, gave my new friend a big-armed friend-hug and walked out the door and made my way down the elevator, into the lobby and back to my car.

I was only too aware from my relationship with Kayla how suddenly intimate you can be in the presence of someone, feeling millions of miles away, then just as quickly, you're back to yourself, thinking about your old problems again.

Maybe it was time to apply for a DamnRight Card. Hell, if it could make me feel better and save me from doing some things I'd regret later, maybe it would be worthwhile.

I still had the nagging feeling it might not solve the whole problem. I mean, despite the initial reassurance you'd get from it, there'd still be the occasional hook-ups and post-coital regrets and denials. Now, maybe if they'd invent an "I'd-Admit-To-My-Friends-I-Actually-Had-Sex-With-This-Guy" card...

# CHAPTER 7

Joel Avigdor had tickets to the Condors' game at the Walmart Center. We met up at the box office and made our way through the crowd inside the arena.

We got flimsy plastic cups with a little beer and a lot of foam and made our way to our seats, which were up pretty high, but still with a good view of the action.

I slurped off a bit of the foam and looked over at Joel. He was staring down at the floor.

"I swear those cheerleaders get younger every year."

"Yeah, and smaller too," I offered.

Joel looked at me strangely. But it actually did seem like they were miniature versions of past years' women. Not smaller in any particular area, like breasts, hips or thighs. But just…well, smaller all over. Perfectly proportioned, but tiny. Almost as though they had once been regular-sized women put through some science fiction-style reduction machine. Probably all former gymnasts, and they're generally small, right? I shook my head, not wanting to spend any more time pondering yet another insoluble riddle that nobody but me would give a second thought.

After an energized acrobatic routine by the Phlight Squad and another dance by the cheerleaders, the game started. The Wizards took an early lead, but I continued to nourish the hope that the Condors could close the gap until the buzzer signaled the end of the first half.

Joel left and returned with another beer and the World's Largest Slice of pizza, and I momentarily regretted my decision to stay put rather than fight the crowd.

I heard the ping reminder and pulled out my smartphone and tapped in the URL from the card Carl had handed me after giving me my new job as a Mover. It was for a Facebook closed group for Brokers only, but Carl invited me anyway, since I was on a fast track to becoming one. Immediately upon logon, I was greeted with a video featuring none other than Carl himself.

"Hey, guys. It's Carl. Welcome to the Brokers Group. You're a member of an elite team of people specially chosen for one of the most important jobs in today's Real Deal Economy.

"You'll be dealing with some very nice, civilized people who just want things they can't get in stores and some other good folks who happen to have those items—new and used. You'll also have to work with cheats, bullshit artists, fakers, liars, four-flushers, assholes, fuck-ups and hard-case types— the full gamut of the lowest forms of human existence. People who want something for nothing and others who think they should get ten grand for their garden shovel.

"It'll be your job to convince them that compromise is the only way the deal is going to happen. Do it well, and you can make a shit-ton of money.

"Now I'd like to turn it over to Josh Weldon, our top earner last year, to tell you a little bit about how he's done it."

"Hey, what's up, guys? So, Carl asked me to say a few words to you new Brokers about the job. I'm here to tell you it's the best thing that's ever happened to me. You get paid what you're worth. And you're worth whatever you put into it. You eat what you kill. No more, no less.

"At the beginning of every year, every month, every week I make it my business to decide—notice I said DE-CIDE—how much I'm gonna make. I write that shit down on this little three-by-five card here [holding it up], and then, as I close a deal, I subtract the amount I made from my goal. And I keep it in front of me, see? So, when I'm dealing with some dirtbag and all I can think about is how can I get this fucker off the phone, I take a look at my little card, and I say to myself, *'Hold on, Josh. You gotta hang in there till you can get a $200 spread on this one.'*

"Another point—and I can't stress this enough. You've gotta make sure you take care of your Movers. They are critical to your success. Yeah, I know they get a regular cut. But serious Brokers are going to be paying them extra, and if you want them to *really* work for you, you're going to have to do it too. Part of the game. You're going to get a reputation with them. Remember, they've got a Facebook group too, and your name will definitely start coming up. And it's up to you to decide what they're going to be saying about you. Straight shooter? Easy to work with? Good payer? Tightwad? Dickwad? Who do you think they're going to work their asses off for?

"I'm sure you guys have lots of questions and will have plenty more as you get into the work. That's where this group will come in handy. You should check in often. I'm here looking around at least once a day. And I know most other experienced Brokers are too. Chances are one of them's already dealt with the thing you're wrestling with at any given time, and has written something about it in the FAQ. Or, just go into the open forum and put your question up there. Someone—probably a few guys—will probably have something for you. Well, that's about it from me. I'll turn it back to Carl."

"Thanks, Josh. Tomorrow we're going to get a special treat. The man himself is gonna join us. Yep, we'll get a special visit from Roebuck during our next call. You don't want to miss this. Tomorrow morning, oh-eight hundred hours. Be there. Ok, Brokers. Time to go to work. Get out there and find some Buyers. Find some goods. Close some deals. Make some money! See you around campus. Carl out."

Carl's face froze on the screen and the little "Go" arrow inside the circle appeared in front of it.

*I guess I can do that,* I thought. *Why not?*

I could see Joel making his way back up with another cup of beer foam and another big, floppy pizza slice. I momentarily wondered again whether it was worth the trip, remembering that even bad pizza is actually pretty good.

The game was back on, and I watched a few possessions. To me, instead of the Wizards vs. the Condors playing basketball, it was a primitive battle between lazy giants. Big European and African guys loped up and down the court while coaches urged them on with instructional and motivational yelps. The giant Euros would somehow get into the lane, take a pass and try to muscle their way to the hoop. Once in a while, somebody would take an outside shot for a three-pointer. The pace lagged, and the game seemed to go on and on. Owners and team execs in suits sat courtside, arms folded and watching without much animation or interest.

Maybe it was because it had been a while since I'd been to a game, but I was struck by the absence of even a basic level of conformity to the rules—a scarcity of calls by the refs; guys slamming into each other, with and without the ball, shooting or not—and not a peep from the officials. And not once did I see a call for traveling. Moving around the court, players would tuck the ball under their arm like a loaf of bread and throw in an occasional token dribble. What happened to the requirement of keeping the hand on top—not under or along the side of the ball?

Overall, it was a sluggish, if violent, display and not really worthy of what I'd always thought of as pro basketball, but it eventually—mercifully—came to an end. I can't even remember who won.

I thanked Joel for getting the tickets and we fist-bumped our good-byes, then I made my way back to my car and drove home.

Shit! I had totally forgotten I was supposed to meet Tao at Crenshaw's tonight. Emily had said, "He wants to meet with you before I take on these new responsibilities as his assistant. He does that with the spouses of everyone who starts working for him, so they understand up front the kind of commitment their significant other will be making that will involve working late and a lot of travel, sometimes on weekends."

"Hang on a sec," I had replied when Emily told me about the meeting. "I thought you were going to be his yoga assistant, running yoga classes and handling phones and administrative duties. Where's the need for late nights and travel in that? How are you going to fit that in with your regular day job?"

"I'm not sure, really. He asked me and I said yes. Look, can you just for once say 'ok,' and meet with him without having to analyze everything?"

"This isn't analyzing. It's a man wanting to know why his wife—who already has a full-time job—wants an admin assistant's job for a yoga instructor, and why it's going to require her to be away from home during weird hours, that's all."

She had waved me off before I finished that last bit and was already on her way down to the basement and into the garage. I heard her car start.

I had looked at the paper on the fridge. "Meet Tao at Crenshaw's Grill, Tues at 10 p.m."

I started my car and headed to Crenshaw's.

There was a small but lively crowd at the bar when I walked in. I gave my name to the hostess and told her I was meeting someone named Tao, last name unknown. Taking a stool, I stared at the elaborate tap handles for about ten different draft beers, and settled on a pilsner. The bartender—big smile, tattooed arms, neck and head—tried hard to ignore me, preoccupied as he was with the important work of giving fist bumps, high fives and bro hugs to the regulars as they came up behind and all around me.

I was getting a flushed feeling, starting in my chest and

creeping up my neck to my face—that long-ago feeling I'd get as an invisible newbie approaching a kids' game, the participants totally ignoring my presence. It was my own fingernails digging into the palms of my clenched hands that brought me back to the present moment. I heard my own voice croak, "Hey, can I get a pilsner?"

"Hey, man. Gimme a sec, ok?" he said, frowning, genuinely offended, like my simple request was a serious intrusion on his quality time with his homeboys. He put down a paper coaster in front of me, accompanied by an annoyed smirk, and quickly resumed dispensing his special brand of *bon homie* as he greeted the rest of the crew and some chatty girls who were showing lots of white teeth, long hair (invariably blonde) and tanned arms and shoulders, and who had by now taken the remaining seats at the bar.

Finally, the bartender set down in front of me a foam-topped pint. "No pilsner, man. We're serving Angry Bear Lager tonight."

"What about all those tap handles?"

"Yeah. Well, when was the last time you were in a bar? Nobody's got those anymore. Wake up, dude."

No sooner had my beer been placed in front of me—a little too firmly, I had noticed—than I felt a light tap on my shoulder. Turning around, I came face-to-face with a blonde woman in her mid-thirties, looking like she'd come directly from a yoga studio, decked out top to bottom in pink and orange athleisure wear. As she approached, I picked up a strong, flowery scent on top of faint notes of girlish perspiration.

"Hey," she said, smiling. "You're Raf, right?"

"Yeah. That's me."

"I'm Nikki," she said, extending her hand, holding onto the smile. "I know you were expecting Tao, but he sent me in his place. He had a thing that came up the last minute and didn't want to leave you hanging. He wanted me to tell you Emily's doing a great job and he'll sure be happy to get her on full time."

*I'll bet he will. Shit! I had been all set to fuck with this smarmy shithead my wife seemed so smitten with, but now here's Nikki instead.*

She quickly caught the eye of the bartender, who took a break from rinsing beer glasses and exuberantly greeting his homies to tilt his shaved, tattooed head in our direction, signaling it was ok for her to call out her drink order.

"What can I get for you?"

"I'll have the house white, rocks on the side."

That agonizing business out of the way, I thought I'd get right to it. "Now what was it you—or Tao—wanted to talk with me about concerning Emily's new job?"

"Oh, yeah. Sure. That's why we're here, right?" She giggled and gave me a little-girl eye-roll and shrug.

"Right."

"Well, I just want to be sure you're on board with picking up the slack at home since she's going to be tied up a lot of nights. You have a young daughter, right?"

So, she was up to speed on our family situation. No surprise there. But I was pretty sure Emily's rendition of the home story inflated her role and diminished mine, and I was damned if I was going to spill my guts with a whole new set of alternative facts. Let her (and Tao) think whatever they wanted to.

"Well, maybe you can tell me a little more about what she'll be doing. Meanwhile, I'm kinda hungry. Are you ordering anything to eat?"

"I think I'll just have another one of these," she replied, lifting her glass and tapping the side and smiling at it like a new toy.

I waited till the bartender was looking in our general direction and raised my hand. After a few more of his patented LOLs and smirks, he made his way down to us and gave me the shiny-head tilt indicating he was in receiving mode. I wasn't too sure how much more of this walking art gallery I was going to be able to tolerate.

"Can I get a cheeseburger, medium, lettuce, tomatoes and pickles, with fries and another Angry Bear? You do have the cheeseburger, right?"

"And another white with side rocks," added Nikki, her smile on auto-pilot.

I'm sure she kept talking to me, but I didn't really pay much attention, especially after my cheeseburger arrived, choosing instead to focus on it and just getting through the encounter. Surprisingly, it seemed to be a real, honest-to-gosh burger, like in the old days, cooked just right—pink in the middle, still juicy, and the lettuce and tomatoes were fresh, the pickles nice and crunchy. The price on the menu was hard to swallow at $29.50, but I had to marvel at the apparent effectiveness of their supply chain. It occurred to me that I might have sold the bartender short. Hell, he might be moonlighting, putting in some rounds at the Depot, collecting Chits redeemable for burgers for the house to earn extra comp from his boss. Who knows?

"So, what exactly do you do at Tao's studio?" I managed between bites.

"Oh, well, I'm sorta his chief of staff. Technically, I guess, Emily will report to me. I mean, Tao's got a lot on his plate so I'll be the one giving her direction on the day-to-day."

*Gee, wonder whether Emily knows about that.*

"So, what's with the night work you mentioned?"

"A lot of our classes are at night, and Emily would be the one to check people in and collect their payments and then lock up after the class is over."

*And I wonder whether she knows about that.*

The rest of the "meeting" passed without incident. We said our good-byes and I walked out into Crenshaw's parking lot, which looked different from when I first arrived, now that it had filled up, and it took a moment to remember where I parked my car.

I was weary from the day's activities—and the evening's

revelations—and looking forward to getting home, doing my night stuff and falling into bed. I had just clicked my remote to open my car door when I was shoved from behind and slammed into the door. Somebody kicked my feet out from under me, and I slid down to the asphalt. The weight of at least a couple hundred pounds was suddenly on my back and a hand pulled my head up by the hair. Cigarette breath whooshed close to my face as my head was jerked around.

"See that curb over there? What do we do with a smart little shit who, all of a sudden, thinks he can move goods?"

I wasn't sure whether or not it was a real question so, in view of my compromised status, I kept my mouth shut. My new friend clarified the situation by yanking on my hair again and giving me another dose of cigarette breath as he exhaled, "I'm talking to you, Dickhead."

I figured I ought to say something. "The curb? What curb?"

More jerking of my head and directing my attention to the nearby curb that separated the parking lot from the sidewalk. The pressure on my back didn't change, giving me to understand there were two of them, one to deliver the message and the other just to sit on my ass and legs.

"What we do is drag his candy ass over to a curb just like that one, place his head carefully on the curb and then stomp the shit out of it. Sometimes we break an eye socket, sometimes we break the neck. We're not too particular. I can promise you for sure you'll either be dead or wind up in the ER, wishing you were. As long as you keep it small, you should be fine. Start getting too big for your britches and we might decide it's time for a curb job. Got it?"

I did my best to nod and I felt the weight lifting off me as he released my head to the asphalt with an extra bit of force for emphasis. I lay there motionless as I listened to them walk away. Gradually, I tested my legs and arms and finally got into a sitting position. The side of my face was smarting and my neck and head felt like—well, like you'd think they'd feel after getting worked over by a couple of goons who sneak up on you in a parking lot and knock you around.

I got into my car and locked the door, then looked at myself in the rearview mirror. Not too bad, considering. My head hurt like hell and I was dizzy and disoriented, but I took a moment to consider what just happened. Apparently, my recent entrée into the world of Movers had attracted the attention of some bad mo-fos. Message delivered. I wondered who they were and figured I'd talk with Carl about it in the morning. I switched on the car, croaked out "Home." But before we headed out, the thought of Kayla jumped into my mind.

I checked my watch and saw that I still had some time before I had to relieve Maddie at home. So I called out Kayla's address. There were times when I needed some consolation and TLC after some setback or disappointment, and there were also other times when I was fresh from a victory and felt like celebrating with someone who seemed to like and appreciate me. Today was a real up and down day—with some progress and some setbacks, with some weirdness thrown in for good measure, like my conversation with Nikki and my encounter with the goons in the parking lot.

I texted Kayla and she got back immediately with a "Sure, come on over." In a few minutes I was in her building's garage.

I shut off my engine and instead of just hopping out as I usually did, I sat there a moment and reflected on where I was and why. Sure, things weren't going great between Emily and me. And who knows what she had going on. But my marriage promise meant I had to hold up my end of things, and my thing with Kayla was clearly not doing that. I paused for a moment to let that swirl around in my brain, which normally at a time like this would have been on pause while other parts of my anatomy took over speculating how I'd feel with her arms around me, pressing herself into me in a welcoming embrace.

Well, yeah. Validating me just because I'm me. Not the employee who can take some work off the boss's plate. Not the dad who can be counted on to protect and provide for a child. Not the husband who brings in a paycheck or who can erase the pain of having a father who didn't work hard enough. The fact was, Kayla was the only non-transactional thing in my life and to me that was worth all the risk I was taking.

Kayla greeted me as usual, with a smile and warm hug as only she knew how. She expressed appropriate concern for my new wound and held a bag of peas from her freezer against my head for a little while to ease the pain and reduce the swelling while we told each other about our days. And for an hour or so, I forgot all about the other things in my life that were coming apart at the seams.

Later, pulling into my driveway, I saw that Emily wasn't home.

I was keyed up and exhausted at the same time from my interlude with Kayla, but I composed myself to greet Maddie Ackerman, who stood up from the couch when I walked in. My initial notion that I could slip by without her noticing anything was quickly dispelled.

"Whoa, what the heck happened to you?" she said, walking up to get a closer look at the side of my head.

"I, uh, guess I tripped over one of those concrete wheel-stops in the parking lot and fell..."

"...I'd say you did. And hit your face in the process. Did you go to the ER? You should get checked out for a concussion."

"No, no. Thanks, Maddie, but I'm fine."

She looked dubious and even offered to drive me to the hospital, but I convinced her I was ok, and asked her to tell me her hours for the day. She said she arrived around six, so I rounded up and paid her for five hours. She got her coat while I opened the door to let her out, and she gave me one last look of concern and a slight shake of her head as she headed down the walk.

I stopped in the kitchen and stood at the sink drinking a twenty-ounce glass of water. My head hurt like a sonuvabitch, so I got a bag of peas from the freezer on my way to my work room, holding the peas against my face. I had left Crenshaw's eager to get started on my next search and my little parking lot experience hadn't dampened my desire.

I fired up my computer and there was an email from Carl with a link to a new site I hadn't seen before. It was an Assignments Board and I was surprised to see my name already on it. I clicked the little icon next to my name and, to my surprise, up popped my next mission: A guy named Amory was looking for twelve restaurant waitstaff jackets, the short kind with brass buttons. Wow. I hadn't seen one of those since I wore them myself as a summer-job waiter. Most places had their servers wear vests and had given up on these little jackets decades ago.

My face was still smarting and I wondered momentarily whether my sudden appearance on the board could have triggered my little parking lot tune-up, but I seriously doubted the fuckers who jumped me would consider chasing waiters' jackets as going for the big time.

I immediately thought of the old Toren Hotel in Toren Beach. Fashioned around a faux tower, the name paying homage to some of the town's early Dutch settlers named Van Toren, the hotel had served as my introduction to the hospitality industry as I waited tables in the hotel's on-site restaurant. The waiters had worn these short, gold jackets that were just the kind Mr. Amory was looking for. I got on their website and noted the phone number and the names of the manager and kitchen steward so I could call tomorrow.

I wanted to find more seekers and more goods, but frankly I was beat. So, I sort of absent-mindedly went to YouTube and pulled up another one of those foreign language tutorials where a young woman from another country—Poland, this time—would model the pronunciation of speech sounds in her language that English speakers might find peculiar.

I randomly typed in "L in Polish" and up came a short

video featuring the young woman speaking into the camera: *"Thees sound should be quite easy for ewe to prodewce seence eet ees seemilar to your dobble u sound—as een wwwwoods and wwwwork and wwwwild."* The speaker was young with shoulder-length blonde hair and horn-rimmed glasses, and she puckered up nicely to make the "W" sound out of an "L." She maintained a little half-smile for most of the 1:15 video. And the look she gave the camera matched her tone of voice, which was kind of ironic, I thought. As if to say, *"I don't know why ewe are so eenterested een learning our language bot I am weeling to make a veedeo to show you how."* l found myself wondering about the town she grew up in, the schools she went to, the house she lived in. What was it like at her family's dinner table? I'm not sure why I found these videos such a captivating and entertaining diversion. It's not like I had a burning desire to learn Polish or any other of the languages featured, but hearing her voice was like a little vacation to a foreign land.

Pushing myself back from my computer, I allowed my mind to wander some more: What would she report to her girlfriends if she could see me sitting here now watching her? *"So, thees guy, not so old, he seets een front of hees computer screen just watching me say the 'L' sound. No, hee's not doing anything creepy. Just seeting there holding thees bag of frozen peas to the side of hees head."* And they would frown and giggle and shake their heads at the story of the crazy American speech-lesson voyeur.

I know this probably sounds like a crazy way to spend a few minutes at the end of the day, but it provided a way to take my mind off my treatment at the hands of the goons in the parking lot. I played her little video a few more times, and finally shut down my computer, her blonde, bespectacled and puckering image still in my mind and her Ls that sounded like Ws ringing in my ears. I know they say you shouldn't take NSAIDS if you suspect internal bleeding, but the throbbing convinced me to take the chance, so I popped a couple of Advils. Then I washed up and went to bed. After reading a few pages from a book I had bought about street magic, card sharps, con artists and grifters, I drifted off to sleep.

# CHAPTER 8

I was whipping up one of my new breakfast concoctions featuring butternut squash and walnuts when Emily breezed into the kitchen. We murmured what passed for greetings and she poured herself a cup of coffee. Olivia came in a few seconds later toting a full backpack.

Emily informed me, "I won't be home for dinner. I have yoga at five and then Parvathy and I are going to grab something at the Green Guys salad place."

"No problem," I replied. Then to Olivia, "How 'bout if you and I hit Armando's for spaghetti?"

"Sounds good, Dad."

Emily added, "I've got an early meeting, but I can drop Olivia at school so you can get started on that new job."

I had told her about getting the Mover job, but frankly was surprised she remembered. I thought it might be getting a little over my skis to tell her I already had my first trial Broker assignment.

Nobody wanted much breakfast. Olivia had a bowl of oat cereal and some apple juice and Emily had a piece of Ezekiel bread, toasted with almond butter. The clinking of spoons and crunching of toast seemed especially loud against the absence of conversation at our table. Olivia got a quick laugh with "Uh, did I miss that we're doing an 'In silence' retreat here?" Emily and I both said at once, "No, we can talk." But nobody said anything else. Minutes later they were both charging out the door and into Emily's "cute-ute." Neither one had seemed to notice the new scrapes on my face.

I took my coffee and a small dish of the squash and walnuts into my work room and fired up my computer. It was almost eight and I didn't want to miss Carl's live broadcast with Roebuck as special guest.

Moments later, Carl's face was on the screen and I turned up the volume.

"Hey, what's up, Brokers. As promised, we've got none other than our main man, Roebuck, here. And he's got some important messages for you guys."

Roebuck suddenly appeared full-face in the screen. It was the first time I'd seen him up close, his features magnified that way. He had the kind of slick-bald head that seemed an extension of his face, smooth and almost khaki-hued. Shiny brown eyes under full but sculpted brows and a confident smile showing even white teeth.

"Carl told me about you new guys, and it's exciting to see all that potential out there.

"I want to talk with you today about the importance of getting in touch with your true, inner self and then aligning everything you do with that."

*Oh, boy. Better buckle up for this ride.* He droned on about how "authenticity"—understanding who you really are at your core, setting personal goals and then making sure you spend all your time pursuing activities that move them along—was the key to everything good in life. I hadn't seen or heard any of Roebuck's "philosophical" presentations before, but this was clearly a bunch of warmed-over bullshit from the old school of self-centered, self-absorbed living that I thought had played out a few decades ago. But here he was, serving it up like creamed chipped beef on toast he'd tell you he made from an original recipe.

He droned on a while longer, piling cliché upon cliché, but

finally he wound down and turned it back to Carl, who signed off. I'll admit I was puzzled seeing this "deeper" side of Roebuck, and it occurred to me it tarnished rather than enhanced his bad-ass image. But I had more practical things to do than ponder the guy's personal brand management. I wanted to see whether anyone at the Toren Hotel had any gold waiters' jackets with the brass buttons. I dialed the main number and asked to speak with Josiah Wheatley. He'd been the steward when I worked there.

The operator gave a percussive laugh. "You just missed him—by about ten years. He's been gone at least that long."

"Gone as in passed away, or gone as in no longer working there?"

"Oh, he's still alive, as far as I know. But he left here a while ago."

"I'm sorry, I didn't ask your name."

"It's Brianna."

"Brianna, do you have a cell phone or email for Mr. Wheatley?"

"Hang on a sec...Here it is. It's jwheatley@gmail.com."

"Listen, while I have you on the line, would you happen to know whether they still have any of those gold waiters' jackets lying around anywhere?"

Brianna treated me to another of her cymbal-crash laughs. "Last time I saw one of those, it was hanging with some others in the closet of Room 106. That's the room the waiters use to change clothes. Our servers haven't worn them in some time. They wear paisley vests now."

"I guess that's progress."

Brianna let loose with another short burst. "I guess."

"I'm real familiar with Room 106 from back in the day. Mind if I stop by next time I'm down there? I have a need for some and I'd be happy to buy them from you guys."

"No worries. Just come right to the desk and ask for me. I work days, eight to four. I'll show you right where I saw them last."

"Terrific. Thanks so much, Brianna. Bye."

It was still early, so I decided today was as good as any for a trip down to the Toren for Brianna's tour of Room 106. I closed down my computer and headed out through the garage, started my car and pointed it in the direction of Toren Beach.

The drive took me about forty-five minutes, but it was pleasant enough. Frankly, I was glad to be away from the computer and human contact, and my mind was filled with dueling thoughts of how to make the most of my new opportunity with John and the gang at Omega, and my other new opportunity as a Mover-and-soon-to-be-Broker for Carl and his crew at the Depot.

I pulled up at the street parking area near the kitchen entrance to the Toren and walked around to the boardwalk side, and into the main lobby.

A young woman with shoulder-length brown hair and round horn-rimmed glasses was standing at the front desk, looking down, presumably at a computer screen sunken into the counter. She was dressed in a lightweight blue business suit with a white blouse underneath.

She glanced up and smiled automatically. "Good morning and welcome to the Toren. Checking in?" And then, doing a double take, "Omigosh, is your face ok? Looks like it hurts."

"Oh, this. Yes, thanks. It's fine. Just took a spill in a parking lot. Not watching where I was going. Kinda embarrassing is all."

Looking sideways, dubious. "Well, ok. Are you checking in?"

"Actually, no. I'm here to see Brianna about some jackets."

"That'd be me. Are you the gentleman I spoke with earlier?"

"That's right."

"Ok. Well, I can take you down to 106 in a couple minutes when Raina gets back to cover the desk. Just have a seat and I'll be with you shortly."

"Thank you."

I retreated to the small seating area in the lobby. Checking my email, I saw there was something from Barb DeMinter. I could only see the first two lines of her email, which started with "Hmm."

When I opened it, I could see the rest of it was short and none-too-sweet—"One and done!"—and ended with "We can discuss tomorrow morning if you have questions."

After three attempts, I settled on a simple reply of "Talk with you at 9 tomorrow." Then Brianna appeared before me, apparently ready for my little look-see.

We walked together down the familiar hallway. The carpet and wallpaper were different, and the lighting had been up-graded to LEDs, but there was that familiar musty aroma I'd become accustomed to years ago.

"Well, here we are." She whipped out her keys and un-locked the door.

We walked in and I went straight to the closet. At first I thought it was empty save for a couple of dozen wire hangers, but when I looked deeper, behind the wall to the right of the closet door, I saw not one but six gold jackets. I couldn't be-lieve my eyes.

"Whoa! Here we go!"

"This what you're looking for?"

"You bet. Wonder whether there are any buttons anywhere."

I reached into the inside breast pocket of the first jacket and found one of the familiar red trays waiters used for pre-senting dinner checks at the end of the meal. As I put it back, I heard a little click as it touched something at the bottom of the pocket. I pulled it back out again, stuck my hand in and retrieved two sets of brass buttons.

"Schweet!"

"This is your lucky day!" cried Brianna.

Rifling the pockets of the other jackets, I found seven more sets of buttons.

Thinking about the order for twelve I had to fill, I asked her whether there might be another cache somewhere.

"You know, there just might be one or two in the coat closet behind the front desk. Why don't you bring those six and let's go see?"

I grabbed the jackets and followed her back down the stairs into the lobby and behind the front desk. Sure enough, there were three more gold jackets shoved way to the side of the coat closet.

"Hey, that's nine!"

"Any other secret stashes anywhere?"

"Hmm," she frowned. "I think that's going to be about it. No other places come to mind. I'll keep my eyes and ears open and let you know if I come across any more."

"Ok. Great. Now about these. How much do you want for them?"

Brianna looked around with mock furtiveness. "I don't think anyone's going to be looking for them any time soon. I doubt anyone even knows they're here. But I've gotta check with my manager. Hang on a sec."

She slipped into the corridor behind the front desk and around the wall. I heard her murmur something and another voice answered. They talked for a few minutes and I heard some tapping on a keyboard. I couldn't make out what they were saying, but soon she was back followed by another woman, mid-forties, frowning under a mouse-brown blunt cut, old-fashioned two-piece business suit with floppy tie over white blouse.

"This is my manager, Ms. Wellstone."

She cut to the chase. "You're interested in our old jackets?"

"Yes, ma'am. I'm a Broker and I have a client who wants to buy them. I'm happy to pay you a fair price."

"I just did a quick search and couldn't find any like it on any of the sites. That means they must be pretty rare, right?"

"I'd say so, yes. Look, whatever you think..."

She held up a hand and nodded, eyes closed momentarily, her expression almost pained as in *"Spare me the bullshit."*

"Right. I hear you. We've got something you don't see every day and you want to buy it from us. I figure your guy, whoever he is, is going to be willing to go at least a grand for the lot. You're talking to a gal whose family had a main street retail business for decades before the economy went to shit. I knew about *keystone pricing* before I could count to ten. Fifty dollars apiece sounds about right, don't you think? And I'll throw in the buttons."

I gulped. "Well, yeah. I'm good with that."

She watched as I counted out $450 onto the desk, then picked up the bills and expertly thumb-counted them in half the time it had taken me. Reaching under the counter, she pulled out a receipt pad and quickly scrawled a makeshift bill of sale. Handing it to me, she managed a half-smile and said, "Nice doing business with you."

"I appreciate your help and your time." I walked out of the lobby with the jackets and the buttons.

Back in my car, I thought for a minute. The guy says he wants twelve. I've got nine. Now what? I was tempted to go back to my computer and start digging to find someone who knows someone who might know someone who might have them. Sure. And I could dick around for the next few days trying to come up with the other three or I could go to the guy with what I have. Maybe he had found a few more from some other source.

Pulling into the driveway, I called the number I had for Mr. Amory, the prospective buyer for the jackets.

He answered on the second ring.

"Oh, hi, Mr. Amory. My name is Raf Vella and I'm a Broker. *(Slight exaggeration of my status, but I was acting in that capacity, right?)* I understand you're interested in some gold waiters' jackets."

"Why, yes. I did put an order out there a couple weeks ago.

You're the first person I've heard from. Do you have them?"

"Well, I'm working on it. If you don't mind my asking, what's the setup there at your restaurant?"

He laughed. "Actually, there's no setup yet. We're still in the planning phase. We figure we'll need twelve total staff, ten waiters on at a time—seven for the dining room and three more for the bar area."

"What if I could get you nine gold jackets for the dining room waitstaff and three more of some other color for the bar area?"

"Hmm. I hadn't thought about it, but I guess that would work."

This was definitely a "Hmm" kind of day for me.

"Ok. Let me see what I can do, and I'll get back to you."

"Fair enough," said Mr. Amory.

I hung up and dialed The Toren's main number, hoping I could catch Brianna before her shift ended.

She answered right away.

"Hi, Brianna?"

"This is she."

"Hey, it's Raf, the waiters' jackets guy. After I left, I got to thinking: Do you think you have any other jackets in any other color?"

"You know, I think we just might. Hang on a sec."

She put me on hold and Shaggy's "Angel" came on to keep me company: *"She was there through my incarceration, I wanna show the nation, my appreciation."*

Just as Rayvon was about ready to come in to sing the chorus, Brianna came back on the line.

"You won't believe this. I found three in red with buttons in the pockets! And yes, you can definitely have them at the same price—$50 apiece."

"That's incredible! Ok if I stop down to pick them up tomorrow?"

"Sure. I work the same hours and I'll have the jackets here for you."

"Great. Thanks."

I called Amory back and told him I had twelve jackets for him—nine gold and three in red. He was ecstatic and didn't hesitate when I told him the price was $1,050 for the lot, with the brass buttons included.

I hung up feeling very good about my day's work. I headed back toward home and decided to swing by the Depot to see about my pay for the recent transactions.

I guess Margot had picked up my newfound brio as she gave me a combo smile-and-quizzical look as I drove through the gate and parked near the entrance. It was early for the night crowd, and the parking lot was mostly empty. I walked in and headed for Carl's office.

"What's goin' on, Bro," Carl said without looking up. He was head down, frowning at his laptop.

"Hey, Carl. Just thought I'd stop by and see about my comp for the beach chairs deal."

"Whoa, Captain, you just closed that deal a couple days ago..." Then he did a double-take when he saw my face. "What the hell happened to you? Looks like somebody took a belt sander to the side of your head."

I told him about my run-in with the goons in Crenshaw's parking lot.

He grimaced and shook his head. "You get a good look at 'em?"

"Nah, it was dark and they jumped me from behind. I couldn't tell you anything about them. Except maybe one guy had this tattoo on the inside of his wrist."

"Uh, what kind of tattoo?"

I grabbed a pencil from the mug on his desk and the notepad next to it, and did my best to draw the tattoo from memory: a fist holding what looked like crossed sewing needles with thread dangling from them.

Carl leaned back and smiled. "Looks like you found a couple members of the Seamsters Union."

"SEAM-sters? You mean TEAM-sters, right?"

"Nope. These guys are members of the union of tailors. They've got a shop right here at the Depot, making men's shirts and slacks from patterns from the old days. Pretty good workmanship."

I shook my head. "Not too sure about that, Carl. These guys sure didn't look like the 'Angelo' I remember from the men's store where my dad used to take me to get suits every couple of years."

Carl allowed himself a little laugh. "Well, a lot of things don't look like they used to. Get used to it, bro. As you've just learned, they don't like it much when it looks like someone's trying to muscle in on their business, either by making or trafficking in men's clothing. They monitor email accounts and our posting boards and they have bots that flag transactions like that. They find out who the account belongs to and send out their muscle to give the guy a tune-up or maybe a little extra if he's already been warned and doesn't seem to be listening. They must have found your waiters' jackets deal even before you did and thought they should give you a little tap to introduce themselves."

"Geez, I guess I have a lot to learn. Anyway, I figure I'm due $275 on the beach chairs and some money on my first deal as a Broker for the waiters' jackets which, by the way, cost us only $600, and I'm selling them for $1,050. Any way you can advance me some on that?"

"Damn, boy. You're taking this real serious, aren't you?"

"As a heart attack. Plus, I really need the cash flow. Just like the rest of your guys. Don't you have some way of advancing people the money on deals they close so they don't have to wait for all the paperwork to get a little cash in their hands?"

Carl pushed himself back from his desk and looked at the ceiling. "You're talking about an advance on business actually sold. Closed. Done deals, right? I'm not looking to put out money to guys and then have to chase them down if something goes south."

"'Course not. This is just *potentializing* the commission on deals where the case is closed but the money is just not yet in the house. I'm surprised nobody's asked you for it before. I'm telling you, Carl, you should be doing this for all your guys. They'll love it. Plus, you'll be able to recruit a higher class of Broker with a better comp plan like this."

"Po-ten-tial-izing," he repeated slowly, the way you do when you're trying out a word you've just heard for the first time. Then, scratching the side of his head and starting to nod, he said, "Maybe something could be arranged if I knew how to work it out."

"I've done this before in my prior life," I said. "Who handles the programming for your compensation systems?"

"Guy named Aubrey Workinger. Long-haired, geekish-type guy. Smokes like it's in his job description. I'll introduce you if he's here."

It turned out Aubrey was indeed in the house, and he responded *"B rt thr"* to Carl's text. Next thing I knew he was standing in the doorway, accompanied by an invisible cloud of cigarette smoke aroma, looking every bit as advertised—lank brown hair framing a gaunt face, a half-smile revealing tar-stained teeth. He started nodding before anyone said anything, as if to communicate eagerness to solve any and all manner of "what-ifs" to be tossed his way.

Carl introduced us and then gestured for me to tell him what we wanted.

As I talked, Aubrey resumed his nodding (if he had ever completely stopped) and said, "Well, sure, I can do that. No worries. Can you write up exactly what you want it to do—'if-this, then-that?' You know, sorta business specs?"

"Sure. But then I want to go over it with you in person. Talk it through. Use some examples. Have you sharp-shoot and ask questions. Then maybe put together a little worksheet and put my examples in and see whether it gives me the answers I was expecting."

Aubrey straightened up and smiled more broadly. "I can see this isn't your first rodeo, amiright?"

"I did this kind of thing when I was a sales manager, setting up and managing comp plans. We had a high-performing type of rep and they expected to be paid ASAP on business they closed without waiting for the mouse to go all the way through the snake, if you know what I mean."

Aubrey was nodding again, and Carl was too. Nodding and smiling. He could see where this was going. I told Aubrey I'd get an "if-then" email to him by close of business and we made plans to meet the next day to review it. He gave Carl and me a little half-bow, raised up onto his toes, executed a service-member-worthy about-face and marched out of the room.

Carl was ecstatic—or at least as excited as I had ever seen him. "This is going to be great—just what we need, man! Thank you."

"If you want to thank me, wait till we're ready to go live and let me intro the program on one of your Broker calls."

"Sure thing. Easily done!"

"Meanwhile, let's see how fast we can get this set up. I'll need to coordinate this with your disbursements people."

"That's Rob Gutschman. Been here since day one. Doesn't know dick about the front of the house, but he's damn good at what he does."

"Sounds like he's my guy. Can you let him know I'll be reaching out to him later on today or early tomorrow?"

"Damn, you're not letting any grass grow, are ya?"

"You wouldn't want me to, would you?"

"You got that right. I'll text you after I've talked with Rob."

I was already on my feet. "Well, I guess I'll take off."

"Right. Call me tomorrow after you meet with Aubrey and talk with Rob."

He gave me a thumbs-up. "See ya."

I walked out with a little spring in my step, feeling good that I'd impressed Carl with my idea and might be helping him with an important aspect of the Depot's operation.

# CHAPTER 9

I was back home in my kitchen, late afternoon, Olivia at the table doing her math homework, when my phone buzzed. Emily.

"Hey, what's going on."

"Hi. I just wanted to let you know I'm not going to be home for dinner. Tao has asked me to get together over dinner to discuss a master class he's thinking about offering. This would be toward a certification as an instructor, and I'd be his assistant as well as a student in the guinea pig group."

"Oh, ok. I'll probably order Chinese for Olivia and me. Where are you going anyway?"

"Buxton's, I think. They have sort of a diner menu and we can each get what we want."

"Ok. See you later."

"Don't wait up. I'll be late. Bye."

This time the "Hmm" was a silent one and it came from inside my head.

I ordered the food and, when it arrived, we ate while Olivia told me about an assembly that day where the kids were asked to share their feelings about co-ed games at recess. She said she was in a minority that favored separate-gender games.

After we cleaned the plates, put leftovers in the glass containers in the fridge and tossed the boxes, she wiped the table and resumed her math homework.

I sat there with her for a while and checked my phone a few times.

Olivia finished up her work and said she was going to her room.

✖✖✖✖

For about fifteen minutes, I just sat there, my mind racing. I absently picked up my phone again and realized I had half-consciously pulled up the Buxton's site on my phone and had their number on the screen in front of me. I tapped it.

"Good evening. Buxton's."

"Oh, hi. I'm sorry to bother you, but I wonder whether you can help me find a couple of people there having dinner. The woman has short brown hair and a short, blue leather coat. Not sure what the guy looks like."

"You know, normally I'd tell you to call 'em on their damn cell phones or just go jump off a cliff, but things are really dead right now and you sound like you need a little help. Hang on."

I waited for what seemed about an hour. It was actually about sixty seconds till she came back on the line.

"Uh, sorry, nobody here like that now. Like I said, it's slow so I'd see them right away. But the other server said she saw a woman with hair like that and a guy with a stingy-brim hat. She said the woman came in first and ordered chamomile tea and said she was waiting for someone. Guy came in about five minutes later. Then they left together right away. He didn't even sit down."

"This guy—what'd he look like?"

"Hang on a sec."

I heard her ask somebody but couldn't make out the response. She was back in a few seconds.

"Average height and build. Jeans. Light jacket. He came and went pretty fast so she didn't really see the face."

"Ok, thanks for your help."

"I hope you find 'em...if that's what you really want."

I hung up and realized I had a bellyache and my face was throbbing.

The rest happened in a blur. I was on automatic pilot and had to remind myself to breathe a few times. My chest was tight and my teeth were clenched. My finger somehow pressed Emily's cell phone number. She answered on the first ring.

"Hi. Is something wrong? I'm in the middle of my meeting."

"Uh huh. Where are you?"

She let out a sigh of exasperation. "Like I told you. I'm at Buxton's. Meeting with Tao. Look, what's so important it can't wait till I get home?"

"You're there now?"

Another sigh, signaling one of her eye-rolls. Then "Yeh-ahh."

"And you've been there since you left home?"

"Look, Raf, I'm kinda busy right now. I'll talk to you when I get home."

"Emily, I know you're not at Buxton's. Come home now. I'm leaving. I've got my shit packed. In twenty minutes, I'm calling Ginny from next door to come stay with Olivia if you're not back by then."

I disconnected and sat there with the phone in my shaking hand for a few minutes, my brain on fire. After a while I got up and went to the bedroom and started yanking clothes out of my drawers and throwing them on the bed—underwear, socks, shirts, pants, a couple sweaters. I went to the closet, got out my clunky suitcase and threw everything in. I stopped in the kitchen to pick up a plastic freezer bag, went to the bathroom and put my toiletries in it.

I closed the suitcase and took it into the living room, then put on my coat and sat down to wait.

Ten minutes later, I heard Emily's car. Without waiting to talk with her, I walked out the door, got in my car and started it up. I caught a glimpse of her open-mouthed stare from the driver's side window as she pulled in while I was backing out.

Where I was going, I had no idea.

I ended up at the Marriott by the airport. I parked near the lobby and walked in, leaving my suitcase in the car. The name tag told me it was "Jen" on duty at the front desk.

"Yes, sir. How may I help you?"

"Do you have anything for tonight?"

"One person for one night?"

"Right."

"Let me see. Ok, sure. Here we go. Second floor ok?"

"Sure. So long as it's not by the elevator or ice machine."

She frowned at her screen and did a little typing. Then a smile.

"Room 238. Here we go." A few more taps and she activated a key card, slipped it in one of those little envelopes with the room number on it and handed it to me with another smile. "Have a good night."

I went back out to the car, retrieved my suitcase and went up to the room. Dropped the case on the bed, pulled out the few things I wanted to hang up, and then went down to the bar. Not much action there, which suited me fine. There was a basketball game on the big screen in front of me, but the volume was off and I didn't even notice who was playing. I ordered an IPA on draft. In other circumstances, I would have been amused that what they served me was Angry Bear Lager.

At that moment I think I honestly believed things between Emily and me would somehow get worked out in a couple of days. I had made my statement, which I thought would suffice as a protest of her actions and duplicity, and I figured she'd cut the crap after she thought about what was at stake.

I paid up and went back up to the room. I flicked on the TV and got ready for bed. I watched a little bit of an old *Baywatch* and fell into an uneasy sleep.

109

I was up early the next day, went downstairs for the buffet breakfast in the lobby—coffee and a toasted English muffin with peanut butter seemed the least offensive option—and then went back to my room and switched on my computer. It was almost time for my conference call with Barb DeMinter about the presentation at Brancati Financial, so I reviewed my outline, happy to have something to occupy my mind. Satisfied that I was ready, I punched up Barb's direct dial number at Omega.

She answered on the first ring.

"Hi, Barb. It's Raf Vella."

Long silence. Then, "Uh, ohh-kayyy."

"Yes, to go over the Brancati presentation?"

"Right, well, it's done. Like I told you, I got it over to John and he said it was fine. I asked my assistant to get it over to you. Did you get it?"

"Well, actually, I sent *you* a draft earlier. Did you get it?"

"Yeah, well, I think I did see that and, while I can't recall the specifics, I do remember thinking it wouldn't cut it. Let me check with her. Can you hold a minute?"

"Sure." I was starting to get that hollow feeling in the pit of my stomach, accompanied by a coppery taste in my mouth—the same one I used to get all the time in the final days leading up to my leaving Omega—when everyone around me was acting like an asshole and everything was politics, positioning, undercutting, sidewinding, backbiting, sabotaging and other assorted bullshit.

She came back on the line and said her assistant was emailing me and then we could discuss. In about thirty seconds I got the email, opened the doc and saw that it was virtually the same document I had sent her with a few cosmetic changes.

"We sent this over to John so he'd have it at the same time we're talking about it. Do you have any general comments? Do you want to go over it line by line or is it good to go?"

My first impulse was to say "Ok," but something else grabbed hold of me.

"You know, Barb, I don't think this is going to work. I've gotta go right now. I'll get back to you when I have more time."

And then I disconnected.

I was not in the mood for the corporate fuck-around dance, so I quickly punched up John Flanagan's number, and he answered after a few rings.

"Hi, John. It's Raf."

"Oh, Raf. Glad you called. Barb's here with me. Did you get a chance to review her draft outline? Looks pretty good, don't you think?"

"John, it's not her draft. It's mine. I sent it to her so we could discuss it this morning prior to getting something over to you. But instead of waiting to talk with me as we agreed, she got her assistant to take my doc, make a few minor changes and send it over to you, passing it off as her work. That's the kind of weird shit you've got going on over there in your shop, John. And frankly, I don't want anything to do with it. Translation: There is no fucking way I'm working with Barb on this or anything else. If you want my help on this, I work directly with you or not at all."

"Raf, wait a sec. You're obviously upset here..."

"No, John. Don't make this about my being upset. This is about Barb pulling a fast one and stealing my work product. I've seen this movie before and I'm not going to be part of it. I don't have the time or the inclination to play corporate jujitsu. I'm out of that game, remember? I'm hanging up now, John, and you can decide whether you want to work with me or not. Let me know. Bye."

And, just like that, I disconnected the call. I could imagine Barb shrugging and expressing complete surprise and dismay at my "unfounded" accusations. No good could come from any further talk.

In the space of about twelve hours, I had put my marriage on the table and basically told John to stuff the contracting job he'd offered me.

I saw that Emily had called while I was on the line with John, and she had left a voicemail message, so I punched it up.

*"Raf, I don't know where you are. Olivia is asking questions, so I told her you were on a business trip, but I'm not sure whether she believed me. What's going on? When are you coming back? Let me know. Thanks."*

Practical. That's the only word—or thought—that came to my mind. Emily was all about the logistics. Practical to the end. No thought to what she might have done to precipitate my abrupt departure. No expression of concern about me, about us. Just when will things get back to the way they were, when I will get back in harness. Nasty. I was by no means ready to get back to her.

I did have to talk with Olivia, though, and made a mental note to call her right after she got home from school. Maddie Ackerman, the sitter, would be there and I wouldn't have to deal with Emily just to get to talk with Olivia.

I packed up my computer and headed downstairs, stopping at the desk to tell them I'd be staying at least another couple of nights.

Traffic was light and I got to the front gate in about twenty minutes. I flashed my new pass and Margot waved me through.

I stopped at the door to Carl's office, seeing he was on the phone. As soon as he saw me, he nodded and motioned for me to come in and take a seat while he kept talking.

"Brett, hold on a second. As luck would have it, the guy I was telling you about just walked in. I'd like to put you on speaker so we can all talk."

He punched the speaker button and said, "Brett, you there? Great! This is Raf Vella, our newest Broker." Raising his eyebrows and cocking his head as he heard himself trying the title on me for size. "Raf, this is Brett Rollins, one of our very best clients. Brett, Raf may be new, but I've gotta tell ya, he's already kicking some serious ass. We think he's gonna add a lot of value."

Brett said, "Hey, Raf. Nice to meetcha."

"Same here, Brett."

"Raf, Brett here has a need for some uncommon goods, and I'd like to find a way to help him get 'em."

"You guys up for a short course in fat and bone?" asked Brett.

"Say whuh?" Carl scrunched up his face.

I was as mystified as Carl but I said, "Sure. Go ahead, Brett." My curiosity was already firing, impressed that Carl was starting to see me as a go-to guy for unusual deals.

"Guys, my clients here on the East Coast are companies that use animal fat and bone from pigs and cows. A lot of the products they've been making using petroleum derivatives have had to be reformulated, since petroleum is on the X List, completely outlawed by laws and regulations. They're back to using animal fat for animal feed, fatty acids, soaps, personal care products, biodiesel, paints, lubricants and greases.

"They also use the bones for a number of things. As you know, a lot of the fertilizers people have been using have been outlawed. So, they're back to using animal bones for that and as a swap for petrol products—superphosphate fertilizers, boneblack, 'bone oil' as fuel for factory boilers.

"Next, the pitch from the tar-stills is used to make black varnishes such as Brunswick black.

By this time, Carl had done a face-plant, his forehead on the desk. I might have thought he was unconscious, but he was softly pounding both fists alongside his head. I figured we'd lost him, but he may still have been listening.

"The residual charcoal is employed as a decolorizing and refining medium, chiefly in the sugar industry. The fine dust charcoal is sifted out and used in the preparation of blackings and 'ivory black.'

"Then there's a market for the spent char as a source of superphosphate; or it may be calcined in air to bone ash, which is an important ingredient in the paste used for English bone china. When treated with sulfuric and phosphoric acids, bone ash also yields a substitute for cream of tartar in baking powders."

Carl had finally raised his head and pushed back from his desk, stood up and was pacing the room, tossing an orange from one hand to the other. "Brett, I gotta tell ya, my head is about to explode. But I'm guessing Raf here's absorbed enough of all that to be up to speed." He spread his hands in the universal "Help!" signal and nodded hopefully at me.

I knew what was coming next. Brett wanted us to find some sources of fat and bone and move it from Point A to Point B, probably in huge quantities, maybe surreptitiously.

He paused for a moment. "Uh, is it just you two there in the room hearing this? I need to know if I can speak freely."

Carl was quick to assure him. "Yep. Just us."

Brett continued. "My clients have continued to buy petrol products on the black market, but the price and the costs of security and paying off the inspectors have increased their costs to the point of being prohibitive. They've run the numbers and they've decided animal fat and bone is the way to go. We just need a source and a safe way to get it from there to here. That's where I'm hoping you guys can help."

Carl raised his arms, palms up, and raised his eyebrows in a silent question to me: *"Can we do it?"*

"Brett, I think we can help you," I said with more assurance than I could back up if pressed for details. But I could already see how it might be done.

Hearing that, Brett was eager to move to the implementation stage. "I'm gonna send over a graph I think will help explain our situation. Let me know when you get it."

Carl and I watched his big monitor until Brett's email with the attachment came up. Carl clicked on it and it filled the screen.

"Ok, we got it," said Carl.

"As you can see, while production of chicken has been rising and pork has been holding its own, beef production has been in some decline over the years. Don't get me wrong, there's still plenty, but what I'm saying is, it's less than it was. And while the demand for beef as food has been going down, the demand for fat and bone has been increasing. Hence the shortage.

"The main problem can be summed up in two words: *boxed beef*. In the old days, they'd ship a whole side of beef to the East Coast. Nowadays, most of the dressing goes on right there in Nebraska and Texas, and the ready-cut roasts, steaks and chops get shipped east in boxes. The fat and bone stay out there. What we need is a cheap, reliable way to access that and get it from out there to here."

"Why not just hire some long-haul truckers?" offered Carl.

"Sure, we could do that—if we could buy it in the first place. But the big slaughterhouses have sweetheart contracts with our competitors who buy their entire output. On the off chance we get to buy a little, our truckers get hijacked before they cross the state line. We need two things: 1. Some new contracts with the slaughterhouses, and 2. Security for our trucks to bring the product to the East Coast."

Carl gave me his best *Any ideas?* look.

I jumped in. "Brett, let us huddle here a bit and get back to you. I'm thinking we can do something, but I want to talk it over with some of our folks here. We'll have a plan to you by the end of the week."

"Good deal," said Brett.

We clicked off and Carl asked, "What the fuck do we know about fat and bone?"

"Nothing. But we *do* know something about negotiating contracts and a shit-ton about security. That's what they need. We can do it."

"Who's going to do the negotiating?"

"Uh, that would be me. And you can activate some of your Depot hard-case types to put together a security detail. I'd say let's get back to Brett with a proposal that starts really small. One contract with one slaughterhouse. Arrange the first few shipments. Make sure the security is good. Get some success under our belts and see what we learn."

Carl nodded and got quiet for a minute. Then he said, "I think we've got to get hold of some bad-ass truckers we know for this trial run. And make sure the security trucks are unmistakable so the bad guys know not to fuck with em."

I shook my head. "I'm pretty sure the competitors know those guys and will be monitoring their activities. I'm thinking we go the other way—get the tamest, mom-and-pop semi operator we can find. Folks the bad guys would assume are carrying your basic groceries. Winners of the Least-Likely-To-Be-Hauling-Fat-And-Bone contest. And make the security real low-key and following at a safe distance."

Carl showed me his best jack-o'-lantern grin.

I responded with a grin of my own. "And I think I know just the right folks for this run."

"Seriously?"

"Yep. Remember a few years ago when they closed off the whole financial district for a week after that last big terror attack? Nothing coming in or going out? Well, there was this restaurant down there that was trying to stay open serving rescue workers, but the guy was running low on supplies. I got Costco in North Jersey to donate some food, and then I had to figure out how to get it over the river and down to the restaurant.

"Costco had no trucks anywhere around, but I asked them whether they knew any independent truckers who might be en route to somewhere close. Sure enough, the second guy I called was on his way with a load from New Hampshire. He was dropping it off near us and his pickup was in South Jersey in a couple days. He'd be dead-heading the next morning by the time he was passing through.

"I met him at 6:00 a.m. behind the Costco—driver, his wife

and a little dog. You shoulda seen this thing. Rig was all set up like a little house. They were more than happy to contribute to the cause. We loaded up and got an NJ State Police escort to take us to the GW bridge, then NYPD picked us up from there and led us down to the restaurant.

"I wish I had a picture of the look on this restaurant guy's face when we pulled up with the goods. One of my best days ever."

"Good little story, Raf. Think that guy's still driving?"

"Well, he's gotta be late sixties by now, but I can call him and see. I still have his number in my phone."

I looked up Orville Donovan in my contacts, and tapped the number.

"You got the O," said a gravelly voice.

"Orville, this is Raf Vella."

Long pause, then "Ohh-kayyy."

"You might remember me from that run we made from the Costco in North Jersey to the restaurant in the financial district a couple years ago."

"Remember? That's a big 'Hell, yeah!' Not too good with the names, but I remember the runs real good. How the heck are ya, Dude?"

"I'm good, Orville. How's Marlene?"

"She's fine, man. She's right here."

"Hi, Honey. How you?" Throaty and Southern-tinged, she chimed in to let me know she was indeed there.

"Great, Marlene. Gee, it's terrific to hear your voices again."

I told them what we had in mind, and they seemed eager. When I mentioned security, I could sense a little hitch in their enthusiasm.

"Why we need that, man? Thought you said this was some meat scraps we'd be haulin'."

I explained the value of the goods and why we'd need to protect the shipment.

"I'm good with it, but you know I don't like my woman or

my dog here bein' exposed to any rough stuff."

"Understand perfectly, Orville. This isn't going to be like a caravan or anything. It would be unmarked—real subdued and hanging back. We're not expecting any trouble, but we want to make sure if there is any that you'd be protected. We'd have real top-drawer security talent on this one. Guys with experience as contractors in war zones."

"Guess I should ask. What are you guys payin' on this little venture?"

"Orville, we're willing to pay you double your normal rate."

"Keep talkin', Kemo Sabe. Your signal's comin' in louder n' better."

"You all electric now, Orville?"

"Heck, no! You checked out the plug-in auction for trucks lately? Your chances of winning any decent spot in line are somewhere between slim and nil, and the thing's corrupt as hell. You wanna charge any time soon, you gotta pay this guy and his brother and his uncle, too. No, this here rig is one of the last of the hybrids. I make my own electricity to charge my battery with every mile I drive. That makes more sense to me anyway. I mean, why should I be a further drain on the power grid that's groaning under the weight of all these pas- senger cars—er, more likely, passenger pick-ups? People with those gigantic Fords are guzzling up the power like there's no tomorrow. Whose idea was this all-electric mandate anyway?"

Orville was clearly a holdover from an earlier age of road vehicles. He was also stubbornly clinging to the CB radio age and was determined to keep on using the lingo, regardless of the particular communication technology of the day.

"Great. Listen, I'll get back to you with more details by the day after tomorrow. Good?"

"Fine. Look forward to hearin' from ya."

We hung up. Carl was on his feet and smiling ear to ear. "My MAN! This is great. We got transportation, and I'm not worried about lining up the security detail. But there's still the little matter of accessing the goods."

"I'm on it, Carl. You saw the info Brett sent over. Might as well start with this gem, a family-run business—AmCo Meat Products in Omaha. Can you front me a plane ride out there?"

"Easily done. When you want to go?"

"How 'bout tomorrow morning?"

"Book it now and put it on the Depot's credit card."

We got the best fare we could find, which was still sky-high, but you "gotta do what you gotta do." And in ten minutes I had a seat on the 7:15 a.m. to Omaha. I wouldn't need a hotel or rental car for this quick in-and-out venture.

"Raf, if we can pull off this bitch, it would make our whole quarter."

"Quarter, hell! This'll make your damn year by the time we're done! I've got a feeling this fat and bone thing'll be huge if we can get a handle on it. Shit, with Brett we've already got a buyer for all we can deliver. That's the tougher side. And by tomorrow night, if all goes well in Omaha, I'm gonna have our first supplier lined up."

Carl was ecstatic. "Schweeet!"

By the time I got back to the hotel, it was 3:30, so I thought I'd try to talk with Olivia before Emily got home. She answered the phone in a hesitant little voice, and I knew she'd been crying.

"When are you coming home, Daddy? I miss you."

"I've got to go out of town for the day. Then I'll be back and we'll go out to dinner. Just you and me."

"Out to dinner? Heck with that. When are you coming home, like, to sleep? You know—for good."

I told her as best I could that her mom and I were having some problems and that I wouldn't be sleeping there at least for a while, maybe longer.

"Are you guys getting a divorce?"

"We have to see what we can work out. Whatever it is, you don't have to worry. There's always going to be a way we can see each other."

"This doesn't sound very good to me. When am I going to see you next?"

"Day after tomorrow."

"Where are you going to be?"

"Just out of town on a business deal I'm working on. I'll tell you all about it when we talk. Take care till tomorrow. Ok?"

"Ok, but I want things to be like they were. Soon. Now."

"I'm not sure what's going to happen between your mom and me, but you and I are solid."

"Ok. I'll see you Wednesday."

"Ok. Bye."

I truly felt like shit after that conversation and I went down to the bar and ordered a beer. I sat and drank and made notes about what I was going to say when I got out to AmCo Meat Products. The person I was to meet with was named Cindy Danzger. It seemed like a pretty simple deal. I was going for an arrangement where we'd buy her entire output of fat and bone. We'd pick it up on a regular basis, and pay her with each pickup.

I made my to-do list: Look at the numbers to see what my max offer could be. Who was she selling to now? How much were they paying her? What kind of people were they? If they were rough types, we'd better be prepared for some physical stuff once they got the word their deal was over. Better check with Carl to see whether we had anything in the budget to make AmCo whole in case there was some kind of penalty for termination of their contract with the folks they were currently selling to. See when Orville could make the first pickup.

My head was starting to ache when my phone buzzed and I saw that it was John Flanagan. Before answering I reminded myself not to say anything I didn't want Barb DeMinter to know. Hell, she was probably sitting right next to him having rehearsed this call with John before he dialed my number.

"Hi, John."

"Oh, hey Raf. Glad I caught you. Thought I'd have to leave a voicemail at this hour."

"Well, I'm right here, right now, at your service. What's going on?"

"Well, I sure hope there are no hard feelings about this mix-up on the Brancati presentation."

"John, it's not about feelings. And there was no mix-up. We all know what happened here. I don't think I can work with you guys."

"Look, Raf, is there anything I can do to get us back on the right track?"

This is the guy who basically reorg'ed me out of a job, then called me out of the blue to work on a project, then lets his kiss-up chief-of-staff steal my work product, and NOW he wants to make nice? I took a couple of deep chest breaths to ease the tightness and cleanse my brain of angry thoughts, trying to think of a way forward with John.

"Let me think about it, John. I'm sure if we put our heads together, we'll come up with something, but I'm just going to say this once more: I will have no more dealings with Barb DeMinter, period."

After three full beats of silence, John said, "Raf, listen carefully. I'm willing to give you a shot at some work here. And I'm willing to be flexible on terms. But there's one non-negotiable: You WILL get along with Barb."

I started to respond, but John interrupted. "I get that you're upset. Don't say anything right now. Think about what I just said. And put something in an email and send it to me. Do it soon."

Taking another deep breath and refocusing on my trip the next day, I decided to put Omega and John and Barb on hold. "I gotta go. Take care, John."

I got to the airport early for my flight to Omaha, checked in, made my way through security and went to the gate. I had some time to kill so I sat in the boarding area and thumbed through my messages.

I pulled out my notebook and started jotting down notes for my meeting with Cindy Danzger. We were going to start out by meeting for breakfast. I knew the stage would be set by what was said there.

- The fat and bone story: Sustainability, the EPA regulations, scarcity of petroleum products.

- Why we need it. Touch lightly on Brett's company on a no-name basis for now.

- Why you should sell to us: Price, ease of doing business, stability, security, a good business partner.

- Ideal client relationships we have and what makes them great.

- Work flow, point people, how we'll communicate.

- Problem-resolution process.

I had to assume they'd know all about our client's proposed uses of their product and why they needed it, but I wanted that to be part of the presentation anyway. They ought to hear it from me.

I checked my watch. The flight was scheduled to take off at 7:15 a.m. and we were to get to Eppley Field at 9:40 Omaha time, which was actually a three-hour-thirty-minute flight.

It was about a fifteen-minute cab ride to Lula B's on Dodge Street where Ms. Danzger proposed we meet for breakfast. I paid the driver and a young blonde woman came out the door and met me as I exited the cab. Blue Dickies work slacks and a gray tailored blazer over a crisp white shirt, flashing me clear blue eyes and white-toothed smile, she grasped my extended hand. "Cindy Danzger, Mr. Vella. Welcome to Omaha."

"Hi, Cindy. Please call me Raf."

"Ok. Raf it is then. I've got a table for us. This place has the best breakfast in town. Best coffee, too. I figured we'd talk here for a while, then head over to the plant. We're over on G Street and it's only about a ten-minute drive from here."

"Sounds good."

I followed her to the table. The server brought coffee, which I sipped gratefully as I looked at the menu. I was hungry as hell, but I didn't want to spend a lot of time looking at the menu. I passed on the specials like chicken-fried steak and biscuits with sausage gravy, and ordered eggs over with bacon, toast and potatoes.

"Raf, let me give you some quick background on us. My dad, Ed, is technically President of AmCo but I've been running things the last five years. This is a family business that's been here in Omaha since the '60s when my grandfather opened our first plant here. We're not like the big guys that do five hundred head a day. They buy the cattle, butcher it and sell it under their own name. We have a different model: custom slaughtering and fabrication for smaller ranchers. We have the capability to re-set our facilities for kosher and especially halal which, as you might imagine, is becoming a bigger share of the market. We also process for farmers who raise grass-fed and hormone-free."

As much as I wanted to hear the whole story, I was eager to jump into the fat and bone part.

"Cindy, I'm interested in buying as much of your fat and bone as you're willing to sell me."

She nodded and chuckled, looking down with raised eyebrows, my East Coast impatience not lost on her. "We get quite a few folks up here interested in taking our fat and bone off our hands. What makes you different?"

Now that I had opened the door, I knew she was as eager to get to the "What price?" part as I had been to talk about the product itself. Her Midwest practicality was not lost on me.

"All I want to do today is to just agree to do a little business together. See how we like working together. Let's start with a small order. I'll match whatever your best buyer is paying right now. You're going to like the way we do things. We're on time. Courteous. No goofs, gaffes or foul-ups. Your guys will like working with us."

Before we'd finished eating, we agreed to get started with a get-to-know-you first order. Cindy wanted to show me the plant and facilities, so we paid the check and drove over, gratefully carrying our coffee refills in paper cups.

Her little tour lasted thirty minutes during which she introduced me to six of the guys we'd be getting to know as we worked together. They seemed friendly enough, but I caught some wary looks on their faces: "who's-this-new-guy-and-how's-he-gonna-complicate-my-life."

What she showed me was a gleaming labyrinth of stainless steel, the most modern meat processing facility of its kind anywhere, she said. And I believed her. We ended up in her office, one of those glassed-in cubicles up on the catwalk overlooking the plant. She said she'd have her lawyers email me some papers to sign.

"Cindy, let's not get bogged down in a bunch of paper. We're not getting married here. This is just to see whether we like each other. I'll have our first truck over here Monday morning to take our first delivery. Our driver and one other guy will load up, give you a cashier's check for the full amount and be on their way."

"I like that!" I could see she was warming to our way of doing things. "But what do I tell my regular guy who normally picks up Monday?"

"Does he have an exclusive for your entire output?

"Oh, no. He's just one of several outfits I sell to."

"Well, just call and tell him you don't have anything for him this week and to check back with you next week."

I glanced at my watch and saw I could still make my 1:20 p.m. flight home.

"Let's talk in the morning. How about calling me a ride

and I'll be on my way."

"Sounds good."

Cindy tapped a few keys on the laptop on her desk. "Your car's about two blocks away. Better get down there."

She stood, we shook hands and climbed down the steps to the ground floor and then she showed me to the door.

"I'll call you tomorrow morning around nine your time, Cindy."

"Sounds good. Hey, your car's here."

The car slowed to the curb, popped the door and I got in, waving to my host, who gave me one more look at the blue eyes and nice smile as we pulled away.

I thought about what we had just agreed to and started making notes about all the things that had to happen to get Orville, Marlene (and Skippy, their dog) out here by Wednesday morning.

# CHAPTER 10

Back in Newark I picked up my car and drove to my home-away-from-home—the Airport Marriott.

I watched the news for a few minutes before drifting off to sleep. A five-wide panel was dissecting President Stapleton's presser of a few hours ago, where she focused on the need for renewable energy. She had shared the podium with a professor from the University of Colorado Mining and Energy Department who talked about the alarming strain on the power grid caused by the sudden ubiquity of auto battery charging stations, price gouging, long lines at the stations and some resulting rioting. I awoke about an hour later to a blaring commercial featuring some singing and a woman doing a "happy dance" about lower car insurance rates.

I knew I had to get Orville on the line to confirm arrangements for Wednesday morning in Omaha. Hell, he'd have to leave Tuesday night to get there on time, and I wanted to give him as much lead time as possible to arrange other loads along the way to minimize dead-heading.

He picked up on the first ring. He was fine with the 9 a.m. pickup time at AmCo.

I drove to the Depot, tipping my imaginary hat at the gate to Margot, who permitted my entry without comment—or smile.

Carl was eager to hear what had happened, and I filled him in.

"What do you think about security, Carl?"

"Already got that bitch figured, Cap'n. I got a couple ex-Special Forces mo-fos standing by. These boys did a couple runs for me a while back. Nothing big as this, but enough so I know I can trust 'em. What time's the pickup in Omaha?"

"O-nine-hundred Wednesday morning."

"My boys'll be there."

"What kind of ordnance they bringing?"

"Why you wanna worry about that shit? That's their end."

"Carl, I intend to let them handle it, but we're the quarter-backs of this team and we need to know every little detail. Get them on the horn and let's walk it through."

Carl winced and rolled his eyes a little, but he punched up some numbers on the phone, and a voice answered with, "Blue. Go."

"James, this is Carl..."

"Whoa, Dude. No names, ok? State your business."

"Ok. My guy's back from Am...er, the job site, and he wants to talk logistics."

"Gotta call you back." And he clicked off. Five seconds later he called back.

"Ok. Whatcha got?"

We filled him in on the details of the run. He said he and his "associate" would be traveling with an Aubrey-June-July-One-Six and two Burton-August-May-Three-Sevens. He waited while Carl wrote down the numbers and scribbled alongside the first sequence "M60 machine gun" and next to the second "M1 rocket launchers, shoulder mount." He pushed the pad over to me and looked up for a response. Truthfully, I was surprised at that much firepower as well as its vintage, but with the next-to-dick level of knowledge I had about ordnance, what could I do but shrug and nod?

I had to consciously refrain from the usual intro and pleasantries that front-end most phone calls with people I don't know. It was time for me to set the stage. "On its face, this is hauling meat scraps about 1,200 miles through six states. Maybe twenty hours with breaks for bio and food. But this is a new business relationship, and we're essentially muscling in on existing deals some competitors have with the supplier. I'm not expecting any trouble, but it wouldn't surprise me."

On the other end, there was a pause of about three beats. Then: "With all due respect, sir, I'd expect a full shit-down. We checked these competitors you're talking about—the guys who've been buying the stuff from your supplier? It's going to take them about a minute to learn about your little deal and they've got some hard boys doing their security. Hell, they probably heard about it before you left your little getting-to-know-you meeting out there. Soon as we pull onto the highway they'll be on our little convoy like white on rice. Is your trucker traveling with any hardware?"

"No way. It's just a guy, his wife and their dog. They're expecting an uneventful day on the road."

"Well, you'd better let them know things could get rough. Tell him to be alert for the signal from me, at which time he's to calmly and slowly start braking and pulling over. If there's a rest stop nearby, that's where he's going. If not, just over to the shoulder. We'll take out their main tailing unit, and then our hang-back team will watch for a secondary unit and neutralize their asses. Then "Clyde, Moms and Scooby-Doo" can just as calmly get back on the road and resume their journey. We don't want to start the real fireworks till their truck is out of the way, so it's critical that they move smartly on my command. You getting all this? This is some serious shit right here, and I don't want any foul-ups on D-Day because somebody got all confused about what he's supposed to do."

Carl was beaming, excited that James seemed to have things in hand. Me? I was thinking ahead to the can of worms we might be opening. Any picture I had of this being just another smooth and uneventful chapter in my adventures in Broker-world had been rudely replaced by images of an ambush and firefight with battlefield-worthy ordnance—and maybe some bloodshed. Shit was about to get real.

"Uh, assuming you're successful in—er, *taking out their units*, won't they be looking to come back at us?"

This must have struck James as funny, because he allowed himself a short chuckle.

"No shit, Sherlock. Let's go back to kindergarten. You're the business guy. You know damn well you start messing in someone's shit, you're starting a war. I didn't say I was going to solve *all* your problems for you. You're hiring us to help you get *this* load from Point A to Point B. End of story for us. Shit that happens after that is a whole new day, and it's all on you. You decide you need our services further, we're available. Carl knows how to reach me."

My mind was racing by this point. "What if we preempt any reprisals by just showing up at the HQ of the competitors that order the hit and let them know they'd be wise to sit tight rather than come after us?"

"All kinds of things can be done...for a price. But now you're talking about going beyond road security and into T and I—threats and intimidation. That's a different kind of work which we—I guess you'd say—*outsource* to another firm that specializes in that sort of thing. I'm hearing a little hesitation over the line from your end. Is this bitch on or not?"

"Oh, yeah, it's...on. I'm just trying to do a little what-if planning here."

"Sure. Do all you want. We're gonna be there Wednesday at o-nine hundred, locked and loaded. Oh, and by the way, we get our money in full—cash only—before we hit Start."

I looked at Carl, who spread his hands and nodded, like *"What choice do we have?"*

I said: "We can wire the money to your account."

"I'm hearing my kind of music." He actually sort of sang that part. "I'll have my guy call you with the instructions. Soon as he says the money's good, me and my hombres will saddle up and ride. Money gets funny, the deal's off and you and I suddenly develop relationship issues. Got that?"

Carl nodded and so did I.

"Did I hear a 'roger that'?"

"Oh, right," we said in unison.

Carl added, "You have our phone number to give your accounting person, right?"

"That's a roger, boss. Out."

Carl and I tidied up a few housekeeping details, and I headed out to my car and started the engine. Before putting it in gear, I just sat there and took a few deep breaths. I think it had been a while since I actually breathed. The activities of the next few days were sure to challenge my stress management capacity, and I couldn't afford to lose my focus.

I had to see Olivia, even for a few minutes. I called her cell, and she picked up on the first ring.

"Hi, Dad." Suddenly she sounded strangely teenaged. Guess the recent antics of her parents were accelerating her maturation process. And probably not in a good way.

"You available for dinner?"

"Sure, if it's quick. How about the new salad and stir-fry place?"

"Whatever's good for you, Honey. I'll pick you up at 5:30."

"Ok. See you then."

I still hadn't left my parking space at the Depot. For the next few minutes I let the engine run and my mind wander. And what popped into my head was the name "Dick Jones." Dick—that wasn't his real name, but he didn't look or act like the Bernard or Bernie his parents gave him, and people had always called him Dick. Plus, he seemed to like it, or at least went along with it. He was a guy I had known back when I was in the Army Guard. Came in out of nowhere and took over our unit. Brought in some new ways of doing things and a wacky new vibe to what had been a staid and hide-bound operation. I'd describe him as crazy-but-competent. (When we were in the field on maneuvers, he'd wake me early every morning by coming into my tent, puffing on a freshly-lit cigarette, two steaming coffees in hand, the commodities auction blaring on his cell phone speaker.) He always had interesting and unconventional ways of looking at things, and I wondered what his take would be on our little operation. I hadn't cleared it with Carl—the idea of bringing in any new players—but I was willing to take a chance. I knew I was in over my head, and I felt I had to bounce the plan off someone I could trust and who might know a little about an operation like we were planning.

"Captain Vella, I presume." He had seen my name come up on his phone, and naturally used my Guard rank in his greeting, same as always. "Been too long. To what do I owe this unexpected pleasure?"

"Hey, Dick. I've got something I want to run by you. First, what the hell are you doing these days?"

"You are talking to the mayor of Diffle Beach, South Carolina."

"Where the hell is Diffle Beach? How long have you been that?"

"In reverse order, got elected two years ago, and at this moment running for state legislature. Go to Google Maps. Don't make me waste my time on a geography lesson, Fucknuts. I spent most of the years since you last saw me fighting in one Tee-dub or another. I finally had enough of the action and squirreled away a little nest egg so I could settle down here. The weather's nice and it's real quiet. What's this all about?"

I told him what we were doing, starting with a very abbreviated primer on fat and bone and ending with a no-names description of our upcoming first mission.

No answer for a full five seconds. Then "Oooh. Do the words 'walking into an ambush' mean anything to you?"

At this, I really did stop breathing for a moment.

"Well, I guess I'd better hear what you're thinking. That's why I called you."

"You guys are obviously not the first to the party on this fat and bone thing. And the way things are going now with all petrol products on the blacklist, the folks who are currently buying it are going to be jealously and carefully guarding their supply sources. And there's an abundance of muscle with military experience coming home from the Terror Wars looking for security work. And I assume you know that, thanks to the recently-rejuvenated NRA, it's no problem for every one of these guys to have his own small arsenal with all kinds of high-end field-grade goodies most civilians have never seen. It's easy for every company to have its own private army and, believe me, most of them do."

"Wait, you mean my old employer, Omega Financial, is likely to have its own armed security force?"

"I'm sure they do. It's probably pretty small, since their products are financial instruments rather than tangible goods. But any firm that's moving stuff like you're talking about has bigger, better and more lethal. But they may have enough, depending on what you need."

The wheels started to turn. I had been thinking about a role in this for John Flanagan, my old boss, who definitely owed me one. We were going to need some source of funds to front the acquisition of fat and bone and provide operating capital. If I got Omega involved in the money end of things, it would be a natural for their security guys to help us with the movement of product to protect their investment. Maybe we could get them to lean on the competitor's head-shed to preempt their retaliation for our intrusion into their contract with AmCo. I quickly filed those thoughts away to get back to the business at hand.

By the time we were done, I had briefed Dick sufficiently on the plan, and he graciously agreed to be my point man to check out the Omega security force and to enlist them for the side mission, if needed. He seemed good with it, and grateful for the prospect of a little excitement. I promised to get back to him by the next morning with next steps. Before we hung up, he had a helpful heads-up tidbit to share.

"Coming east on 70, you should be fine all through Missouri. But once you cross over into Illinois, things could get dicey. You'll be going through a total of six states, and there are some leased sections of roadway with tight connections between the cops and the business community. They go to great lengths to protect their own, so keep your eyes open and your weapons locked and loaded."

I knew about the leased highways, the aforementioned Kovaleski Skyway near us being one of them, but I hadn't thought we might be passing through any of them. I assumed James and his boys would be aware of it and would take any necessary precautions. I thanked Dick for the tip and then decided to take a flyer. "You know I'm doing this for the Depot, right?"

"I figured. Hey, does that guy Roebach still run the thing?" He pronounced it Roe-BACH, but that didn't mean anything to me at the time.

"Yes. Know him?"

"I guess you could say that. When I was with the County Detectives, another guy and I went all the way out to L.A. to bring him back on an extradition. Fucker really put us through the wringer."

"Extradition? You mean like he was wanted on an out of state warrant for some sort of crime?"

"It was on a weapons charge that came out of a routine traffic stop by the patrol division. I didn't get involved till he failed to show up for the arraignment. This was the Friday before Easter. We expected it to be no big deal. My partner and I flew out there and picked him up from the L.A. Sheriff's lockup and boarded a plane from LAX. Plenty of time to get back home for the weekend, or so we thought.

"Soon as we got in our seats, the fucker throws a shit fit—hollering and cursing at the top of his lungs, kicking the seat in front of him and generally causing a ruckus—and we get thrown off the plane. We had to rent a car and drive the whole way. He knew he wasn't going to win, but he did it just for shits and giggles and so we wouldn't be able to enjoy our weekend. Spiteful and resourceful. That's your boy, Roebach, in a nutshell." He said it that way again, and this time I took note of it. "Did eighteen months out of a five-year sentence and apparently has kept his nose clean since then and sure did land on his feet at the Depot. Must have some kind of connections."

"Well, he calls himself Roe-BUCK now."

"Whatever. Still an unconscionable prick by any other name, I'm sure..."

"Thanks for the history lesson."

"Always nice to know who you're working for. Take care, m'brother."

Next on the agenda was to bring Carl up to speed and get his buy-in. I was still in my car in my parking space at the Depot, so I got out and walked back in and told him in person. I guess it was becoming clearer to him—and maybe even to me—that I was finding my way and sort of knew what I was doing and could be trusted.

It was time to pick up Olivia for dinner. I pulled out, giving a jaunty, confident salute to Margot on the way out. This time she smirked and shook her head. Was that progress?

Olivia was waiting outside when I pulled up in front of the house.

"Take it from me, you don't want to go in there right now. Mom's in a real shitful mood and, when I mentioned you were coming to pick me up for dinner, I got the feeling she'd like nothing better than to unload some of it on you if she got you in her sights. This new job at the yoga studio is more full-time than part-time and I'm getting the feeling the honeymoon with that Tay-o character has just about played out."

I held up my hands in mock confusion. The old cliché crossed my mind: *"Who are you and what have you done with my daughter?"*

"Look, you and Mom are the ones who've gone nuts. I don't understand why you guys can't figure out how to stay together. Heck, you did it for twelve years. This war you guys have started is going to be expensive and take an emotional toll on all of us, and that includes me."

Shaking my head at the burst of adult wisdom, I mumbled what little reassurance I could muster. "That's the last thing I want to happen. You know we both love you and this has nothing to do with..."

She held up her hand in the universal "talk-to-the-hand" gesture.

"Don't start with a bunch of old twentieth-century psycho-babble. This is going to be a shit storm and you know it."

"Well, you and I are going to stay close, as long as you want to see me."

"Goes without saying, but don't forget, I'm getting busy with school and soccer and music. I've started singing with a band Josh and Eamon put together. Josh is really good on guitar and Eamon's been studying piano since before he could reach the pedals. Eamon's got a few tunes, and I've been putting some words to them. We're working up a little set we can do at breaks in the recorded music for the next school dance."

"Say wuh?"

"You know how a band plays a forty-five-minute set and then they play recorded tracks while they take a fifteen-minute break? That's great for an established band with a lot of songs in their bag. Well, we're just starting out and have just twelve songs. So, we're just going to flip it: they're going to play tracks for forty-five and we're going to play the other fifteen. Cool, huh? My idea!"

"Wow, that's great. Just let me know when it's going to be so I can stop by."

"Will do. But if you show up, can you kind of stay in the

back? Now, what's this about another trip to Nebraska on Sunday. What's in Omaha?"

Over dinner—salad with tofu for Olivia and a vegetable stir-fry for me (they had a couple pathetic chicken offerings on the menu but the prices were ridiculous)—I told her a little about the chapter in my career as a Broker and our sudden interest in the meatpacking industry and the Omaha connection, leaving out the "by-the-way-Dad-might-get-shot-at" part.

"I guess you're glad to be working again and making some money. It's gotta suck big-time, Mom, with the important job and you not doing much."

"Not bringing in decent money is no fun, for sure. But this new thing is good. I've already impressed the people I've been working with, and it looks promising."

We were back at the house and I'd pulled up outside. "I'm off to Omaha tomorrow. Should be back home by sometime Thursday. I'll give you a call."

"Well, be careful."

"You know I will."

She got out and we exchanged I-love-yous and good-bye waves and I drove back to the Marriott wondering just how much trouble I was really getting myself into.

# CHAPTER 11

I slept late, pulled on my running shorts and long-sleeve tee shirt and got some coffee at the lobby bar.

"Guh-mornin', Mr. Vella."

"Hi, Yolanda."

"You got a worried look today, Mr. Vella. Hope nuthin' wrong."

"Well, we'll see. I'm flying out this afternoon."

"Hope it all work out for ya. Take care."

I gave her a half-hearted thumbs-up as I retreated to one of the lobby chairs, sipping my coffee and scanning the news feed on my phone. After a thirty-minute run, I was back in my room. I'd decided to leave for the airport early, thinking it would be better to kill time there rather than look at the four walls of my hotel room the rest of the day.

But for a few short minutes I just stretched out on the bed and let my thoughts drift to Kayla. On the one hand, I missed her sweet ministrations and our energetic couplings. On the other, the last few times were marred by arguments, no doubt fueled by my jealousy and anger.

It had started a few weeks back when I went to use the shower in the guest bath as I usually did, but she intercepted and firmly directed me to the one in her master suite. I took my shower there, but when I was drying off and it was her turn in that same shower, I made a beeline for the one she'd kept me away from. That's when I saw dark body hair—the extra-curly kind—on the soap in the dish and stuck to the bottom of the empty tub. Blood pulsing in my ears, I started prowling around madly, looking for more evidence. I went to her fridge and found two bottles of grape soda and a six-pack of Heineken—beverages neither of us drank.

I waited till she emerged from her shower and was toweling off. "Uh, what's with the 'public hair' in the guest shower? Sure ain't yours or mine. And grape soda and Heineken? Seriously? I mean what the fuck, Kayla?"

"Raf, you don't get to tell me what to do. You're married, remember? You have a life—I have a life. Have I ever denied you anything?"

And it sort of just hung there. And things haven't been the same since.

I finally roused myself from my daydream, took my shower and got dressed for the trip.

Traffic was sparse and I made good time going to the airport. Along the way, I thought about my role in this. I had set it up and got the bases covered by other people who seemed like they knew what they were doing. So why was I going out there? To make sure it went according to plan, that's why. I had seen enough good plans go up in smoke the moment the action started. I had decided to ride along with Orville and, as soon as I got to the airport and through security and settled in at my gate, I punched up his number on my phone.

"Hey, Orville. It's Raf Vella. Just checking in to be sure we're all set for tomorrow morning in Omaha."

"Hey, Buddy. No problem. We're in Cedar Rapids, where I just made a delivery. Marlene and I are in a nice little hotel, and we're planning a relaxing day and an early dinner."

"Listen, man. Is it ok if I ride with you tomorrow?"

He paused a few beats and said warily, "You know, we usually ride by ourselves. This is kind of like our home and... well, you get the picture."

"Orville, I'm thinking maybe Marlene should sit this one

out. Skippy, too. I'll get her a plane ticket from Cedar Rapids back home, and she can meet you after you finish our little haul."

"Mmm. Seems like there's something more I ought to know about this deal."

I told him about my conversation with James and Dick Jones.

"Don't worry though. We'll have that security escort I was telling you about. I don't expect any rough stuff but, well, you never know."

Orville agreed I'd ride shotgun and Marlene (and their dog) would fly back to Newark from Cedar Rapids.

We got to Omaha on schedule, and I got a cab to my hotel. I was tired and ordered a room service hamburger and a beer and, after my little meal, drifted off to sleep with the TV on. A news team was reporting from the scene of a fire that had broken out at what was thought to be an abandoned warehouse, but which turned out to be a covert sweatshop making tee shirts. There were rumors that the blaze was the work of members of the Seamsters Union.

I was glad when morning came, and wanted to get to AmCo early to meet Orville for the load-in. His semi was already backed into position at the loading dock when I arrived.

"Hey, Buddy. Already got my coffee and an egg sandwich, and I'm sittin' here lovin' life. I'm ready to load soon as they open the door."

I vaulted up into the cab of his truck and we talked for a few minutes until the loading platform door opened. Cindy Danzger stood there looking like a million bucks in her crisp, trim-fitting blue Dickies work pants and long-sleeved white Dickies shirt, holding a clipboard, blonde hair pulled back in a ponytail. She smiled and waved and I jumped down and we shook hands.

"Looks like you're all set." She seemed impressed to find us there and ready with Orville's rig and an empty refrigerated trailer. "My guys'll start loading right away."

Inside of about forty minutes, we were ready to roll with our first official load of fat and bone. Now where were James and his security boys?

About that time, a black Suburban with tinted windows rolled up and came to a stop near Orville's truck, and a guy got out the shotgun side—about six feet, close-cropped brown hair, thick neck and body, upper arms filling the sleeves of a black tee. There was another hard-case type in the driver's seat and one more in back.

The shotgun-side roughneck flashed me a half-smile and asked, "Ready, Guy?"

"James, I presume."

"You Raf?"

"That's right. And this is Orville."

James nodded. "We all clear on the route? Same one you sent me, right?"

"That's the one."

He signaled and the others got out of the truck. "My guys'll just take a quick look-see in back, ok? We like to make sure we know what we're protectin'."

I looked at Orville, and he nodded and got out and unlocked the back door of the trailer. James' boys hoisted themselves up and into the trailer and opened a few of the cans. Screwing up their faces at the wafting aroma of fat and bone, they seemed satisfied, closed the cans, hopped down and gave a thumbs-up to James.

He flashed me another of his big grins. "Time's a wastin'."

Orville and I remounted the truck and James got back in the passenger side of the Suburban. I waved at Cindy as she disappeared behind the lowering loading dock door.

Our little caravan pulled out of the parking lot, and we were on our way.

Our route looked to be about 1,200 miles over about 21 hours driving time, and called for us to spend a lot of time on

I-80. The first leg was about 443 miles—we expected to hit Joliet, Illinois after about seven and a half hours.

We had taken a bio-and-food break about three hours in and were making good time to Joliet, when I heard a whining sound and we started feeling a jerkiness in the engine. I glanced over at Orville, whose expression had turned from what had been a placid steady-state to a frowning and wincing look of concern.

Turning an ear to listen more intently, he said, "We gotta stop ASAP and take a look." I phoned James and gave him the news.

Luckily, the turn-off to the rest and service area came up after about another couple of miles and Orville pulled into one of the designated parking spots for tractor trailers.

Orville got out and looked at the engine. "Looks like it might be the fuel pump. Gotta get 'er over to the service area."

By this time, James had exited the Suburban and was looking into the engine with Orville and me. "How long's this gonna take?"

"Let's find out."

We drove over to the service area and talked one of the mechanics there into taking a look. "I can get a new one over here in about two hours, and then it's four to five hours of work to do the job."

While Orville thought about this, James motioned me over and spoke softly. "This is not good, Cochise. If my gut is right, the bad hombres have probably just learned about the timing of our little venture, and this may give them the jump they need to do an intercept. I think we need to get another truck pronto, pay Orville for his services and let him go, hook up your trailer and be on our way."

I was kind of surprised at the confident way he said it—that our enterprise here had been compromised—and that the enemy was already on the way. "Wait, how would they have found out?"

"You're shittin' me, right?" James pointed at his head. "At least one of those guys at AmCo who loaded us up is most likely on the payroll for the regular buyer of their product, and you better believe he was speed-dialing his contact as soon as he saw an unfamiliar truck at the dock."

It dawned on me if I was going to honcho any more ops like this, I had to be doing better what-ifs to prep for a quick change in plans. I shrugged and, lacking any better ideas, punched up Dick Jones' number.

He answered on the first ring. "What up, Cap?"

I told him our predicament, and he said he'd be back to me in fifteen. He was back in ten.

"Got a guy comin' at ya out of Joliet with a new truck. Be there directly. And he'll be fortified. Ex-Special Forces guy riding along."

"Not sure we need that..."

Dick laughed. "Trust me, brother. You need it."

I told him we already had security.

"Raf, one mo' time: I'm sending my driver plus one. Both should be considered armed and extremely dangerous. Jones Out."

I thanked Dick and rang off. It felt good to have the cavalry on the way, but I couldn't help but think about the expenses piling up. After all, I was the leader of this expedition, and that meant the budget was mine. Security was critical, but I had to be careful not to blow our profits on cost overruns.

I went over alone and talked with Orville, who at first seemed disappointed, but I got the feeling he was also relieved to be out of this one.

There was nothing more for us to do but wait for Dick's new truck, so we went in and got coffee at the Starbucks in the food court.

The news was on and President Stapleton was doing a victory lap for the return of the last troops from the Ivory Coast. As soon as that was over, the announcer came on and reported 10,000 more troops sent to Nigeria, which had blossomed from a half-baked terrorist outpost to a full-blown capital for training of operatives. That made a total of twelve fronts in the War On Terror.

I must have dozed off, because I was awakened by the buzzing of my cell phone, Dick Jones' number flashing.

"Look alive, Raf. My boys are fifteen minutes out from your position. Where exactly are you?"

I told him.

"Good. Be on the lookout."

"Will do."

In what seemed like only a few minutes, I felt the shadow of two guys standing in front of me: one young and stocky with a buzz cut and a trim, fit, middle-aged guy, weathered-looking with a tanned, shaved head.

"You Raf?" said the older one.

"Yep." I introduced James and his two associates.

"I'm Creek. He's Lawson. Dick Jones said you fellas are in need of a semi-truck."

I explained the situation briefly while they nodded impatiently, interrupting me before I was finished. "Ok, we get the picture. Let's get that trailer hooked up and back on the road."

Leaving Orville and his truck and his coffee at the rest stop, we were rolling inside of thirty minutes, Creek driving the truck with me in the shotgun seat and Lawson in the back, James and his boys following in the Suburban.

After about an hour on the road, we saw a sign that said a weigh station was up ahead and I expected us to slow down and pull over. Creek must have seen the questioning look on my face.

"Weigh station is a great place for an ambush. No, thank you. We keep going."

"Yeah, but if we get stopped a cop's gonna look in our log-book and pull us off the road. Then we've got real problems."

Thirty minutes after passing the weigh station, we saw a police cruiser closing fast in the rear view behind the Suburban, lights flashing.

Creek's jaw tightened. "If he pulls us over, let me do the talking. James and his boys have seen them too and they'll know what to do."

About that time, James' Suburban pulled out, passed us and kept going.

The cruiser seemed to ignore the Suburban, and got right behind us, leaving no doubt it was us he was interested in. We pulled over and he angled in right behind us with his flashers still on.

"Afternoon, fellas. Can I see license, registration and your log book, please."

While Creek reached for his wallet and I went for the log book and the registration, the cop shined his big flashlight around the cab.

Then he surprised us both by asking, "Where's the old guy?"

Creek frowned and said, "Uh, say what?"

My head started to spin. How the heck did this cop know an "old guy" was supposed to be the driver on this trip? And what would he care about *who* was driving anyway? I figured I ought to say something, so I just said, "Uh, he wasn't feeling too well and we were lucky enough to get a sub here to fill in."

The cop seemed not to pay too much attention to my response and was shining his flashlight inside the cab. Then he turned to me.

"You. Please step out of the truck and open up around back so we can have a look around." Then, to Creek, "Sir, you sit tight please, hands at ten and two. We good?"

"Roger that," Creek said, then wiggled his fingers, already in the position.

As soon as I opened the trailer and the cop got a whiff of our foul-smelling fat-and-bone payload, he quickly decided he didn't want to spend a whole lot more time back there. He motioned to me to close up.

"All right, boys. That'll do it. Be careful getting back into traffic."

He went back to his car and pulled away, dousing his flashers as soon as he hit the highway. I walked back to the cab and got in.

"What'd he say?" Creek wanted to know.

"Nothing, really. You know, it may sound weird but I think he lost interest in us when he found out Orville wasn't aboard."

"If you say so, Bud. Are we good to go here? I'd like to get home sometime this year."

A few miles down the road, we saw James' Suburban parked on the shoulder and as we passed, it pulled out behind us. As we barreled down the highway, I thought about the cop's unexpected knowledge of (and interest in) who was driving our rig.

The trip went smoothly after that. We pulled into the Depot parking lot and unloaded our cargo in the big walk-in around back. I checked in with Carl, who was delighted to see us—and especially the payload—and he gave me the cash to pay James and his guys and Creek and Lawson.

We unhooked the trailer and said our good-byes and I went back inside to call Orville. I was hoping he got his truck fixed and was back on the road. It went right to voicemail, so I left a message that we had made it back and asked him to call as soon as he got the message.

Carl and I agreed we wanted to be rid of our fat and bone cache as soon as possible, so we punched up our buyer, Brett Rollins, on the speaker phone. He answered on the first ring.

"Ah, Carl, I presume. May I assume you are calling with good news?"

"Like a gravy sandwich," Carl bragged. "Raf is here with me. He was on the truck."

"Oh, ho! Nothing like a little road trip to chase the cobwebs, right?"

I wasn't particularly amused at his poking fun at what he imagined was my normal role as desk-jockey, but I played along and forced a laugh. "Yeah, it's good to be home, though."

"Well, when can I get my goods?"

"Tonight, if you like," Carl said through a smile and raised eyebrows.

"Good. My boys will be there with a truck by seven. Will you guys still be open?"

"Is the Pope Catholic? We will accommodate the needs of our esteemed client, and are at your disposal."

"That's what I like to hear. Two stalwarts with vehicle will be dispatched forthwith."

Carl rose from his chair and gave a jubilant, Rocky-style double fist-pump. "We'll be waiting. You'll wire the funds forthwith?"

"Uh, as soon as my boys see the goods and report back here."

"Understood. Until later."

Carl sat down and leaned back, his hands laced behind his head. "This looks like a very good deal. I think we are going to be a couple of happy guys tonight when this bitch is done."

But my mind was still working on the loose end of not yet hearing from Orville and our brief interaction with the cop. "I sure hope so."

I told Carl about my concerns and punched up Orville's number. Again, it went right to voicemail. I looked at my watch. It had been about four hours since we left him at the rest stop. Surely Orville's truck would be fixed by now and anyway he'd have his phone handy.

My phone rang in my hand. An unfamiliar number showed up in the display.

"Raf, honey, this is Marlene. Have you heard from Orville? It's not like him not to call. Last I heard from him, he'd just had his truck fixed and was getting back on the road without his trailer. That was a couple hours ago."

"I'm sure everything is ok. Give him a little more time. He'll call."

I gave her whatever reassurance I could muster. I had to get out of there and clear my head.

"You got it here?" I asked Carl. "I'd like to head out, if you don't mind."

"Be my guest. I'll text you when the deal is done."

I was still worried about Orville after I got in my car and started my engine. I felt my phone buzz and was surprised (and relieved) to see his name on the display.

"Boy, am I glad to hear from you..." I stammered into the phone.

But it was a different voice that interrupted with, "We got the geezer right here, Shithead."

"Who is this?"

"It's like this: You wanna see your old boy, wire fifty K to an account I'm gonna give you an hour. Now would be a really good time for you to get a pencil."

I had one in my hand. "Ok. Go."

He read me some numbers and I read them back to him. "Don't mess this up ,'cause I assure you, we won't hesitate to go to Plan B."

"How do I know he's alive?"

After about three beats, Orville's voice came on, a little shaky. "Raf, I hope you can do something for me. These are pretty rough boys who seem like they mean business."

"Are you ok?"

"Yeah, I'm good. They banged me around a little. Nothin' I ain't had before. Hey, can you call Marlene? I'm sure she's worried sick."

"Will do. Any idea where you are?"

No response. Then the unfamiliar voice was back. "Right. Like we're going to let him tell you that, asshole. Just get the money and call me when you're ready to wire. Once it's in the account I gave you, we'll tell you where you can pick up your guy."

He disconnected, and I just sat there in my car for a full sixty seconds looking at the blank phone display in my shaking hand, trying to calm myself with deep-chest breathing.

We had been just about ready to celebrate our successful first fat-and-bone deal, and now I felt miserable. I had gotten Orville involved in this and then, when I figured things might get rough, thought I had got him out of it.

I knew I'd better talk with Carl right away. I sure hoped he'd agree to front the fifty K because there was no other way I could raise that kind of cash right away.

**✕✕✕✕**

I got out of my car and walked back to the Depot building and into Carl's office. He was just hanging up the phone, and flashed me a big smile.

"I was just going to call you with the good news. Our buyer's boys are on their way over as we speak to pick up the goods. Congratulations, Broheem!"

I held up my hand. "Popping the cork has to wait awhile, I'm afraid."

I told him about our new predicament. Strangely, he didn't seem surprised.

"Shit like this happens all the time. Only thing that's weird is that they picked your guy."

"What do you mean 'all the time?' This is a fucking calamity! A man's life is in jeopardy because of me, and time's running out!"

Carl leaned back and laughed, holding up a hand. "Whoa. Slow down, Big Guy. These assholes don't really want to kill anyone. They just want some money. Give 'em what they asked for and you'll get your man back. Easy as pie. Or, we can get our own bad asses to saddle up and go after 'em."

I wasn't thrilled with any options that involved a potential shoot-out and maybe some deaths, including Orville's.

"And where exactly are we supposed to get fifty thousand dollars?"

He shrugged and answered predictably, "Sounds like you've

got yourself a personal problem, m'man."

So, while my brain was burning up, trying to come up with a fast solution, Carl seemed to be in no particular hurry. I sat back and forced myself to take a couple of deep breaths. I had a coppery taste in my mouth and a creeping sensation up the back of my neck that told me Carl and I were on different pages. I had to take the initiative, and do it now.

"Carl, how much is my share on the fat-and-bone deal?"

"Hang on a sec." He punched a few keys and raised his eyebrows at his computer. "Looks like $17,500. Not bad for a few hours' work, eh?"

"Any chance you could pay me that now and advance me $32,250 as a loan against future business?"

"You seriously thinking of paying the ransom on your own?"

"Do the words 'as-a-heart-attack' mean anything to you?"

Carl shook his head and punched some more keys. Then he sat back and, after a few moments of staring at the screen and more tapping, said, "Ok. Fifty K is now in your account ready for you to draw on."

"Let's do it now. Can I borrow your computer?"

He got up and I took his seat behind his desk and set up the wire transfer. In about sixty seconds, my phone buzzed with a message from an unfamiliar phone with an address and time. I called James and told him what was what and asked him to pick up Orville at the rendezvous point. Then I called the kidnapper back and told him we were ready. He said he'd dispatch his guy and Orville, and that they'd be in a black Suburban. I called James back and relayed the info and asked him to call me when he was in position and saw the other Suburban.

He called back in about nine minutes, and I stayed on the phone as they delivered Orville and drove away. The whole thing was done in about twenty minutes. I asked James to take Orville directly to his home, and called Marlene to give her the good news. Then I sat down and closed my eyes and shook my head.

As harrowing as it was, the deal was done quickly and without a hitch, but I was spooked. And I was weirded out by Carl's nonchalance about the whole thing, like it was no big deal.

"This was too fucking close for comfort, Carl. We cannot put people's lives at risk like this."

Carl was listening but looking down and away, and his hands were fidgety. He was not buying into my level of agitation at all. "I hear you, man. But this kind of thing is par for the course when you get into the bigger-money deals. This is the world we live in, ya know?"

"Just like that? How 'bout some compassion?"

I was still sitting in Carl's chair and he walked up in front of me, put his hands on the desk and leaned over into my face.

"Who the fuck you think you're talkin' to? I'll tell ya who. Two hundred pounds of rompin' stompin' Airborne Ranger hell. That's who. Yours truly's done four tours in the wars, and that's on the ground, dick. Not in some fucking head-shed. Know why I'm not still there? Because some raggety-ass trainee pushed me too far. I'll tell you about a day five years ago, just the way it happened.

"I was pretty sure I knew why the CO had summoned me at 0530.

"Sergeant Witham reporting, sir."

"At ease, Sergeant."

"The CO's face was red, his head down, moving side to side, taking in the stacks of files at the corners of his desk and finally landing on the one opened in front of him."

"Carl, this thing with the big Mississippi kid..."

"I'm sorry, sir. The guy got right in my face. Shoved me. He was askin' for it."

"Sorry won't do it this time, Sergeant. And I don't give a shit what he was doing. Nothing gives you an excuse to deck a trainee and you damn well know that. And it's not like it's your first. Today you have officially given me a case of the ass..."

"I'm ready to accept whatever you're going to tell me, sir."

"No, Carl, I don't think you are. Not this time. You've got your twenty in, right?"

"Roger that."

"The boy's parents want your head, and I don't blame them. I'm putting you in for retirement. You're done."

"B-but."

"The CO held up his hand in the universal 'talk-to-this' sign, officially cutting off anything more I might have wanted to offer in my own defense."

"It's that or a court martial. And not a summary deal, either. This would be at least a special—the whole nine yards. If I were you, I know what I'd take. And frankly, I don't have the time or the inclination to do the paperwork involved in charging you. That's all, Sergeant. Now get the fuck outa here so I can get back at it. The XO will be in touch."

"I saluted, executed a crisp about-face and took the four steps to the door. I paused for about three beats, thinking I might get in a few more words that might save me, but I thought better of it and walked out into the first light of day.

"My first thought was that my life as I had known it for the past twenty years was officially over. The second one was 'what now?' Until this moment, I hadn't given much consideration as to what I might do after retiring, but now it was 'go time' on that.

"It took me two years of shuffling around at dead-end civilian jobs to finally connect with Roebuck and get into this place.

"Raf, you've shown some useful skills and all, but you don't know shit about how things really work. You bring your pussy-boy privilege down here on day one—for what? Some lamb chops! Whoopee shit. Who the hell eats lamb chops? These other guys, what kinda lives you think they've got at home? At least your old lady's bringin' in some income. Lotta these guys are the sole so-called primary breadwinners, with no real jobs to go to. So, they gamble and fight to try to get enough Chits for white bread and hamburger meat. The ones with some higher aspirations and a little more to offer, they're willing and able to go out and do a Mover's or Broker's job. Sometimes people get hurt and yeah, I've seen some very good people end up dyin'. Get over it. You see enough of that, you get immune to it. So, if I'm not expressing the right amount of—com-PA-shun—for your buddy's near-miss, I'm real sorry about that, fuck you very much."

I stayed quiet for what I believe was about five beats, but it seemed longer.

"Believe me, I get all that, Carl. And, I respect your service to this country and the work you've done down here. But whatever you think about me, know this: I bring stuff to this party too. The Depot may be 100% of the world for you and for some other people too, but there's a lot more reality out there. You guys may kid yourselves into believing that just because of the hard-ass nature of the way things happen here, your Real Deal Economy is some kind of self-contained universe. But shit happens out there every day that affects your Depot-reality more than you realize. I have a lot of regard for you, Carl, but with all due respect, your immersion in this environment has deadened you to matters of life and death. Like it or not, I'm your link to the surface world, which is something you need and have been sorely lacking, fuck YOU very much!

"So, yeah. I'm open to learning from you and other Depot-dwellers, but I hope I can count on you to be just as receptive to things you might learn from me."

Carl nodded slowly. "Raf, you spent some time in the Guard, right? So, you know how the military works—relative roles of the officer corps and the NCOs? Well, down here it's the same thing. You're like a brandy-new LT: lots of smarts and plenty of energy. Me? I'm the fucking top sergeant. I know how to fight this war—and how to make shit happen. I've seen plenty of guys like you come and go, and I'm still here and will be long after you're gone. So, when you talk to me about com-pa-shun, here's another word to keep in mind: per-spec-tive. Don't forget it, ok?"

Carl sat down slowly in one of the guest chairs and we both just sat there for a few minutes, letting the steam settle from our little exchange. After a while, I figured I'd said about all I needed or wanted to say, and I guess Carl felt the same because he stayed quiet too, head bowed, examining his fingernails.

I wanted to get back to the business at hand.

"It bothers me that they'd pick an old truck driver like Orville to kidnap. Usually you hear about kidnapping victims being rich people or corporate execs with deep pockets behind them."

Carl must have been thinking similar thoughts because he got right in step. "Sounds like we need to do a little research on this Orville. How much do you know about him?"

"Very little, other than that he helped me out big-time a few years ago."

"Well, I've got a guy who can take a look for us—Jason Weisbrod."

Carl picked up the phone and punched in some numbers. Somebody answered in a couple of rings.

"Hey Jason, it's Carl down at the Depot. We need a quick background check on a guy and, of course, I immediately thought of my main man. Can I put you on speaker? I'm with my associate, Raf Vella, and he's gonna give you more details. We good?"

Carl pushed the button and said, "Jason, this is Raf. Raf, say hello to Jason, the best background man in the entire world."

"Hey, Dude, how can I help?"

"Jason, we need everything you can find on Orville and Marlene Donovan. He's a truck driver, lives up in Denport. We need to know his family situation, kids, his work history, associates and friends, financials—bank and credit cards. All that."

"I'll be back to you in one hour." The phone went dead.

Carl said, "This guy does what he says he'll do. Better go get yourself something to eat and be back here around five."

I didn't need any more prompting on that. It had been hours since I'd eaten, so I saluted Carl and went back to my car and drove straight to the Texas Roadhouse.

I sat at the bar and ordered a large club soda, whereupon the dark-haired lady bartender's welcoming smile quickly turned into a wince. She offered me a menu, but I waved it away.

"I'll have the six-ounce filet."

"No filet these days. I can give you a six-ounce eye-round. We tenderize it, so it's not too tough."

"Uh, ok."

"Do you want the mushroom sauce? It's awesome."

"No, thanks. Just plain. And a baked sweet potato. Oh, and the mixed green salad with oil and vinegar."

"And are you good with cinnamon butter on the potato?"

"No, thanks. Just plain. And bring it all at once." Now she was flashing full-on disappointment, and looked at me strangely. I mean, who turns down "awesome" mushroom sauce and cinnamon butter?

"How 'bout some rolls and butter? They're amazing."

"No, thanks. I'm fine."

She shook her head and went to the keyboard to tap in my order, which was devoid of any of the upsell opportunities she probably counted on to make the transaction worthwhile.

While I waited, I stared robotically at the TV behind the bar. Full screen close-up of a boomer-aged couple: *"We thought we had done all we needed to do to prepare for a comfortable retirement. But when it came time for both of us to leave our jobs, we didn't have enough. Then someone told us we could sell our life insurance policies and get cash. We didn't need the coverage anymore, so it was a slam dunk for us..."*

I had seen this commercial dozens of times. It was one of the few steady-Eddies you could count on seeing regularly these days. But, for some reason, this time it struck a new chord in my brain. My food came, and I ate quickly and without tasting anything. And then that line hit me again, this time like a ton of bricks. *"We could sell our life insurance policies for cash..."*

I passed on dessert (piling on more disappointment for my bartender) opting for a coffee to go, and quickly paid the check with a nice addition to the tip to make up for the absence of up-charges for "awesome" extras on the dinner check.

I was back in Carl's office within fifty minutes. He gave me some more positive feedback about our recent closed deal, and I wanted to be receptive, but all I could think about was how I could validate the new hunch about what might really be going on.

The phone rang on Carl's desk. He picked it up quickly and put it on speaker.

"Jason, you are a man of your word. Less than an hour."

"Ok, here's what I've got."

I had my pad and pen ready, but Jason spit it out so fast I could hardly keep up. It was the usual list you might expect of someone who had lived into his sixties. Mortgages, jobs, debts incurred and paid.

But now I was looking for something very specific. "Jason, listen. Can you tell whether he was involved in one of these deals where you sell a life insurance policy you no longer need? You've seen the ads on TV."

"Hang on. Let's see... Yep. He sold a policy with a $100K face amount and got $47K cash."

"Who bought it?"

"One of those consortiums—those guys that advertise on TV. Let's see, they're called Broadview Life Settlements, LLC."

"So, who's behind Broadview?"

"Whoa, Hoss. This is after less than one hour's work. Getting the info on the principals might take a little more work. What else you need?"

"Get back to us with that and we'll be thinking of what else we might need to see."

"Later, guys." And he was gone.

Carl shrugged. "What can I say? The guy is a worker, not a talker."

The next two hours seemed to take about twenty to pass. I paced for a while in the little waiting area outside Carl's office drinking coffee and munching on trail mix. Finally, Carl motioned me in.

"Here's your list of shareholders of Broadview."

I quickly scanned the list of about a dozen names on an excerpt from a company filing and one jumped out at me: Barbara A. DeMinter. *What the fuck?*

I felt I had to move fast and that meant taking some chances. I punched up John Flanagan's number at Omega.

"Hey, Raf. How's it hangin', buddy?"

"Uh, real quick, John. What do you know about Broadview Settlements?"

"Ooh. Name sounds familiar. Don't they have some commercials on TV?"

"Right. Life settlements. They buy life insurance policies from older people and then package them and sell them as investments. When the insured dies, the investor collects the death proceeds tax free."

"Oh, yeah. Remember, we were approached a bunch of times to get into this business ourselves during your tenure here? It takes advantage of a loophole in the insurance laws. An insurable interest has to be present only at the time of the original application. The owner/applicant must be someone with a financial interest in the continuing life of the insured—wife, kids, employer. But once the policy is issued, the owner can sell the policy to anyone he wants. That's why they call it stranger-owned life insurance, or STOLI. Of course, the seller doesn't get the full amount of the policy death benefit as a sales price because who knows how long the new policyowner is going to have to wait for the insured to die so they can get that death benefit? Depending on the age and health of the insured, it could be years or months or days. Say the death benefit is $100,000. The sale price might be, say $60,000 for an older guy or $25,500 for a younger insured. The longer you have to wait, the greater the opportunity cost of tying up your money. Guy dies soon, you did well. Now, owning just one of those policies is kinda risky. But if you bundle up a bunch of 'em on different lives with different ages and health profiles and you spread and manage that risk, then sell that as a package—voila, you've got yourself a new form of security. Think sub-prime mortgages."

"Uh, not sure that's such a good example. That sure didn't end very well, did it?"

"Yeah, but this is different. These people are all going to die sometime, right?"

"True, but I recall there being some senate hearings where one of our actuaries testified that this was against public policy—having strangers with a financial interest in someone's death."

"Yep, and that's why Omega passed on it."

"Well, this Broadview Settlements is all-in on it. Did you know Barb DeMinter is one of its main stockholders?"

There was a full three-beat pause. "I don't think so, Raf. She's not allowed to be a principal in any other company while she's working here. I think you've got some bad info there. What's this all about anyway?"

"My source is pretty good, John. I can fill you in on the details later. But this is pretty important. Can you ask her now?"

"Not with you on the line, I can't! That's basically accusing her of an ethical violation and I'd want to have a private conversation where this is handled—uh, delicately."

"Well, do it any way you want, John, but do it now. I'll hang up and wait to hear back from you. I'm calling you back in five minutes if I don't hear from you before then."

I hung up without waiting for a response.

Carl was busy talking on his phone when I got back in his office, but he waved me in and finished up his call. Now he was curious, too.

"What'd he say?"

"Well, naturally he said it must be some mistake because it would be really outside the lines for her to do that. I pressured him into talking with her about it right now. I sure hope your guy Jason is reliable, 'cause I've lit the fuse on something based on his say-so."

"You may rest assured Jason has it right. He's never steered me wrong. You saw the printout from the company's filing with the Secretary of State's office, right?"

I sat and stewed quietly while Carl handled some paper-work in his office. And then it hit me: If John confronted Barb right now and if my hunch was right, she might panic and alert others, canceling some options I didn't even know about yet. I had to take a chance with John, so I hurriedly called him back and told him the story of the kidnapping and my hunch.

"You're hallucinating, Raf. Barb is headstrong and all that, but she is not a criminal..."

"I'm not saying she is. But she may be hooked up with some people who are. Have you talked with her yet?"

"Heck no. I'm sitting here thinking about how I'd bring it up."

"Well, don't do it yet. Look, will you walk this thing down with me a little bit further and see where it goes before you talk with her?"

"Sure, I'm more than happy to delay that conversation. What do you want me to do?"

In the next five minutes, I laid out a plan to John that I basically was making up on the fly. I think it must have been my intensity that covered for any flaws or weaknesses he might have picked up, because he didn't say much and seemed to go along with it.

I hung up and knew I had to work fast. I opened my computer and went to ZillowPlus, where you could input a person's name and it would show you any real estate purchases. I wasn't surprised to see Barb DeMinter had bought a place in Jupiter, Florida for $1.2 mil. Pretty good for someone on an exec assistant's pay. Oh, wait. The thing was in foreclosure. Sounds like Barb's in a bit of a cash crunch.

It was time to play a few cards just to see what kind of hand I really had. I called John Flanagan back.

"John, what do you know about Barb's personal life—finances, friends, boyfriends?"

"Well, she's divorced, no kids. She was seeing this guy—a yoga instructor."

"Did you say yoga instructor?"

"Something like that."

"What's his name?"

"Well, she used to call him Tao—she pronounced it Tay-o."

I thought my head would explode.

"You got a last name?"

"Nope."

"Is she still seeing this guy?"

"I don't think so., He's fucking some married woman, and Barb is rip-shit about it."

"Woman's name?"

"Who knows?"

# CHAPTER 12

With all the excitement of the past couple of days, I had to remind myself that this was the day for our trip to see Norm Brancati. I was knee-deep in trying to solve the mystery of the connection between the life settlements business, Barb DeMinter and the kidnapping of Orville Donovan, so my heart (and head) were not in any way focused on this trip. But I had said I'd go and, heck, I might learn something worthwhile.

I met John at the station, and we boarded the train for New York. After we settled into our seats, he got absorbed in some email on his laptop while I looked at the news feed on my phone.

When we arrived, I ordered an AutoZip which took us to Brancati's office, only a few blocks away in Midtown. Settling into the back seat of our ride, I punched up Norm's number.

After one ring, it was answered by a soft, young male voice. "Ms. Calabria's office."

"Oh, I must have the wrong number. Is this Brancati Advisors?"

"Yes, it is."

"Well, can you transfer me to Mr. Brancati's office, please?"

"Actually, Mr. Brancati is working out of this office temporarily. Do you wish to speak with him?"

"Yes, thank you."

The phone went to music and then an older man came on.

"This is Norman."

"Oh, hi, Norm. This is Raf Vella. I'm here with John Flanagan of Omega, and we're in town for our meeting."

"Well, sure. Yeah. Come on up. Gina's here and we'll be glad to see you."

"Ok. We're almost there. See you in a minute."

*Who the hell's Gina?* I didn't say it, but that was the headline question in my mind.

We pulled up in front of the building and spent a very-long few minutes at the security desk getting our pictures taken and temporary IDs issued by three extremely polite folks in security uniforms. They appeared to be moving in slow-mo, looking tentatively at each other while they went about this task so simple one of them should have been able to handle it in a fraction of the time. Finally released with the obligatory "Have a goo' one," we entered the elevator which took us to the thirty-fourth floor where we were met by a young man (the same one from the phone?) who escorted us down the hall to a corner office.

The first thing that hit me was the decor. The paint scheme, carpeting and window treatments looked like photos from a women's magazine—maybe accompanying an article entitled "Your Dream Workspace"—with big portraits of famous women from history like Clara Barton, Susan B. Anthony and Harriet Tubman, and posters featuring heroines from pop culture including Wonder Woman, Katniss Everdeen from Hunger Games, and Rey from Star Wars.

The second thing I noticed was that there was a woman sitting behind the desk and a guy I figured was Norm on the other side, perched on the edge of one of the guest chairs. Kind of *leaning in* toward the woman at the desk—literally and figuratively—appearing to pay rapt attention to whatever it was she was saying.

The woman looked up blank-faced as we got to the doorway, which prompted Norm to turn around toward us. He stood and smiled broadly, motioning us in with hearty and welcoming hand gestures. Together there in that moment they made quite a tableau: The "Old School" and "The New School."

"John, Raf, it's a real pleasure to meet you. I'm looking forward to telling you about our operation here and hearing about how you guys can help us do more life business."

Norm stood about five-feet, five inches, and was built like he might have carried the ball in college. He flashed us another million-dollar smile as we shook hands.

Turning to the woman, he said, "This is Gina Calabria. She's the new CEO and she'll be sitting in for our meeting today. Actually, this is her office now."

I tried not to show my surprise, but was privately blown away, hearing for the first time about an apparent "regime change" at a company where the players were usually closely watched and reported very publicly by the financial press.

At this, Gina stood and smiled and blushed politely, giving us firm handshakes, saying evenly, "Nice to meet you. I've heard good things and I'm eager to see what we can do together."

She was about five-four with long blonde hair—mid-thirties, I figured. Her attire was updated Women in Management dress-for-success style—a plain, gray business suit over a creamy, collared blouse, open at the throat to reveal a small gold cross and matching chain.

I jumped in. "Well, from what I hear, you've got clients with some needs and some money. We've got the products and the people and the systems to help those clients—and, hopefully in the process, help you guys make more money."

Norm laughed and Gina held onto her smile while I handed out copies of our little agenda—(and, er, Barb's?). Norm and the new CEO seemed content to roll through the items one by one, asking questions from time to time, and half an hour passed quickly.

I was about to get into the details about our process when

Norm raised his hand and shook his head and smiled. "Can you give us a minute, guys?"

"Uh, sure." The young man who had escorted us in must have silently entered the room because, as we turned to leave, there he was again, waiting with a smile. He showed us to a small carpeted waiting area just outside the office. He got us each a bottle of water and we sat and drank and waited. In about five minutes he returned and beckoned us to follow him back to the office.

Gina was still seated, but Norm was on his feet. "We can get into the details later. We've seen all we need for now, and we're ready to work with you guys. Why not send over whatever documents you want us to sign to get this thing rolling."

Before we knew it, we were shaking hands again and were shown back to the elevator by the same young man.

John was genuinely enthusiastic and generous in crediting me with what appeared to be a positive outcome. "Wow. That was awesome, Raf. You haven't lost a step!"

I barely heard him, occupied as I was unrolling the tiny wad of paper Norm had surreptitiously pressed into my hand on the way out. It was a phone number.

Coming out of my distraction and looking at John, I shook my head. "Too early to start celebrating, John. Lotta stuff has to happen before any money starts flowing. And uh, aren't you just a little weirded out by what we just saw? I mean, Norm Brancati has been 'The Man' in this company—hell, in this *business*—for years. How all of a sudden is *she* in his chair and *he's* huddling on the other side of the desk, looking like he's begging for crumbs?" Then, holding up the little piece of paper, "Maybe this will give us a clue."

John stared at it momentarily, raising his eyebrows, surprised he had missed the covert hand-off from Norm. Then he shrugged and spread his hands. "Who am I to question? We deal with what's in front of us now."

Our AutoZip was waiting at the curb and we got in. I whipped out my phone again and keyed in the number on the paper, but it went right to voicemail. Then a text message came up from Norm: *"Meet u at trn sta."*

I showed John the little paper again. "I guess we'll learn more in a few minutes."

We got to the station in less than five minutes and had about half an hour before our train. We went into the Pret and grabbed sandwiches and coffees. We carried our food to the table, and John got right to work unwrapping his and diving in. I was about to do the same when my phone buzzed.

It was Norm, his voice low and conspiratorial. "I'm at the station. Where are you?"

I told him and, in less than a minute, he slid into our booth with his own cup of coffee.

He wasted no time getting into it. "Sorry I couldn't talk earlier. I've built my career making quick decisions about who I can trust and you seem like straight shooters so I've decided to level with you. Here's the deal: As you've probably already figured, I've been seriously, royally fucked by my own company—the one I founded and built from the ground up. It's been brewing for some time, but the shit really hit the fan about a week ago. They've held off the reporters while they get their cover story straight.

"I'm still reeling from it, but I'm determined to stay focused—keep coming to work, head down, doing what needs to get done. The new people have absolutely no idea what they're doing and, if I don't stay involved, the whole thing will go down the tubes in a month. They've given me plenty of incentive to keep it going. The funny thing is, they actually want me to stay and continue as before and they're paying me some serious money. I'm off the Board and I'm no longer an officer of the company and, as you've seen, I'm out of my corner office, but it's still my name up there."

"It all started about six months ago with a call from our HR rep, the one that's assigned to the Executive Office, saying they had this young woman whose job in one of our divisions was being eliminated and asking whether I could use her as my Chief of Staff. I laughed at first. I mean, I never needed anyone to write my emails or prepare my speeches or run my calendar. And anyway, those kinds of positions had been phased out in most companies, including ours, about ten years ago in the endless rounds of cost-cutting. I thought I had nipped it in the bud, but before the end of the day, I got another call, this time from the head of HR, more strenuously suggesting I *really* did need a Chief of Staff, selling this woman really hard, and telling me I should seriously consider her for the job. He was really pressuring me and I heard myself say 'Send over her resume.' He said he would do that and asked whether I could interview her that very day. Geez, I thought, they really want to find a place for her. She must really be good.

"We agreed on four p.m. and at three fifty-five on the dot, she's right there fresh as a daisy, like it was eight a.m.

"We talked about the jobs she'd had, what she had done at each one and then she started telling me what she could do for *me*. She was prepared—had done her homework. I'm not sure how she actually knew so much about what I did, but the way she talked it was like she had worked in my office shadowing me for months. She knew the tough spots, things I had struggled with and where I really needed help. She was very specific about what she would do, starting right away. She said she wasn't looking to make changes, just to make me better at the things I was already doing. Yeah, right.

"The crazy thing was, by the time we were done, I didn't need any more convincing that she was exactly what I needed. She started the very next day. At first, she was doing the things you'd expect of a Chief of Staff: preparing memos and reports for my signature, setting up meetings for me with key people. But after about a month, she started sending these memos—even ones I had written—over her own signature and attending meetings with me. Pretty soon she was drafting memos and sending them herself with copies to me. I know it's weird to say this, but in that short time, it started to look more like she was the boss and I was working for her. Suddenly, here she was, taking credit for everything that came out of my office and actually doing a lot of the work on her own initiative.

"Then last month I got called into a meeting with our Board Chair and the Chief Legal Officer and they lowered the boom on me—told me she was going to be the new CEO. They were very upbeat and positive about how my title would change to Executive VP, Special Projects. I'd keep my comp plan and be expected to keep doing what I was doing, and the company name would stay the same. I didn't have long for another shoe to drop, because within a few days of the reorg, Gina brought in some new people and before you knew it, we were in the life settlements business. I don't have to tell you that stuff is a far cry from any kind of business I ever wanted to be in."

He leaned forward as if for emphasis. "And get this: Her salary is about the same as a Level Four Executive Assistant."

I was trying hard to piece this whole thing together. "So, she's got the title but being paid like a secretary, and the company gets to say it has a woman CEO. And, the focus of your business has moved away from selling new policies for estate and business planning and more into life settlements. Is that pretty much it?"

He nodded and gave me a rueful smile—more like a wince— and took a sip of his coffee. "The Chief Legal Officer told me confidentially they had been under intense pressure from the EEOC and the Board to have a woman at the top, and the time had come for them to move on it.

"But don't get me wrong, the new stuff is an add-on. We still do plenty of the tried-and-true and that's where you can help us."

Norm was sitting directly across from me, with John on my right, and Norm had been looking at me the whole time he spoke. John had been quiet, and I wondered whether he was really paying attention. A stranger looking at us would assume Norm and I were having a conversation with John just along for the ride, looking straight ahead at nobody in the chair across from him.

But all at once he seemed to come alive after my summary. "Sounds like some of the shit going on at our place."

I shot John a look, trying to warn him off sharing any kind of confidential info about the inner workings at Omega. I guess he got the message because he let his last statement lie there in front of us like a slab of lox, none of us saying anything more.

The silence lasted for maybe a long fifteen seconds. Then Norm downed the rest of his coffee, looked at his watch and said, "Gotta head back, guys. Let's talk soon."

We stood and said our good-byes and Norm headed back toward the subway. John and I sat back down and didn't look at each other right away.

"I get why you didn't want me to go on about the musical chairs at Omega. No need to blab to Norm about any of that. Do you think there's any connection between what we've got going and Norm's situation?"

"Not sure I know exactly what's going on at Omega. I mean, I do know a woman named Tamar Bolisar is listed as the CEO, but beyond that... Look, you know I haven't been full-time there for a while but I can tell there've been major changes, including integrating—shall we say, faith-based practices—into the daily routines. Norm's thing seems different. Somebody—specifically his Board—thought it was critically important and urgent that this Gina be moved to the CEO spot. It's almost like it's just so they can she's in the chair. On its face, I'd say 'no connection' with our thing, but maybe. When did Tamar take over at Omega?"

"About nine months ago. Before that she was on Jack Winslow's senior leadership team. Then, before you could blink, she's the CEO."

"Hmm. Same sequence as at Norm's, only way bigger on the corporate scale. What happened to Jack?"

"He hung around a few weeks, working out of a little room no bigger than a closet, then he was quietly packaged out."

"John, I think I'll get a guy to look at a few things to see if there are any dots to connect here. I hope you'll keep this part of our conversation just between us for the time being. We good on that?"

"Absolutely."

It was getting close to our train time, so we got up and headed to the platform.

## ✖✖✖✖

"Now, tell me again why I need to hear all this."

I was back at the Depot, sitting in Carl's office going over what I'd learned about the recent people-shuffling shenanigans at Brancati Advisors—strictly on a no-name basis—and my musings about a possible connection with Omega. I could understand his puzzlement as this seemed to have nothing to do with the Depot business. He was responding by leaning back, hands laced behind his head, eyes half closed, his face betraying his best *"This is out of my wheelhouse so I don't need to give it my full attention."*

But he could see I needed his help and maybe he was a little flattered that I had chosen to take him into my confidence on a matter of such importance to me.

"I'll give you that it looks like the same move, but I wouldn't go so far as to say there's a connection. That same pattern is playing itself out in virtually every company of any size in the country. But you already know that, right? I mean, that's the new Story of Work in America. Hell, if ole' Studs Terkel were alive today and wanted to update his book on *Working*, ninety percent of the people he'd find to talk about the regular, legit workplace would be female. It's no big revelation. That's just a fact everybody knows. But this thing's obviously a burr in your saddle, and I'd like to help you. What can I do?"

"Well, thanks. For starters, you can find out whether this Gina Calabria woman has anything to do with any of the other players in this little drama."

We both said the name at the same time—Jason Weisbrod, the guy Carl had tapped to help us get the lowdown on Barb DeMinter. Carl was already getting him on the line. He must have picked up on the first buzz because Carl launched right into letting him know what we needed.

"Yep. The name is Gina Cah-LA-bree-ah." He said it, exaggerating the second syllable for clarity. Then to me, "He wants you to spell it." Which I did.

For confirmation, Carl said back to the phone. "You get that? Good. How long? I know, I know. Yesterday. Well, as soon as possible, then. It's urgent, man. Yeah, I know. Sorry about that. Ok, buddy. Thanks a million."

"He hopes to get back to us by the close of business today."

✗✗✗✗

We were back in Carl's office around five p.m. and he was looking at a short stack of papers that had come off his printer.

"This Gina grew up in Westchester County. Top grades in high school. Got into Barnard, early decision. Majored in theater. Left in her junior year to marry a guy from Minneapolis. Lived out there for a while, doing entry-level clerical work for a life insurance company while he took classes to—get this—join the fire department. Divorced after three years. Moved back to New York and lived in Brooklyn with two other girls. Tended bar while taking classes at night at Hunter College. Got a job at Arnie Goldoff's big Guardian agency in the city. Her co-worker, bestie and roommate at the time was someone named Barbara DeMinter. Mean anything?"

I gulped and sent Jason off to do some background on Barb.

169

He learned that she was Arnie's main go-to person at the time.

"Apparently Arnie gave this Barb a lot of responsibility early on. My guy talked to a couple of other people who worked there at the same time who told him one of those responsibilities was doing whatever Arnie needed her to do. Who knows?"

"All that's very interesting, but..."

"Hang on, buddy. There's more. And here's where it gets *really* interesting. Barb's there about a year and a half and then suddenly she's gone and nobody knows why. Just up and left one day.

"From there she pops up at another agency, the New England Mutual office in Brooklyn run by Tony Giordano. Apparently, she's there for like fifteen minutes and the home office in Boston is starting to make noises about why she isn't being promoted to Assistant Manager. So, Tony promotes her—under duress, one assumes, because she and Tony were not on the best of terms. Certainly they didn't have the kind of joined-at-the-hip thing she had with Arnie. She's in that job for about a year and then guess what? The Home Office promotes her to co-manager. Tony, who was already in his early sixties, just about has a shit-fit and takes early retirement, leaving her to run the shop.

"But back to when she worked at Arnie's Guardian shop in the city. You know how these big field offices have their own Case Design and Underwriting Departments? And guess who was running Underwriting? Barb again. She also headed up the Faithful Women chapter there."

Faithful Women was a women's support organization founded by Bob Westbrook, a TV evangelist out of Dallas, and his wife, Taffy.

"An evangelical group at Arnie's?"

"Yeah. Arnie encouraged all his employees to join a Bible-centered church and to apply Christian principles in the workplace."

"Thought Arnie was Jewish?"

"Well, that's how he was raised—in New York. But he went to Baylor undergrad and then SMU grad school. There are a lot of evangelical youth groups on those campuses. Maybe that's where he converted."

"I think we should look into Arnie's book of business, especially those cases written during the time Barb and Gina were there. Might tell us something."

"Like what?"

"Like the profile of the clients they wrote. Target markets. Every shop gets a reputation for certain kinds of business. I'm thinking maybe Arnie's market focus was owners of closely-held businesses. That would lead him to *specialize*—if you will—in fifty- and sixty-somethings with heart issues. Maybe a lot of substandard business."

"And...your point is?"

"Somebody working in the Underwriting department of one of these big shops spends her time pulling together lots of medical information and packaging it to shop around to various carriers to see who makes the best offer. She would soon learn what the home office underwriters thought were the better risks, and she'd figure out the best way to present a case in a positive light. She'd also learn what makes a *bad* risk—the people who are going to die soon, the things that cause underwriters to decline or charge extra premiums."

"You're fadin' out like a distant station, Bro. I've got zero idea what you're talking about. I'm the Depot guy, remember?"

"Sure, but hang on. That kind of experience looking at all the medical info in those underwriting files—talking with doctors' offices to get the reports to actually put together those files—would be valuable when the business switches from writing new cases—where *better* health and fewer risk factors is a *good* thing—to the life settlements business where the name of the game is to find and bundle up the *sickest* lives you can find. You want them because presumably they'll die faster and that makes for quicker cash flow, which means you can sell that package for more than one that's made up of healthier lives. See?"

Carl frowned and nodded slowly, and I could see the wheels turning. "That part I get. So, what's that got to do with the Depot?"

Carl sat back and we both just stared at each other for a long ten seconds, trying to put these new puzzle pieces together. I went up to the white board and picked up a black marker and wrote: "Evangelicals—Life settlements—Old, sick lives."

"Don't forget 'women.' Accomplished, powerful women."

I added that to the list.

"I can't help but think the cash flow that's generated out of here is always looking for new and obscure parking places—like life settlements paper. And what better place to find the muscle for the dark side of that business—like kidnapping and extortion and maybe murder. I'll bet with a little digging we'll find a Depot connection to the life settlements business Omega is doing...Get Jason back on the line."

I almost said "Let's get him to check out Roebuck." Up till now I had been alone with my suspicions, and bringing Carl into my thinking made me feel like he was kind of a "bud" and I had let my guard down. But I remembered that he *works* for Roebuck and mentioning his name as a "person of interest" in all this would have been a very bad move. I'd have to find another way to get that info.

A background check on Roebuck would have to wait, but meanwhile I liked the idea of checking on Miss Tamar and wondered what her work history would reveal—how she had come up in the insurance business.

Coming-to from my little reverie, I realized Carl was already on the line with Jason and was looking at me for some details to help him get started looking into the back story on Tamar.

"It's Tamar, not Tamara. There can't be too many of those. And the last name is Bolisar." I spelled it for him. "She seems like early fifties, maybe."

Jason was back in two hours. "Can't find the last name Bolisar in any language. The word 'bolish' means 'pillow' in Uzbek. The verb 'bolichear' is used only in Argentina and Uruguay and it literally means 'go to bars.' Guys, I think she made up the name."

"Sorry to put you through this, Jason. Let's think for a minute. I don't know how you do your magic, but I'm thinking if your system allows a first-name search, that might be easier. Hell, how many people named Tamar can there be, right?"

"I'm way ahead of you, Chieftain. I think I've got her. There's a Tamar Bolisarian who'd be about fifty-two now. Born in Summerville, South Carolina. That's not far from Charleston. Father and mother came over young from Armenia, and ran a diner in Summerville. Tamar was an only child. Went to local schools and did well, grade-wise. Active in sports and school activities. She called herself Tammy all through school.

"After graduation, she wasted no time getting out of Summerville. Everyone thought she'd go to the University of South Carolina, but she joined the Air Force. Had several postings overseas and her last one was in Dover Air Force Base, working on those big-ass C-17 transports. Apparently, she was a pretty decent mechanic.

"It was while she was there that she started selling life insurance part-time to other service members. Got good at it too and, after she left the Air Force, she went to work for a local agent for Metropolitan in Dover, still focusing on the air base market she'd already cultivated. Attracted the attention of some people in Met's home office who recruited her for a training program for field managers. At the time, they were focusing on former service members, figuring they'd come in with some discipline and leadership that would transfer well to running an insurance office.

"Tammy did really well in that program and went from there to an assistant manager position in Met's flagship field office in New York City, run by Manny Ohanian. I guess there may have been some kind of affinity there, since Manny's folks were Armenian immigrants like hers. Anyway, he took her under his wing and taught her everything he knew, as the expression goes. She was an eager student and Manny came to rely on her for just about everything."

I heard everything he said, but part of my brain was stuck on the words "training program" for field managers." Those programs were to insurance sales operations what the Officer Candidate School was to the Army's infantry organization. You were put into pressurized situations, cheek-by-jowl with other people you've never met, faced with a mission, and you had to perform and cooperate. You learned quickly who you could trust. Fast and lasting friendships and alliances (and enemies) were made in these programs.

"Hold up, Jason. This management training program at Met. Can you get me a list of the people in Tamar's class there?"

"Uh, sure. I guess so. Think that's important?"

"It might be. It'd be worth a look anyway. How long?"

"Should have that by end of day."

"Great, Jason. Give us a call when you've got something for us to look at."

He rang off to get back to work. I had to think about how to handle this with Carl in case a name (like Roebuck's) came up. If that happened, I wouldn't want to spook him by showing too much interest. Carl might seem like a work-a-day guy, but he was nobody's fool. And testing his loyalty to his boss at this stage seemed like the wrong move.

Jason was back to us at 4:30 on the dot. There were nineteen last names on the list, but none of them was Roebuck or anything similar.

My head ached, and I was losing focus from fatigue. I was also getting hungry. I folded the list and put it in my pocket, figuring I'd look at it over lunch.

Lunch was a Whopper (the third-generation fake-meat

kind, with cheese), fries and a Coke. Munching away, absently picking out the crispiest of the fries first, I stared at the list of class members hoping something obvious would jump out at me. The first thing I noticed was that, out of nineteen names, twelve were women. (I thought it was kind of interesting that out of those twelve, there were four Megans. Well, one Megan, a Meghan, a Meaghan, and a Megyn. Also, an Ashley and an Ashlee. No surprise there.)

I put the list aside and focused on my Whopper. At the urging of a health-conscious President several years ago, the government had twice outlawed this kind of fast food—high fat, high carbs and high sodium beyond certain levels—but both times they caved in to the weight of public outcry. So now we were free to kill ourselves with lab-created ersatz meat while blissfully indulging in the forbidden treats, provided we were willing to pay a hefty sin tax on top of the purchase price.

I wondered whether there had been a class picture of the Management Development Program for Tamar's year. Yeah, I was pretty sure there would be. But where would it be now, and how would I find it?

It was actually easier than I'd figured. After finishing my lunch, I got on my computer and found the photo I was looking for in about fifteen minutes in the archives section of the MetLife website. It was in an article in the *MetLife Global Review*—their employee magazine—in an issue from about five years ago. That's the good part. The other (bad) part was that there was no Roebuck in the class members listed below the picture.

I looked hard at the seven guys seated with the class. No Roebuck. But wait! Who's that standing in the back with another guy? Not seated *with* the class, but standing *behind* them. Sure looks like him to me.

I called and asked the archivist, Isabela Torres, if she could find out the names of the leadership team—the managers, coordinators, instructors, etc. who were running the Management Development Program that year. She smiled obligingly and started typing on her computer. No one named Roebuck but there was a "Shawn Roebach" listed as Assistant Management Development Coordinator. Close enough. So, Roebuck wasn't *in* Tamar's class, but he was part of the management cadre that supervised the program. Listed as Management Development Coordinator, the guy who would have been Roebuck's boss was one Truman Giddens. That must be the guy standing next to Roebuck in the photo. I asked Isabela if she knew whether Mr. Giddens was still employed. She tapped some more, frowned at her screen and shook her head.

"'Fraid not. He retired two years ago."

"Any idea where he's living?"

Another shake of the head. "We wouldn't have anything like that."

"But you might have an article in the Review around the time he retired, right?"

"Oh, sure." More tapping. She came up with the article announcing the retirement of Truman Giddens. In it, Mr. Giddens was quoted as saying he was looking forward to spending more time with his family in the Outer Banks of North Carolina.

I asked her to print out the article, which she did, and I knew immediately where I was going next—some town in the Outer Banks. But which one? Back in my car, I fired up my laptop. White Pages gave me several addresses for Mr. Giddens in towns on the Outer Banks: Avon, Duck and Nags Head.

Avon seemed like a good place to stay, centrally located with a population of about 4,000, which meant there might be some decent places to eat and maybe even get a good, strong cup of coffee.

The Inn on Pamlico Sound sounded quaint and tranquil, so I booked a room for two nights. I got a flight from Newark to Wilmington for the next morning, and headed back to the Marriott, my home away from home, for an hour of downtime. Then I'd rustle up some dinner and get to bed early.

I got an AutoZip ride to the airport early the next morning. After checking in, I got a medium coffee and a bacon (fake-un?), egg and cheese on a brioche at a Pret a Manger and sat down at one of their tables for my mini-feast.

The flight to Wilmington was smooth and on-time. I flagged down the Avis van, which was headed for the lot. My name was on the screen up near the front, and the van dropped me off next to space number 347. I got out and popped the trunk on the Kia Optima parked there.

I took a chance that the Inn might have my room ready, since it was not the high season. Sure enough, Roger at the front desk was able to get me into number 24 right away. It had Queen Ann furniture and a great view of the lake. I flopped down on the big bed and punched up Truman Giddens' number. He answered on the first ring.

"Hello, Mr. Giddens. It's Raf Vella. Hope you're doing well today. I just got in town and checked into the hotel. As I said yesterday, I have some questions about some of your former students and I'd like to talk with you if you have some time."

"Well, I've got nothin' but time but, before we start talking, I'd like to know a little more about you and why you want to know about these folks. First off, are you the law?"

"Mr. Giddens, I can assure you I'm not any kind of law at all. But I want to make it clear that this is a matter of great importance, maybe even of life and death..."

"Let me stop you right there, Mr. Vella. If this is something like that, why haven't you taken this up with the authorities and let them decide how to handle it?"

"If I were you, I'd probably ask the same thing, but all I can tell you is that if I were to alert the authorities, it might put some people at risk—maybe a lot of people. And I can make you a promise: If we talk and you don't want your name involved, I'll keep you out of it. Fair enough?"

He paused for about three beats and then said: "Where are you staying?"

"The Inn on Pamlico Sound."

"Meet me in fifteen minutes at Stu's Donuts. It's right on Route 12, same road you're on, about fifteen minutes away."

I pulled into Stu's parking lot just about the same time as another car—a late-model Toyota Camry. A lean, sixty-something guy looked over at me as we came to a stop next to each other. We got out and I smiled and extended my hand. "You're Mr. Giddens?"

He flashed me an easy smile. "My students called me that. I'm Truman to my mother—Tru to everybody else."

We went inside and walked up to the counter. We both ordered Americanos, but he paired his with a twisted glazed coffee roll, which looked mighty good.

Sitting down at a table near the window (and out of earshot of others), Truman took the lid off his coffee to let it cool, and glanced down appreciatively at his coffee roll.

"You know, I was packaged out of Met about two years ago after twenty-seven years in various Field and Home Office assignments, and I haven't heard a peep from anybody there about anything since. Nothing, that is, until I got your call asking for information about one of my students and one of my MDCs. Where's all this coming from?"

I had already made the decision to tell him as much as I could without compromising my investigation. The little bit I knew about Truman told me he was a straight-up guy and an old-school insurance man who would not appreciate the industry's move away from regular life sales and in the direction of life settlements. He just might be downright offended at the idea.

"Mr. Giddens—Tru—you're familiar with the life settlements business, right?"

"Read about it. That's about as close as I ever wanted to get. Glad I was never asked to be involved in it. It sure doesn't sound like the life insurance business I signed up for and worked in for my entire career. Bettin' on people to die soon isn't something I'd want anything to do with. Does this business you've come to talk with me about have anything to do with that mess?"

"I think it does."

I told him—on a no-name basis—a little about the shift in the focus of Omega, and my interest in the role of Tamar Bolisarian and Shawn Roebach.

"Tammy was what they used to call 'a real piece of work.' On day one, when we went around the room with self-introductions, she said her name was 'Tammy.' By about the third week, she started calling herself 'Tamara.' By the end of the program, she had let everyone know she was 'Tamar.' She was the one who always had the answer to every question, the first to complete every exercise and the first to volunteer for some special assignment. She was also the one who decided it'd be a good idea to start screwing one of our instructors. That give you any idea what we're dealing with here?"

"That would be Shawn?"

"Yeah. When he first showed up a year earlier, he was fresh out of the Army, cocky and sharp as a tack, motivated as hell. By the time Tammy got done with him, he was trailing after her like a whipped dog, begging for approval. In addition to giving me a morale problem in the class, and the HR shit that goes with it—all of which I didn't need—it kinda made me sick on a personal level. I mean, who wants to see a guy go down like that?

"Anyway, the other thing about Tammy—Tamar—that I think you ought to know is that no matter how much approval she got, no matter how many people told her she was the best, the smartest, the top student, the best salesperson or whatever, it was never enough. She always wanted more. More recognition. More appreciation. More validation. She'd go into everything with a big head of steam, crank up a lot of results, get credit and then quickly lose interest when she didn't get that extra something she was looking for, whatever the hell it was.

"Everybody knows that feeling you get when something turns out not to give you the feeling you hoped you'd get in the beginning. Well, Tammy had that in spades. She'd turn cold on something—or someone—so fast it would make your head spin. We all saw it, the students, the instructors and me. But it was especially hard on Shawn. He taught her everything he knew, and she soaked it up and used it. Then, when she figured she'd learned all she could from him, she tried to dump him. She was always looking for the next big thing.

"Funny thing, though. Even though she let him down hard, she and Shawn stayed friends. She had that rare gift of being able to turn a romantic relationship into something else when it was over. And I hear years later he put in a good word for her with the folks at this next assignment at Met after he left our program. She did some contract work for them, and I assume she impressed them and made some good contacts that helped her get more business later. Smart girl."

"What did she do after she graduated from the program?"

"Worked in one of the Met field offices for a couple of years. Then moved into the home office for a few years. Then she got a big contract on her own and left the company."

"I understand she worked in Manny Ohanian's Met Life office in New York for couple of years."

"Sure did. Manny took her under his wing and, again, taught her everything he knew. But I'm pretty sure it was strictly business with Manny. Nothin' funny goin' on. But I guess you never know."

"Did you know Tammy has a big job now with Omega Financial?"

"I'm sure somebody told me that, but I don't know anything about it. I've been out of the loop for a couple years now, and not really plugged into what's going on in the industry."

"What can you tell me about Shawn Roebach?"

"I thought he could succeed big-time in our business if he put his mind to it. But he always had a couple of other things going on the side. He was into Amway for a while. Then he even got into Mary Kay. Can you believe it? One of the few guys in the system. I hear he did well and worked his way up the ladder to Regional Distributor, all while he was working for us."

He sat back and enjoyed a private moment of recollection that made him smile, then laughed out loud. "You know, they have these regular sales meetings, where the leader gets everyone charged up and motivated to get out there and do it some more. Well, Shawn worked that thing to a fare-thee-well. Had regular parties at places like nail salons where he'd pay for a mani or pedi for everyone, serve 'em a little white wine and then they'd talk business."

He shook his head. "I finally sat him down and told him he had to get out of these other things and focus on the life insurance business, and he did—at least for a while. Then I heard he started teaching yoga, of all things. And, just like with the other things, he built up a good following with the ladies. It took me a while to find out about it, 'cause he didn't use his real name in his yoga business."

*Say what?!* I got that feeling at the back of my neck, the one you get when you think you might have just heard something really important, but it was so outrageous and yet stated so matter-of-factly, you weren't quite sure where it was leading.

"Uh, you wouldn't happen to remember that name he was using, would you?"

"Oh, hell no. That was a long time ago, and it didn't matter to me what he was calling himself. I was just pissed he had gone back on what he had promised me, which was to focus full time on the life business and being my MDC in the program.

"Much as I hated to admit it, the bottom line was that, despite his talents, Shawn was not really a straight-shooter. In fact, I'd say if there were two ways to go about something, one straight and one a little crooked, both with equal chances of success, he'd go for the crooked one, just for the thrill of it. If there was an angle, he'd find it. I think Tammy actually liked that about him, though I never saw her getting personally involved in any of his shenanigans or cutting any corners on her own.

"You know how that goes. Ladies love the bad boys, and I guess you could say Shawn fit that description. People always act surprised when they see somethin' like that, but to me it makes perfect sense: You have your nice guy. Women don't feel too special when he's nice to them. Hell, he treats everybody good. But a rough guy like Shawn, makin' it a habit to con or use most people he meets, makes 'em feel like a queen when he really pays attention to 'em and acts like he's lookin' out for 'em."

He looked down and shook his head, then held up his right index finger. "Had 'em wrapped right around his finger. And Tammy was no exception. Who knows what she'd do for him—that is, before she got all she needed from him and was ready to move on."

I sat there for a minute, wondering where to go next. "Tru, you've been a big help. Is there anyone else you think I might talk with to learn more about Tammy and Shawn?"

He scratched his head and squinted for a few seconds, and finally shook his head. "Not unless you want to start interviewing everyone in the class. But I doubt they'd have much to add to what I've told you."

It looked like our conversation was over, and Tru was well into his coffee roll when he suddenly looked up and said, "I guess you could talk to this guy he was partners with in the yoga studio business. He was initially Shawn's yoga instructor, teachng him all the poses and all. Then Shawn showed him how he could make a real business out of it and make some money."

"Well, I would like to talk with him, yes. What's his name?"

"You ready for this? Name's André Beautaille. You say it

like 'bow-tie.' André was in Tammy's class at Met for about fifteen minutes. Came and went in a hurry. Never really got into it. He thought he could supplement his yoga income by selling insurance. Liked to make a big deal about his name. He wanted to be sure everyone remembered it, so he always wore a bow tie instead of your regular long necktie. Different kinda cat. Operated on a separate plane—used Buddhist and Eastern references all the time. Interesting in his own way. Apparently very serious about yoga, and had studied with some pretty well-respected teachers, including the better part of a year in a monastery in Japan. That's what he said, anyway."

"Was he friendly with Tammy or Shawn?"

"Not Tammy, especially. But Shawn took an interest in the yoga and had already started studying with him while André was still in our program. Of course, it was months later, after he left, that I heard he and Shawn had gone into business together."

"Any idea where I could find this guy?"

"Sure. He's down in Naples, Florida now. Got a good business going, I hear, from some of the old classmates who kept up with him."

"Any idea about the name of his studio?"

"Yeah, hold up a sec." He fiddled with his phone. "Here it is. Prana. It's right on Fifth Avenue, the high-rent district. I think it's on the second floor. Above a restaurant."

"Tru, I really appreciate the time. You've been very helpful."

"Ok. Hope you find what you're looking for, whatever that is."

We said our good-byes, and I left Tru with his coffee and the last few bites of his coffee roll, and was on my way back to the Inn.

I actually hated to check out. It was a beautiful place in a terrific setting, and I could see myself extending my stay for a little R&R. But there was work to be done, and I had to move on.

I got to the airport in good time and caught the next flight from Wilmington to Fort Myers, rented a car and drove to Naples. Sure enough, there was a sign that said Prana right above an upscale Indian restaurant among the many on Fifth Avenue.

It was a clear, sun-washed day, and it felt great to be in Florida. I looked for a parking spot on the street, but ended up in the high-rise garage a couple blocks away. Not far, and it was free.

I made my way back to Fifth and the entrance to the Indian restaurant, opened the door right next to it and walked up the steps to the studio. It was quiet and I assumed a class was in session, so I made sure I didn't make too much noise with my footsteps. When I got about halfway up, I was hit by the heady scent of incense combined with female perspiration under a blanket of girly cologne, and heard the tiny ding of a small bell, presumably signaling the end of the class. By the time I got to the top, I could hear the rustling sounds of people moving around, probably gathering up their belongings to leave. Good timing. Maybe I could catch André between classes.

"Oh, hey," said the small voice coming from the short, trim man who exited the studio door. "You must be Raf. Did I get that right?"

"Just right. Thank you, André. Do you have a few minutes to talk now?"

"Sure. Let's just go to my little alcove over here. The folks coming to class know to enter in silence and there's no chatter before class."

I wanted to make the most of the little time we had, so I got right to the point. "Like I said on the phone, I'm interested in what you might be able to tell me about Tammy Bolisarian and Shawn Roebach."

"Well, as I told you, I didn't know Tammy all that well, but I'm sure you've heard from Tru that she was the top student in the class. She completed all the assignments before anyone else, always did more and did it better, and was clearly a thought leader.

"Shawn was our MDC under Tru. I started with the class but dropped out before I finished, as soon as I realized a career in insurance sales was not for me.

"But while I was there, I got to know Shawn pretty well. When he found out I was into yoga, he started coming to the classes I was offering in the Methodist Church basement on Tuesday nights. He took to it very well. Didn't bother him at all that he was usually the only guy in a class full of women. Wanted to learn as much as he could. After about six weeks, he approached me about going into business together. Actually, he proposed a deal where he'd front me the money to start my own studio, and he'd take a cut of the receipts till he got his money back. And he'd handle the financial aspects while I ran the classes. He had me convinced there was money to be made, and we jumped into a lease and got some classes going. He was very enthusiastic and it worked out pretty well at the start. After about three months, he started getting restless and looking around for something else."

"Hang on a sec. Were you both still working at Met all during this time?"

"Shawn was, yes. I quit to devote full time to the studio. Anyway, by the time Shawn was losing interest, I was doing well enough to hire a part-time bookkeeper and didn't really require as much of his time anyway. Shawn was thinking of starting his own yoga studio, giving his own classes. He'd learned enough from me and a few extra sessions he took with some other teachers around. He was a quick study, and he picked it up fast. It was about that time he quit Met and moved away...to Pennsylvania, I think I heard. I kind of lost touch with him after that. I continued to send him the money to pay off what I owed him and he always acknowledged receipt, but beyond that, nothing. Last I heard, he'd set up his own place somewhere near Philly."

"Anything else you can think of that might be helpful to me?"

He shook his head, then laughed. "One funny thing: Shawn was also into martial arts too. Chinese kung fu, I think. He liked to call himself Tao. Only he pronounced it 'Tayo.' I tried to correct him a couple of times, but he said he liked to say it his way better. I remember more than once he made a kind of joke out of it. Kind of a pun, really. He said, 'Well, it is my *way*, right?' And he'd laugh and slap me on the back to get me to laugh with him."

*What the fuck?!* I heard my voice thank André for his time and information, but my palms were sweaty and my brain had shifted into overdrive, trying to reassemble my worldview in light of this new revelation. I left in a hurry, eager to get back to talk with John Flanagan and Tamar and anyone else who could fill in the gaps for me.

# CHAPTER 13

Immediately after we landed, I drove to Omega headquarters and tried to get in to see John Flanagan. His door was locked, so I sat in the lobby area outside his office and dialed his number. He picked up on the first buzz.

"Hey, Raf. What's going on?"

"John, who's the boss?"

"Excuse me?"

"You heard me, Fucknuts. Who's running the side game you've got going with that little 'cash flow accelerator program' with Barb's life settlements company?"

"Now hang on, Raf. I'm not involved in any back-end stuff. I'm just a basic life insurance guy. You know that…"

At that moment, John's office door burst open and John shot through it like a cannon. I was already on my feet and halfway across the carpet to meet him, and I smiled broadly as he came out.

"Hey, buddy. Where you going?"

Surprised to see me right there, he stammered, "Raf, you've g-got this wrong. Yeah, I ok'd Omega's purchase of some of the life settlements securities, but I don't know anything about the back-end stuff."

I walked him back into his office and closed the door behind us. "Sit down, Shithead."

"Wait!"

"No, John. The boss. I want a name. THE name. Now!"

Holding his hands up, surrender-style, he blurted it out. "You've gotta talk to Miss Tamar about that."

"Where do I find her?"

"Thirty-seventh floor. But good luck getting in there. It's like Fort Knox."

I called the main number and asked for *Mr.* Bolisar, an old Jedi Mind Trick.

The operator laughed. "We don't have a Mr. Bolisar. We have a *Miss* Bolisar. But you can't speak to her. She's in a meeting."

"Well, let me speak to her assistant, please."

"Do you have an appointment?"

"To speak with her assistant?"

"Yes, I'm sorry, sir. That's not possible. Goodbye. Have a blessed day."

I called the operator back and asked to speak with Mandy Wilkinson.

"I'm sorry, sir, there's no one here by that name."

Feigning outrage, I responded, "Don't tell me that! I happen to know that Mandy is Miss Bolisar's executive assistant!"

Then, condescendingly, as though correcting a child, she gave me what I needed. "Miss Bolisar's assistant is Heather Morgan." Like a charm! The only thing some people like better than totally stonewalling you is correcting you—proving you're wrong about something.

"Oh, sure. Sorry. I forgot. I guess Mandy was from a few years ago. Please connect me with Heather then. Thank you."

She picked up on the first ring, and I introduced myself. "Hi, Heather. My name is Raf Vella. I worked at Omega for many years and now I do some work for Mr. Roebuck down at the Depot. It's rather urgent that I see Ms. Bolisar right away on a matter of importance. Can you clear me with security so I can come up now?"

"We-e-ell, I don't know..."

"Look, if you call Mr. Roebuck now, I'm sure he'll tell you I've been working for him, and HR will confirm my prior employment."

"Hold, please."

She was back in about thirty seconds. "You can come on up."

When I opened the door, my first thought was that maybe they had directed me to the wrong place, a nearly-empty room, one that hadn't been occupied for a while. As my eyes adjusted, I could see there were definitely some lights on, but they didn't seem to be doing much. The room was swathed in a cloak of half-night that nicely matched the state of my brain, struggling with the random and seemingly unconnected facts and hunches swirling around in it.

As the door closed, sealing off the sounds of the hallway, I could hear music playing softly. Some kind of piano concerto.

Then a woman's voice. "Do you like Chopin, Mr. Vella?"

I looked around, up and down, unsure about where the disembodied voice was coming from in the dusky expanse.

Her laugh was light and melodic, but confident. "Over here."

I caught a flash of movement. It was just her hand motioning, but that was enough to draw my attention to the corner of the room, where she sat at a large desk, clear of paper and objects except for a small green-shaded lamp.

When she turned up the lights, I could finally make her out, smiling slightly, showing small, even teeth in an expressive mouth. The symmetrical features of her oval face were set off by greenish eyes—or maybe they were gray or hazel—and a cap of close-cropped, salt-and-pepper hair. She was wearing a blue brocade sleeveless top, showing off slender but well-toned arms.

"Did you know that Chopin liked to play his compositions in the dark? So, when I listen to his music, I want to hear it just as he did. But here I am going on and you're still standing there. Please sit down."

She motioned to one of the two guest chairs on my side of the desk. I sat slowly, almost cautiously, like maybe I thought the chair might be rigged or something, and looked around. It was a beautiful room with slick hardwood floors with Persian area rugs here and there, elegant textured wallpaper and more crown molding than you'd see in the ballroom of a European palace.

"In the time it took you to get up here, Mr. Vella, I did speak with Mr. Roebuck who said you are a resourceful worker and a quick learner. We're always looking for people like that."

"Miss, er Missus... Is it Ms...?"

Another of her melodic laughs, and then: "My name is Tamar. Most people call me *Miss* Tamar. As you might know, Tamar was the daughter of King David. Are you up on your Bible stories, Mr. Vella? Here at Omega, we're pretty serious about our Bible study. You can learn a lot about Scripture from Mr. Roebuck and a good many other things, too."

"Oh, well, sure. Always interested in learning something new."

"As you've probably discovered by now, Mr. Roebuck is something of a Renaissance Man—smart and tough and ambitious, with just the right touch of ruthlessness. I admire that in a man. And if he's taken notice of you, well..."

She spread her hands, flashed another big-eyed smile, and I could tell she had uncrossed and recrossed her legs under the desk. Then, finally standing, she said, "Mr. Vella, so I can get to know a little about you, tell me about a time in your young life when you did something you were especially proud of."

Now, that came purely out of left field and, before I could fully process it, I just reflexively answered. "Uh, well, I guess when I made the JV basketball team. I wasn't very good, but I tried hard and was happy to be one of the eleven guys picked for the team."

More of that little smile and holding up her hand in the universal *stop!* gesture. "I'm sure that was gratifying. But I want to hear about some specific thing you *did*—some action or insight or decision, some *moment* you felt good about at the time, and still do to this day."

*Wait. What? I'm here to hit her with what I believed to be the horrific truth about what's going on in the bowels of this ship she's running and she thinks she's conducting a damn job interview!*

I was off-balance and wondering where to go next. It was clear that blurting out what I came to say was not the right option. To buy time, I just tried to answer her question.

"Well, in my junior year of high school, there was this play. And the script called for a character who could be called either *Chubby* or *Slim*, depending on the build of the actor who got the part. But the guy who auditioned best didn't have the physiognomy of either a Chubby *or* a Slim, nor was he likely to play it 'funny.' The director was stumped and everyone was standing around not knowing what to do. All of a sudden, I said 'Hey, he's gonna bring a more serious affect to this role so let's just call him *Ernest*.' Everyone laughed and clapped and the director went with it. It was a great moment for me."

I guess this tickled Miss Tamar's funny bone, for she laughed and nodded approvingly, and it must have even impressed her a little because she raised her arm high, fist pumping in a triumphant salute, flashing me a glimpse of faint underarm shadow.

"Bravo! Wonderful problem-solving on your part. And on the spot, too. I like that!"

I sat motionless, basking in the sudden and unexpected expression of her approval, and grasping to recover my composure.

Thinking back over it now, I see that she was probing, testing me to see what I needed: Maybe an attractive woman to focus her attention on me, listen attentively and approvingly? She came out from behind her desk and sat next to me. The air around her smelled faintly of patchouli.

"Tell me about a time you felt happy and content."

For some reason that was unclear to me then, and still is now, I obeyed like a child. "It was when I was working on the beach, renting out umbrellas and chairs, hanging out with other kids with other summer jobs. It was as if the ocean and the sun and the sand washed everything clean and things could be however you said they were. I didn't give any thought to the fact that in a few weeks it would be over and we'd all go back to wherever we came from and pick up our old real-life lives."

"That must have been a great experience for you that came at just the right time. Would you like to hear a story about me?"

I did want her to go on, hoping she'd say something incriminating—something that would validate my hunches and fill out what John had probably already told the constabulary.

"Sure."

"Starting when I was around eleven years old and into my teens, I worked as a cashier at our family's diner for many years. In all the years I did it, I was never more than a few pennies off in the count-up at the end of the day. Want to know how I got so good?"

I shrugged. "Well, you've got me curious now."

"When my dad and mom came over from Armenia, they borrowed money from some family members who had been here for a while and bought this diner down near the train station. The place was kind of run-down, but they brought in this guy who had been a chef, down on his luck and trying to shake a bad drug habit. But the man could cook. He was putting out first-rate food at diner prices. In no time, they built this business up pretty good, starting with people from the train getting entrées to bring home for family dinner. By and by, people started coming from all over as the good news spread about our menu and prices.

"I'd come straight to the diner after school instead of going home, and I'd do my homework at one of the back tables near the kitchen door.

"My dad acted as a kind of expediter, making sure the orders got out to the tables fast and didn't sit too long and, during slack times, sitting at his own table watching and chain-smoking.

"Mom pretty much stayed at her place by the register and, when she didn't have a party checking out, she'd sit quietly looking out at the train station. The express trains would just rush on by, but the locals would stop and she'd see people getting out of cars, kissing their wives or husbands and running to catch the train. I often wondered what she thought about as she looked out there every day. Maybe she was lost in her own thoughts, or still smarting from the most recent of the tongue-lashings she'd get periodically from my dad about her count being off by a few bucks. I know she never responded when he'd criticize her, but would look down or away, waiting for his harangue to be over.

"We always had two waitresses, girls or women who would come and stay a few months and then they'd leave and we'd get somebody else. My dad had strong ideas about how everything had to be done—how the tables ought to be cleared and washed between customers, how the silverware and napkins had to be set just so, and he wasn't too worried about how he came across and whose feelings he hurt. Sometimes a girl would take the job and work a couple meals and run off crying, never to return. Dad would just shrug and say, 'Guess she don't want to do things right. Better that she's gone.'

"These women would often take an interest in me, asking questions about school and talking about hair or clothes or other things girls like to talk about.

"One day, this new girl, Violetta, she was I guess mid-thirties, arrived on the scene. She was sharp—clearly a cut above most of the others. Dad didn't really have to tell her much. She just seemed to know what to do, and she did it quietly and efficiently. Both Mom and Dad remarked at how good she was and how lucky we were to have her.

"Instead of going out back for her smoke break like the others did, she'd just stand by my dad's table, a cigarette in one hand and the other on her hip, making suggestions for how to make the diner run better. At first, he didn't pay much attention to what she was saying, but after a while he started to see she had some good ideas. Pretty soon he started inviting her to sit down with him. Although I could never hear much of what they were saying, it was clear their conversations had evolved over time to more than just improving things at the diner. I'd often see my dad nodding and smiling, his face flushed and looking much different from the way he usually did.

"My mother noticed them too, and I would catch her looking over at them, her eyes wide and vacant, probably curious like I was.

"After a few months, Mom and Dad started coming to the diner separately, and Dad insisted that Mom leave right after the evening count, and he and Violetta would stay 'to finish with the clean-up.' Mom usually didn't say much as she was leaving, but when he would come home later, I could often hear them fighting behind their bedroom door.

"Mom got more and more withdrawn at home and at the diner, saying even less than she normally did, and taking extra smoke breaks instead of eating.

"One day, a few minutes after Mom went out for her break, I heard the wail of an ambulance and looked out the window to see if I could see it coming. What I saw was a crowd of people over by the tracks. I went outside and heard people yelling. I ran in the direction where the people were, but a man grabbed me and held me back, saying 'You don't want to go over there now. Go back to the diner, Honey.'

"My dad went running over there too, and more than a few minutes later, he came back—his face white as a ghost—and told me what I already pretty much figured out.

"The next few days were a blur, with the funeral and friends and relatives from all over coming by. The next part was the hardest—the part my dad referred to as 'after the circus left town.' We went to the diner every day, as usual, going through the motions, but kind of in a daze. We didn't seem to have much to say to each other. Violetta stayed around for a few days, but one day she just up and quit after an argument with my father about something or other.

"With Mom gone, I was promoted to cashier before and after school, right up till closing. I had been her helper there for so many years, I guess my dad figured I could handle it easily enough.

"And I did. But all day, with every customer, I'd think about the end of the day. As it got later and closer to the time I'd have to do the count, I'd feel myself starting to tighten up, sweating and getting a headache. I saw it as a life-or-death struggle to make the count come out right every night. I started screwing up at school and I had to see the school psychologist, who said I had developed a phobia that my father would stop loving me and I'd end up like my mother if I missed the count.

"Anyway, Violetta was gone from the diner, but she wasn't out of the picture entirely. I didn't know it right away, but my father kept seeing her. He didn't bring her home or any place I was going to be for the longest time. But I'd see him getting ready to go out, checking his appearance in the mirror, sucking in his gut and checking his hair, dragging it from here to there, going for a little coverage since it had started thinning pretty badly. I knew he was seeing a woman, but I didn't know it was her.

"By and by, I started asking him about who it was he was going to see and he finally told me. I said it would be ok with me if he brought her around, seeing as it was probably a strain on both of them keeping it a secret.

"It wasn't long after that she moved in with us. My dad became more and more concerned about his appearance, him being quite a bit older than she was. With the benefit of years, I later came to understand that what was going on was that Violetta was just naturally getting tired of him the way people often do in relationships. The honeymoon was over, so to speak, but he didn't know it yet.

"One day he came home wearing this weird hairpiece. It was really awful, but I guess he thought it looked good because he stood there real proudly, a big smile on his face. Violetta was sitting at the kitchen table doing her nails, watching some reality show on her iPad. She didn't look up right away, but when she finally saw him, she got this strange look and opened her mouth a little, like maybe she was going to say something, but nothing came out. Then her shoulders started to shake, her eyes filled with tears and she just started to sob quietly.

"In my mind's eye I can still see us there, the three of us caught in this strange little scene right there in the kitchen. My dad in the doorway, Violetta sitting on one side of the table next to where he normally sat at the head, and me in my usual place at the other end. We were sort of frozen there, none of us moving or saying anything. It was probably only a few seconds, but it seemed like forever. I could sense some kind of unspoken message passing between them in that moment, but I didn't know what it was until much later. About a week later, Violetta moved out, and it was just my dad and me again.

"Business at the diner started to fall off as Dad stopped coming to work every day. The cook left and there began a series of replacements—each one worse than the last. We thought we were going to go out of business.

"And just then, that's when I found the answer in prayer. We had a regular, a Mr. Joseph. He wasn't a real minister or anything, but he was a real man of God, for sure. And he showed me how if you want something to happen and you speak over it and you pray on it, it will surely come to pass. And, as soon as I started doing that, we got a new cook—a really good one.

Brought with him some recipes from the old country. Business started picking up. I convinced Dad to start praying too, and slowly but surely, things started turning around.

"From that day forward, Mr. Vella, I've made daily prayer an important part of my business life, and I've chosen each and every one of my acolytes here—er, new hires—on the basis of their commitment to the prayerful life.

"So, you see, when I make Him Number One, he takes care of everything else in our business. When the cash flow slows down, we just pray on it together, and it quickly turns back the other way."

I had no idea how to respond to her story. She had told it straight-up and without emotion.

I just sat there, looking down. "You had some bad times for sure."

She smiled tightly. "Don't worry about it. It was a long time ago and I've had plenty of time to work through it. We all have our own sadnesses."

I wasn't quite sure how this had evolved from what she had thought was a job interview into a mutual sharing session, and I was frankly uncomfortable. After about ten seconds, I blindly lurched into what I had come to say. "Miss Tamar, I didn't come for a job interview. I'm sorry if there was some kind of misunderstanding, but I came here to talk with you about some disturbing things I've learned about your business. I've looked at the operating statements of Omega for the past eight quarters. And I think I know why the last few have shown a remarkable turnaround."

She cocked her head and looked at me with a combination of curiosity and concern, and I think she shifted almost imperceptibly in her chair. "Go on. Please."

"Haven't you wondered about it? I mean, you look at these things, don't you?"

Her smile suddenly vanished, and she put her clenched fists on the table and leaned forward. "I've told you how it happens, Mr. Vella. It's prayer, plain and simple. Are you suggesting something else—something nefarious? You come in here on false pretenses, get me to share personal recollections and then you start quizzing me about our cash flow, implying that maybe you know something about us that I don't? That the Devil's work has crept into our business strategy?"

And for some reason, her mention of the word "strategy" stoked a few of the embers smoldering inside me, and I was ready to unload.

"Strategy? We both know Omega's been pursuing a whole new business model, miles away from the sale of life insurance for last expenses and estate and business planning. You're now effectively 80% in the life settlements business, Miss Tamar. Those early quarters of a year and a half ago, the ones with the big cash outflows? That was when you were laying out big wads of cash *to buy up* old people's in-force life insurance policies, and to buy TV time to advertise. Your cash flow officially went to shit with all that money going out and nothing coming in. And when you started seeing lousy operating statements for a couple of quarters, you started pressuring your people for revenue. Maybe you thought it was prayer that did it, but Roebuck and his goons and fake cops sure knew some human intervention was going to be necessary to make it happen. In the life settlements business, the only way money comes in is when people die. So those geniuses of yours figured out a way to make that happen. That and some kidnappings and extortion. You didn't seem to want to know or care where the money came from, just so long as the numbers got better."

"Mr. Vella, I don't like one bit of the implications of what you're saying. Everything we do, our every move, is guided by our faith—the higher truth."

Now it was my turn to use the *Stop!* gesture. "There's no implication here. I'm just telling you the facts of what's going on in your company."

She leaned back in her chair and looked at me for a few

seconds, her face completely blank. And then she leaned over, pointing a finger in my face.

"You think you know what is going on here, the actions of people and movement of money. But our guiding principles are in the spiritual realm and they transcend the laws of men and governments. Those earthly peccadillos you think you have uncovered are mere manifestations of our preordained destiny, and are not to be called into question!"

Okayyyy. That oughta do it. I figured I had enough for law enforcement to take the next actions in the "physical realm," but before I had a chance to answer I suddenly felt a hand on my shoulder—a large, firm hand. Turning around, I saw LeMichael's smiling, beatific countenance shining down on me.

"What up, m'brutha?"

"LeMichael, would you please show our guest to our...special offices," Tamar said wearily and with a weak wave of her hand.

With a little unnecessary help from LeMichael, I rose from my chair and, with his hand firmly at my back, headed toward the door.

Then he was restraining me with his other hand on my shoulder. "Not this time, m'man. We goin' another way today."

With that, he pushed me directly toward the rows of shelves lined with books, which seemed kind of pointless. I mean, where could we go from here? When we were out of earshot, LeMike whispered to me, "Thanks for the help on that Renaissance Lounge thing. They threw out the charges. I 'preciate cha."

I didn't have time to process that because suddenly a whole floor-to-ceiling section of the shelves swung away from us like it was on some kind of hinge, revealing a hallway lit from above with bright LED fixtures. I was quickly moved through the new opening and into the hallway, LeMichael on my left gently urging me along.

"What the heck's going on, LeMichael?"

"You find out directly, Raf. It's gonna be a'ight. Man jus' wanna speak witcha for 'bout a minute."

We turned a corner and, with a bit of guidance and generous propulsion from LeMichael, we entered a door on the right. Waiting to greet us was a smiling Roebuck.

"Why am I not surprised to see you here?" was all I could think of. "Should I call you Roebuck or Roe-BACH or Shawn or Tao?"

Completely ignoring my greeting, he stood, hand outstretched. "Hey, buddy!" he enthused, like he was welcoming me to a regular weekly poker game. "Take a seat. This'll be quick."

I found my seat with more help from LeMichael, who did not sit down but assumed a parade-rest stance just behind my chair.

"You remember those old TV game shows—the ones that required some knowledge on the part of contestants? Like say, *Who Wants To Be A Millionaire*?"

"Sure."

"Well, did you ever wonder how they picked contestants for those shows? It was a multiple-choice test with lots of questions. Only here's the thing: It wasn't the people with the highest scores who got on the show. Nope. If they picked only the smartest people, every contestant would get all the questions right, and they'd break the bank. And they couldn't pick the people with the lowest scores. A bunch of dumb-asses up there would never get any questions right, and what kind of quiz show would that be, right? So, what they did was pick the people who got more than 60% but less than 80% right. So, if you got in that range, you were good. Too low or too high and you're disqualified. Follow me so far?"

Wondering where all this was going, I asked, "What does this have to do with me—with us. Here and now?"

"Uh, well, to put it gently, you've answered too many questions right, Raf. You know too much. You've disqualified yourself. And now we have to figure out what to do with you.

One option here is to simply have LeMichael break your neck and then make you disappear."

I looked over my shoulder at LeMichael, who just shrugged and gave me the faintest of *whatyagonna do?* smiles.

It was time to unload. "Roebuck, you're a day late and a dollar short. I've already told everything I know to some very rough guys who would like nothing better than to break *your* neck. These are guys who have seen real combat and they don't take too kindly to a prick who makes money off killing old people for the insurance money and extorting money from people willing to pay to keep them alive. By the way, Orville has been released because I personally paid the ransom. You may be Miss Tamar's enforcer, but to me you're just a shithead. I've already told my story to the county detectives who've been watching this whole thing on TV. They're on their way in here right now."

I switched off my little lapel camera and mic. "One more item. We both know that behind the tough-guy act and the tees and vest, you're just a smarmy crotch-jockey hitting on lonely women."

He rose and headed for the door, but paused and turned back to me. "You're feeling real proud of yourself, like you've won some sort of prize by taking something from me. But you'll see for yourself." He managed a rueful little smile and snapped his fingers for dramatic emphasis as he walked out—or tried to. As soon as he reached the door, a hand gently helped him walk backwards into the room, followed by a smiling Detective Cantrell. Me? I was headed to Barb DeMinter's office.

She was tapping away on her computer and caught me out of the corner of her eye. Then, without looking up, "Hello, Mr. Vella. John's not here right now."

"Actually, it's you I want to talk with, Barb. Let's go into your office, please."

"What? Well, I think John ought to be present for any..."

I followed her in and closed the door. She sat down behind

her desk, and I was right behind her, wheeling one of her guest chairs around to sit right next to her.

She apparently thought she knew why I had come and immediately launched into her prepared defense.

"I want to clear the air, so to speak. I think there might have been a misunderstanding between you and me, and I wanted to straighten it out."

I had to fight the urge to bring the hammer down right then and there, but I could see she actually thought the magic of her words would compel me to reflexively light the peace pipe. I stayed quiet and let her continue.

"I know you thought I used your draft when I sent the Brancati meeting agenda to John, but that was really my own work. It was strictly a coincidence that it turned out to be similar to what you came up with."

I just smiled and said, "Uh huh."

She went on. "I think we can work well together. Great minds think alike, right?" She managed a small smile. Hopeful.

"Barb, we are not going to be working together—now or ever. It's true you are a compulsive liar and corporate backstabber and you passed off my work as your own. And, while that was mildly irritating at the time, that's not why I'm here. Today the subject is kidnapping and extortion and maybe attempted murder."

Her eyes got big and her smooth forehead was suddenly shiny. "What on earth...?"

"I know about your side gig, Broadview. And I know business was slacking off—not enough of your insureds were dying like you told your investors they would."

Her eyes got glassy, and she seemed to stare at something over my shoulder.

"How am I doin' so far?"

She didn't respond, so I went on.

"Roebuck's goons grabbed my truck driver and held him for ransom. It looked like a standard kidnapping except what could be the incentive to target a sixty-seven-year-old truck driver with no real assets to his name? I was able to follow the paper trail leading from my guy's sale of a life insurance policy on his own life to Broadview, making his death a value-realizing event for your company—and for you, Barb. Your little enterprise has been going south fast, and you're in serious need of a cash inflow. And it doesn't matter to you how it comes—death proceeds or ransom money."

Barb looked down at her shaking hands. "Y-you've got it all wrong, Raf. Broadview is a legitimate operation in a completely legal business. We're licensed in all forty-three states that regulate life settlements. We comply with all requirements, including the waiting periods. We haven't had a single customer complaint..."

I held up a hand, signaling it was my turn to talk. "That's because up till recently, you hadn't done anything wrong, Barb. Your insureds were dying right on schedule, the proceeds were rolling in and your investors were happy. That slowed down, and you became desperate to speed up the cash flow."

She stood up. "Look. I've got nothing to do with anything you're talking about beyond my ownership in Broadview, which, as I've said, is a perfectly legal business..."

"Save it, Barb. We know John's making shit money from his day job at Omega, and that he's way overextended on his credit with that lifestyle of his. John has already talked with the police, and now *they* know what *he* knows about Broadview's cash flow problems and how worried you've been about that. They also know Roebuck is your enforcer. But here's a piece of the puzzle neither you nor John knows about: Roebuck's been screwing my wife."

She stood up suddenly, her "sad face" quickly switching to "angry face." "Well, I'm sure I have no idea what you're talking about. I think you should leave now, Raf."

"Sit down, Barb."

"My personal life is none of your business. I'm going to call security."

"I don't think so, Barb."

She picked up the Bible from the corner of her desk and began thumbing through it randomly, compulsively, her Omega-reborn instincts apparently kicking in.

I walked over and gently took the book from her hands, laying it back down on the desk. She sat down slowly and just looked at her hands, folded in front of her.

More of Detective Cantrell's associates from County were on their way into Barb's office as I was leaving.

I was beat and went back to my car and drove to the hotel.

No sooner had I arrived at my room when my cell phone buzzed. It was Olivia.

"Where have you been, Dad? I've been worried sick and Mom doesn't know anything either."

"I've been out of town...on a business trip...but now I'm back."

In the pause that followed, I imagined her patented eye-roll. "Dad...when are you coming home?"

"We'll talk soon about that, I promise."

# CHAPTER 14

The morning news feed had an announcement from Living Water World Enterprises headquarters in Kansas City. The Board of Directors reported that it had requested and accepted the resignation of Tamara Bolisarian, CEO of its Edgewater, New Jersey-based subsidiary, Omega Financial. John Flanagan, Vice President of Insurance Operations, and Barbara DeMinter, Chief of Staff to Mr. Flanagan, also resigned. The company acknowledged "financial irregularities," and said an investigation would be ongoing.

In an emergency executive session, the Board "approved the hiring of Norman Brancati, an insurance industry veteran as Interim CEO pending the search for a permanent replacement." In a prepared statement, Board Chair Jeremiah Tadlock pledged that operations would continue uninterrupted, and that "a Search Committee will immediately begin the process of finding a new CEO to guide the work of this great institution on a righteous path. We are already reviewing the names of a number of God-fearing women with sterling credentials, any of whom would be well-qualified for this important position."

In other news, the District Attorney's office announced the arrest of Shawn Roebach, General Manager of the Specialty Products Distribution Center (sometimes called "the Depot"). It said Mr. Roebach would be arraigned later today on charges of kidnapping and extortion, and that other charges may follow. Carl Witham, Operations Supervisor, would take over as

Interim General Manager, effective immediately.

And President Stapleton renewed a campaign promise to make our nation completely independent of fossil fuels within five years.

Alone, I sat in my car and felt my mind slip into neutral. I sat there for a few minutes and waited for some kind of urge to do whatever was supposed to come next.

The last few days I had depended on a small voice to point me in the right direction and the rush of adrenaline to push me along. Now there was nothing. I picked up my paper coffee cup and peeked in, expecting at least a swallow of cold dregs, but there was nothing left but the foamy remains. I started my engine and let the car take me where I was supposed to go.

Things were in full swing at the Depot. The games and fights had been suspended temporarily after Roebuck's arrest as investigators and auditors swarmed the place looking for evidence of Roebuck's misdeeds and to interview employees. But now there were a couple of card games and three groups of dice-throwers were crouched at the periphery of the heavier action. There was a fight in the ring with about thirty onlookers and bettors clustered around. Carl was right up close, egging them on. I sat down on one of the stools and took in the scene.

When the bell rang to end the bout, I made my way over.

"Mis-tuh Raf!"

I think it was the first time Carl had called me by my first name.

"Well, first off, congratulations on your promotion."

"Helluva way to get it, though. Jeez, I worked with Roebuck several years and I knew he was a rough customer, but I guess there was a lot I didn't know."

I shook my head. "Guess everybody's got some dark secrets. Got a minute?"

"Sure!" He ambled over and cocked an ear in my direction.

"Not here. In your office."

"Ooh. I can hear the gears turning in that head of yours. Need some security muscle for one of your gigs? A problem blowing up as we speak? Some cool new idea that's going to make me a whole lotta money? I'm betting on number three."

I smiled as we walked down the corridor into his man-cave and sat down. He put both hands on his desk and looked at me, eyebrows raised.

"What do you see when you look out there, night after night, Carl?"

"I see a bunch of meatheads with no jobs, in the doghouse at home, trying to earn a few Chits and a little self-respect, some gambling recklessly, others in the ring trying to fight despite a lack of training or ability. What am I supposed to see?"

"I'm willing to bet some of those guys, maybe more than you think, are a lot more than that. They care enough about their families to be willing to come out here and take a chance on getting hurt badly just to be able to bring home some good food and other nice things their wives and kids might enjoy. That was me the first time I walked in here, remember?"

Carl was nodding. "I get that. And...what?"

"You need more Movers and Brokers. These guys are showing courage and a willingness to step out of their comfort zone. I'm willing to bet more than a few have the creativity and persistence and responsibility those jobs require. We're missing out on a valuable source of candidates, right here in front of us."

He spread his hands. "Problem is how to identify and train them."

"That's the next step. And it's not a problem. It's an opportunity. And we can get started on it right away. Stay with me a minute, ok? I just found an order for some Tecova boots. Authentic western. Cartwright model. Chocolate calf in a size 10-1/2. Retailed for about $450 back in the day. Any of your boys come to mind?"

He scratched his chin and thought for a moment. "Maybe

Leland Atwater? He's originally from Amarillo, and he oughta know his way around cowboy boots."

"Well, let's get him over here and see whether he wants to help me connect a man with some boots."

"That's him over there shootin' dice. Hey, Leland. C'mere a sec, will ya?"

The guy's Texas roots were right on the tip of his tongue. "Hey, Carl. What kennah doo-yah for?"

"Leland, meet Raf Vella. He's..." He stared at me, looking for guidance on how to introduce me, so I helped him out.

"Leland, I'm a Broker and I've got an assignment Carl thought might be in your wheelhouse. Western boots."

The young man stepped up, already nodding and smiling. "W'sure. I oughta know somethin' about some boots, I'd guess."

We shook hands, and I told him about the Cartwrights I was looking for. He said he thought he knew a guy who knew a guy.

"They've gotta be in good shape. Can you give him a holler and see what he's willing to take for 'em?

"I'll text him right now. Shoot. This guy's got plenty 'a pairs of boots. Shouldn't be a problem to get him to part with a pair if the price is right."

We agreed to meet later and Leland said, "Before we text my guy, let's look and see what they're going for these days." As we huddled over my phone looking for Tecova Cartwrights, Leland held up his hand.

"Hold up a sec. Go back. Back. There. See those?"

"Uh, yeah I see western boots but they're not Cartwrights."

"No, they're Townes. Alligator skin. Those babies used to go for $1,200. If they were cars, the Cartwrights you're lookin' for would be a Hyundai entry model; these Townes are the top-of-the-line Genesis. Real hard to find nowadays, but I'm pretty sure my buddy's got a pair. Maybe your guy would like them better. Bigger price tag, more room for a mark-up."

Leland may not have had experience in the Real Deal Economy, but he seemed like a natural for spotting an opportunity, and he sure knew his boots. It didn't take long for me to figure out that he knew about saddles and belts and jeans and duffles, too. I could see him becoming my go-to guy for all manner of western gear and clothes.

Later that day it was Carl's turn to call me into his office.

"Take a load off, man. Listen. First thing they asked me when I accepted this job was 'What's your first order of business?' And I said 'That's easy. Get the right person to fill in behind me as Ops Supervisor.' And, as it came outa my mouth, I knew right away my first choice would be you. Will you do it?"

He saw me look down and my mouth tighten in doubt. He held up a hand. "Before you answer, hear me out. Like you said, you came in here with nothing but a desire to make things better for yourself and your family, and a willingness to do what you had to do to make that happen and meet whatever challenges came up.

"Whether it was getting in the ring, finding goods and buyers, making deals and delivering—from little things like beach chairs and waiters' jackets to bigger things like a truckload of fat and bone. And you came up with some big ideas to take things here to a higher level—like that new comp plan for Brokers, which they love, and bringing in the right kind of outside talent to enhance our hauling capability and our security services. Plus, I can already see you identifying and mentoring other guys to be Brokers and Movers.

"Sometimes in life you choose a job and sometimes a job chooses you. This job is yours today, Raf. I hope you'll take it."

I was still enjoying the role of Broker and was reluctant to give up some real hands-on work. Yet I couldn't deny the lure of making even more of an impact, and I already could see the benefit of magnifying my efforts in a leadership role.

I stood up and extended my hand. "Thank you, Carl. I can't say no. I appreciate your confidence in me."

I was enthusiastic about my new assignment and was eager to begin. But my home situation was a mess, and I had to face it sooner or later. I was in serious jeopardy of losing my family and had already caused some strain with my daughter. I pulled up Emily's cell number and pushed the red Call icon.

She answered on the first ring. "Where are you?"

Ah, loving words whispered in my ear. *Does she talk to the other fool like that?*

"Can you meet me at the Jasmine's Hour Tea Room around five?"

"Does it have to be today? I may have to work late and..."

"Emily, please. I'm asking for about twenty minutes. Ok?"

"All right. I'll be there."

I got to the Tea Room right on time and ordered a Darjeeling and a plain scone with clotted cream and strawberry jam. I poured some tea through the strainer and mixed in some warm milk. I broke off a piece of the scone, slathered on some of the cream and a dollop of jam and popped it into my mouth. I let my mind drift from work and family, forced myself to take a deep breath, let it out, and then repeated the process.

Emily arrived as I was taking my first sip of tea.

"Traffic was a nightmare."

"I'm sure. Want some tea?"

"Sure. What're you having?"

"It's Darjeeling."

"I'll have the Jasmine. No scone for me, though."

"Have a piece of mine."

She broke off a tiny corner of my scone and swiped it through the clotted cream on my dish. "What'd you want to talk about?"

"Things with us haven't been right for a while, and I'm worried if we don't do something about it, we might be sorry later. Even if we don't feel like being together right now, we have a lot at stake with our marriage and with Olivia. Your sliding into...a relationship...complicated things."

"Oh, now you want to talk about it. Where've you been for the past two years? All I know is I needed affection and affirmation and you just weren't available."

"Fair enough. But you know I could use a little affection and affirmation, too. Suppose I get involved with someone. Then it changes from the triangle we've got to each of us squared off with our respective Designated Affection and Affirmation Givers, and everything is even more complicated."

Ever the practical one, Emily jumped in. "Well, we still have issues. You know, things have changed since you lost your real job and I've become the primary breadwinner."

"Ex-fucking-'scuse me? Are you hallucinating? Sure, you have a big-sounding title and an office, but how much are you actually making?"

"You know how much. You see it going into our account every month. Raf, I'm glad you seem to have found some things to keep you busy, but..."

"Some things to keep me busy? You're living in some kind of parallel universe. Stay with me here on earth, just for a sec. You clear about five grand a month. That helps, for sure. But did you ever look at the bills-paid statement on our account? We spend about three times that. Where do you think the other ten has been coming from?"

Emily looked at me quizzically. "Fifteen thousand dollars? A month?"

I nodded. "When was the last time you logged into our bank account to check the payments and deposits?"

"I don't do that. You always handled that stuff before and still do. We have that low-balance trigger thing that sends us an email when we get below a thousand. And that never happens, so, you know..."

"That's what I figured. And those 'things that keep me busy' are what's been keeping us afloat. Exactly what do you think I'm doing while you're off at your yoga class or your poetry group or doing your book club reading in bed at ten p.m.? I'm working my ass off at the Depot or on field trips picking up and delivering goods to keep that money coming in, and even harder to keep from getting the shit kicked out of me or worse."

She frowned and jerked her head back in a mixture of confusion and disbelief. "The Depot? You mean that warehouse-type place where people drive up and get stuff you can't find in stores? I've heard about it, but I don't know anyone who's actually been there."

I spread my hands. "See? I wouldn't even know where to start to tell you about what goes on there and my role in it. But that's what's paying most of our bills. And I've worked my way up to some responsibility there, which ought to translate to some more income for us."

I figured that was enough and didn't get into the Roebuck part. Emily seemed to have recovered from my little takedown and decided she'd endured enough bubble-bursting for one session because she seemed eager to change the subject to something more consistent with her view of our little world. "Are you coming back home?"

"Well, I've been at the hotel, and it's getting expensive, so I guess it's either that or find a place. I'd rather not do that yet so, yeah, home seems like the best option. I can sleep in the study."

She nodded, and we just sat there for the next two or three minutes, looking down into our tea cups, neither of us knowing what to say next.

I broke the silence. "There's something else I want you to know. I understand you are disappointed in me. And I've done some things I wish I hadn't. I am truly sorry for the hurt I've caused you. But your expectations of me—the fantasy person you created and hoped and expected I would be—and finding that I didn't measure up to those expectations are all just concoctions of your own mind. That's all on you. I didn't put those thoughts there, and I don't take responsibility for your hopes or your disappointments. But like it or not, and whether or not we'd make the same decision today about getting married, we have a family now and we share the responsibility to keep it going.

"Olivia knows she has no power in this thing, so she won't tell us how she really feels, but she's hurting and counting on us to protect her and to keep her world together. And you'd better believe if we break up our family, there will be some consequences where she's concerned. I don't want to preside over that kind of mess and I don't think you do either."

She seemed momentarily conciliatory. "I do appreciate the contributions you're making. And I just want you to at least acknowledge that I'm contributing too—in a very big way."

I nodded and spread my hands and sat back, signaling that I had said my piece. Emily found a tissue in her purse and dabbed at her eyes. She took a couple of breaths and a sip of water and forced a flat smile, pushing back her chair and standing to leave. "I guess I'll see you."

"I guess so," was all I could manage to get out around the hard lump in my throat as I watched her get up quickly and clip-clop away fast, her shoulder bag bouncing wildly against her hip.

XXXX

I moved back home, but Emily and I didn't have much to say to each other in the ensuing weeks. One of us would almost always be home to have dinner with Olivia, but the three of us rarely shared a meal together. I honestly don't know how she took Tao/Roebuck's reversal of fortunes, or how it affected their relationship, because neither of us mentioned him. She did tell me Nikki had taken over running the yoga studio. We hadn't yet resumed our tea shop conversation, though I hoped someday we might.

My new assignment rejuvenated me, and over the next few months, I pretty much worked all the time, taking assignments and finding guys to go with me so I could show them the deal-making ropes as I had done with Leland. I had developed a small but powerful network of former fighters and gamblers from the Depot who had some knowledge and experience in some area so they could specialize in handling certain types of products.

The President's pledge of a more aggressive target date for independence from fossil fuels made our fat-and-bone hauling business a lucrative profit center for us. I was lucky to find among the Depot regulars a former meat department manager from the former FoodRight Markets who knew his way around the product and had some connections with slaughterhouses in the Midwest to supplement AmCo's output. Brett continued to be a reliable buyer, and he introduced us to a couple of his friendly competitors who were willing to take whatever he didn't need. I had plenty of hauling work to throw Orville's way, and he brought in a couple of his buddies to do some runs for us. James handled the security and the bad guys pretty much left us alone.

Little by little, I was able to focus more on the strategic issues of the Depot as I brought on more guys who could do the Broker and Mover jobs. It also meant I could be home more, since most of my work was done on the computer and I didn't have to go out on the road.

One day Carl appeared in the doorway to my new office looking down and away from my gaze. I motioned him to one of the guest chairs in front of my desk, and thought the best thing to do was to encourage him to get right to the point.

"I can see you've got something on your mind, Carl, so you'd better come out with it."

"Is it that obvious? Well, you know I really appreciate the kind of leader you're trying to be—all your ideas and suggestions for making things run better down here, and the guys seem to like you. But there's a piece of this you still haven't caught onto yet, and it worries me.

"There's a level of cynicism in this work where people view the whole thing as a game of musical chairs, with the music stopping it seems like every fifteen minutes. Actually, a better analogy is 'King of the Hill.' The only thing worse than being one of the guys trying to knock off the king is actually *being* the king, trying to defend his position. So, in addition to all the administrative shit you have to contend with, you should also be aware that you've got this huge target on your back. What I'm saying is, just like I've gotta watch out for myself, so do you.

"Oh, and even my little 'King of the Hill' analogy only goes so far. It implies it's a bunch of guys in a free-for-all, each one fighting for himself, trying to knock the king off so he can take his place. Actually, it's a little more complicated than that. This thing we call the Depot, you think that's the big fucking prize? It's not. The real power is way beyond your pay grade or mine. People you've never met, and maybe never will meet. Power brokers, you'd call 'em. No official titles or positions. But they're pulling strings on all of us. They watch carefully as our elected officials go about their little dance, outlawing this, requiring that, and as soon as a new law or reg takes effect, they've figured out a way to get around it.

"As long as it's convenient for the string-pullers, they'll let us stay where we are. But don't be surprised if one day your pins get knocked out from under you and it looks like it's the work of some hot-shot newbie lone wolf but if you look closely, you'll see he—or maybe, she—is sponsored by the puppet masters. So, do the work, continue making improvements, constantly learning and building your resume. Enjoy it while you can, but don't get too comfortable. Spend some time getting prepared for what's next, whatever the hell that might turn out to be."

Carl's monologue gave me a chilly feeling up my spine, but I guess it wasn't totally a surprise. I made up my mind to keep an eye out for unusual activity from every quarter, making sure I was building goodwill with the troops and sharpening my skills and, maybe most important of all, developing alternate sources of intelligence to give me early warning of bad shit coming down the pike.

At first, I thought I might ease my home life pain by spending more time with Kayla. We spent a few more Saturday mornings together, drinking coffee and listening to old recordings, but I could see she was distracted. I'd often catch her checking her phone for messages, and there were times when she'd hustle me out of her place in a hurry with some flimsy explanation, and I finally asked her about it.

"You seem kinda eager for me to get going. What's up?"

She looked down for four full beats, biting her lower lip. Then, "Look, Raf, I love you. I really do. But it's not the same. The thing that fueled it—the idea that maybe you'd leave your wife and we could really be together. I know now...I can't handle it."

She was full-on crying by this time, and I had this giant lump in my throat. There didn't seem to be anything else to say, so we just came together in a quick and clumsy embrace and I turned around and walked out the door, down the hall to the elevator without looking back.

I knew she was right. I couldn't build anything with Kayla as long as I felt the strong pull of family life with Emily and Olivia.

I had a hole in my heart as I was coming to terms with the fact that things between Emily and me were never going to be what they used to be unless I took the initiative. And even then, it would be a long shot. Though the writing had been on the wall for some time, it was still no less painful to finally accept the fact. I wondered whether Emily and I could ever actually build something new, and how we might start to do that. Right at that moment it seemed pretty remote.

Olivia was busy with school and activities and, for a time, seemed to have given up on things going back to the way they were. But I sensed she was looking for little signs of hope for the future for us as a family.

One evening when we were having one of our Armando's

dinners together, she brought it up in a kind of roundabout way. "You know, Brittany's mom and dad were separated for almost six months, but they decided to get back together. Brittany said there was a lot of strain in the early going, but it was still a lot better than the separation. And then, little by little, they started getting closer again by doing things together as a family, not taking everything so seriously and gradually her parents even having a few laughs together."

She looked at me hopefully and added, "I bet you and Mom have more in common than you think. And she's even been telling me things you two used to do together. I got the feeling she'd be open to talking with you more, and maybe even spending a little time together."

"You may be right. We'll see." And I meant it.

Some things had settled down, all right. But there was still a lot of uncertainty. I knew there were more challenges to come, maybe just up ahead. But despite all I'd been through—or maybe because of it—I was pretty sure I was ready. I sure as hell hoped so.

# ACKNOWLEDGMENTS

The author wishes to acknowledge several people who helped along the way.

Maria Ceferatti, Joseph Libonati and Cynthia McGroarty read early chapters and urged me to keep going. Mark Spencer read a draft of the manuscript, and provided valuable observations, insights, suggestions and encouragement. Janice Maffei was a constant booster.

Thanks to the people at Atmosphere for taking on this book. Special thanks to my editor, Bryce Wilson, for his helpful comments, and to Meg Schader for her meticulous proofreading.

# ABOUT ATMOSPHERE PRESS

Atmosphere Press is an independent, full-service publisher for excellent books in all genres and for all audiences. Learn more about what we do at atmospherepress.com.

We encourage you to check out some of Atmosphere's latest releases, which are available at Amazon.com and via order from your local bookstore:

*Icarus Never Flew 'Round Here*, by Matt Edwards

*COMFREY, WYOMING: Maiden Voyage*, by Daphne Birkmeyer

*The Chimera Wolf*, by P.A. Power

*Umbilical*, by Jane Kay

*The Two-Blood Lion*, by Nick Westfield

*Shogun of the Heavens: The Fall of Immortals,* by I.D.G. Curry

*Hot Air Rising*, by Matthew Taylor

*30 Summers*, by A.S. Randall

*Delilah Recovered*, by Amelia Estelle Dellos

*A Prophecy in Ash,* by Julie Zantopoulos

*The Killer Half,* by JB Blake

*Ocean Lessons*, by Karen Lethlean

*Unrealized Fantasies*, by Marilyn Whitehorse

*The Mayari Chronicles: Initium*, by Karen McClain

*Squeeze Plays,* by Jeffrey Marshall

*JADA: Just Another Dead Animal*, by James Morris

*Hart Street and Main: Metamorphosis*, by Tabitha Sprunger

*Karma One*, by Colleen Hollis

*Ndalla's World*, by Beth Franz

# ABOUT THE AUTHOR

**MICHAEL SHAPIRO** is a writer and musician who lives near Philadelphia. He has had a career in law and business.

CPSIA information can be obtained
at www.ICGtesting.com
Printed in the USA
BVHW040832100723
666996BV00003B/107